T0196609

"As it happens, widowhood agrees with me. I am my own mistress, in charge of my own affairs."

"And you do not wish to remarry?"

"Why should I? It would only mean forfeiting my independence and allowing some man to make all my decisions for me. Thank you, no," she said with emphasis. "I am content to find happiness for myself."

She seemed sincere in her desire to be left alone, but as Edward looked down at her, the room seemed to fade around them. All he saw was Anne.

"I begged you to wait," he said softly.

Her dark eyes glistened up at him. "And I begged you to stay."

He shook his head ruefully and tried a smile on her. "It would appear neither of us is very good at begging."

More from Mia Marlowe

Touch of a Thief
Touch of a Rogue
Touch of a Scoundrel
Plaid to the Bone (ebook novella)
Plaid Tidings
The Singular Mr. Sinclair

Lord Bredon and the Bachelor's Bible

Mia Marlowe

LYRICAL PRESS
Kensington Publishing Corp.
www.kensingtonbooks.com

First Electronic Edition: April 2019
eISBN-13: 978-1-5161-0662-2
eISBN-10: 1-5161-0662-8

First Print Edition: April 2019
ISBN-13: 978-0-5161-0663-9
ISBN-10: 1-5161-0663-6

Printed in the United States of America

Prologue

A drizzly Tuesday afternoon in London, 1817

Lady Daly studiously avoided looking at the coffin at the far end of the parlor and concentrated instead on the mourners milling about the dead man. She leaned toward the woman next to her and whispered, "What did he die of?"

Her friend did not bother to whisper. "It wasn't of loneliness, of that you may be certain."

No one would fail to recognize the snide voice of the second speaker. It belonged to Lady Ackworth, the self-appointed arbitress of good behavior and the general terror of the ton. She kept a running account of all the rakes and roués making the rounds of the great houses and delighted in naming and shaming their hapless conquests. She knew who owed whom exorbitant gambling debts and whose credit was no long welcomed at fashionable establishments. It was generally accepted that if Lady Ackworth didn't know of something, it couldn't be of much import and, in fact, had probably never happened.

"Sir Erasmus Howard rarely suffered from the lack of feminine companionship," Lady Ackworth went on more softly, "especially when Lady Howard was not in Town."

It was only a whisper, but the unkind accusation seemed to swirl in the air currents above their heads. However, if the gathered crowd of mourners in Sir Erasmus's London town house heard the gossip's unkind patter, they were too well-bred to show it. Shortly, the entire assembly would form a procession from the Howard residence to St. Thomas-by-the-Way, a small church on the next block. St. Paul's was only a few more streets over, but St. Thomas's was where a brief service would be held, followed by immediate interment in the churchyard.

It wasn't usual for ladies of quality to complete the entire ritual, the graveside being considered too stark a reality for their delicate constitutions, but Lady Daly and her friend were not the sort to do anything by halves. They'd see Sir Erasmus firmly in the ground, no matter how soggy the walk to his yawning grave.

How else could they speak with authority on the event in the days to come?

"Sadly, infidelity is not an exceptional failing among gentlemen nowadays." Lady Daly eyed a few peers she suspected of the fault.

"It has always been thus, and frankly, I can't imagine what gentlewoman would have it otherwise. Once one has had children, one needn't be troubled with that marital duty, and good riddance to it, say I." Lady Ackworth made a small moue of distaste. "However, Sir Erasmus would have done well to be more discreet."

Other than that all-too-common fault, the gossips agreed that Lady Howard had little room for complaint in her marriage. Sir Erasmus had provided lavishly for her during their short union. His young wife never wanted for jewels or a wardrobe cut in the first stare of fashion. If Lady Howard wished to improve her husband's home, he apparently trusted her judgment on the matter, for he opened his purse wide to let her spend whatever was necessary.

"In many respects," Lady Daly said, "Sir Erasmus Howard was a fine husband."

"Indeed. But was Lady Howard a fine wife?"

"She's managed his funeral well enough." Lady Daly fingered the delicate black gloves tied up with a sprig of rosemary and a long length of ebony ribbon. Quite correctly, she'd been given the mourning token when she arrived, as had Lady Ackworth. The gentlemen assembled had all been presented with black hat bands and handkerchiefs. The house was draped with ebony bunting, and the servants presented appropriately somber expressions while they offered refreshments which were routinely ignored. No one could fault Lady Howard for not following the prescribed mourning rituals.

At that moment, the widow appeared at the head of the long staircase and made her way sedately down. She seemed to be floating, for her head of raven hair didn't bob a bit and there was a becoming sheen to the whites of her dark eyes, evidence, no doubt, of private grief.

Lady Daly nodded in tacit approval. It was beyond distasteful to express strong emotion in public, but a hint of contained sadness was wholly proper.

The widow didn't smile to acknowledge the presence of the other mourners. At least, not by conscious volition. Everyone who knew the lady was aware that, by a trick of musculature, the corners of her mouth naturally turned up ever so slightly.

The effect was reminiscent of the Mona Lisa, of whose enigmatic smile Lady Daly had only heard rumors. She found it charming. Lady Ackworth, on the other hand, always held that the tiny expression revealed a bit of smugness, as if Lady Howard were keeping a delicious secret and the slight smile betrayed her.

"She looks terribly pale, doesn't she?" Lady Daly said.

"Black will do that to a body." Lady Ackworth smoothed the skirt of the bombazine gown she kept at the ready for just such occasions. "It makes everyone appear wan, which equals boring. Look at me. I'm positively peaked."

However, Lady Daly didn't think Lady Howard appeared wan or boring. She looked far lovelier than a widow ought. There was a huge difference between pale and listless, and pale and...mysterious.

"I've heard her new situation means she'll have to have come down in the world quite a bit," Lady Daly leaned in to whisper.

"I should say so. Not only is Sir Erasmus's mother still living, which means there will be two dowagers splitting that portion, but her stepson, Sir Percival, has considerable debts. Now that he's inherited the baronetcy, his creditors will make short work of the estate's assets, so the dowagers' due will be smaller yet." Lady Ackworth made a tsking sound. "This may very well be the last time London Society sees Lady Howard."

Threadbare gentility loomed in the widow's future. For the first time since Lady Daly arrived to join the mourners, real tears of sympathy pressed against the backs of her eyes. Too many gentlewomen were reduced to penury by the untimely demise of their men. Fortunately, her own husband—such a clever man—had arranged to die before he could accumulate too much debt. Lord Daly had left their son with a solid estate in Surrey and her with a lavish annuity that was the envy of the ton.

"It's a pity all around. Sir Erasmus was quite a bit older than Lady Howard, but he was certainly no dotard," she said. "Had he been ill long?"

"No. Death came to him suddenly." Lady Ackworth narrowed her eyes at Lady Howard, who was accepting condolences with an air of gracious resignation. "It does seem odd, doesn't it?"

"Was it apoplexy that carried him off?"

"Not that I've heard."

"A weakness of the chest perhaps?" Lady Daly wondered aloud.

"The Howards have always had the constitution of a horse."

A ghastly thought crossed Lady Daly's mind. "You don't suspect... foul play, do you?"

"Did I say so? What a distasteful idea!" Lady Ackworth whipped out the ornate black fan she kept specifically for funerals and beat the air with it. "I'm surprised at you for broaching such a disturbing topic when we are practically at the gentleman's graveside."

Severely chastened, Lady Daly bit her lower lip.

"Still..." Lady Ackworth cocked her head to one side, as she always did when deciding to appropriate someone else's idea and make it her own. "For a gentleman as hale and hearty as Sir Erasmus to be stricken so unexpectedly...it does make one wonder if he was hastened to his death somehow."

Lady Daly glanced across the room at the widow, who was seated near the wide front window, looking out into the deepening twilight. A small frown drew Lady Howard's delicate brows together, and combined with that mysterious smile, hers was a face at war with itself. Less charitable souls might misconstrue the expression entirely.

"I wonder what Lady Howard is thinking."

If she could have peeked into the lady's mind at that moment, she'd have been more than disturbed. Only one thought was singing through Lady Howard's whole being.

I'm finally free.

They say money can't buy happiness. I say as long as money is what they take in exchange for a berth on a ship bound for an exotic shore, it buys all the happiness I require.
—from the travel journal of Mrs. Hester Birdwhistle

Chapter 1

May 1822

If the unfortunate pianoforte had a soul, it would surely have made a deal with the devil. Anything to escape being hammered to death by Miss Frederica Tilbury. Not that the young lady, known affectionately as "Freddie" to her friends, was playing the wrong notes. All the right ones were there. The trouble was that all of them were being delivered with the same ruthless conviction of one who was killing snakes.

Edward Lovell, Lord Chatham, shifted uncomfortably in his seat, along with the twenty or so other captives who'd made the mistake of attending the recital. The annual event was sponsored by a group of marriage-minded mamas, each of them hoping that her daughter's performance would capture an eligible bachelor's attention. Year after year, stage-struck young ladies displayed their talents. The program included singing, playing a variety of musical instruments, recitation of poetry, and, in one case of a singularly misplaced notion of what constituted a talent, imitating bird calls.

Edward decided Miss Oglethorpe's pheasant call might come in handy during shooting season, but otherwise, a wife who whistled or twittered with any regularity would dance on his last nerve.

He gritted his teeth as Miss Tilbury's assault on the keyboard continued. It was doubly difficult to bear because the young lady was his sister

Caroline's particular friend, and Caro would expect a report on her performance. Edward decided he could truthfully say that Freddie hadn't missed a note. She pounded them all with equal enthusiasm.

And lack of feeling.

Edward did not suffer from that particular failing. He felt more than most, and still bore a black armband for his father. For the past half year, a longer time than most gentlemen wore such remembrances, the band had been a daily item in Edward's ensemble. That small sliver of mourning had become a part of him, as much as his sandy hair and piercing blue eyes. It went part and parcel with his newly acquired earldom.

Since his father's death, Edward had managed the Chatham estate's business with methodical coolness. In fact, for the past few years, the old earl had accepted his help with the workings of the estate, though he would brook no major changes while he was alive. Sadly, the economies Edward had wished to implement had come too late to keep the Chatham ledger book from tipping dangerously into dun territory.

But Edward had conceived a plan to manage that, however personally distasteful he might find the notion. He took the responsibilities that went with his station very seriously. It was a matter of honor that he be able to provide for his large family and many retainers.

Seeing to the needs of those who depended upon him was part of what nobility meant to him. Gone were the days of pleasing himself, with no thought for how his actions would impact others. He was a tree beneath whose shade many could shelter in safety.

Even to his own mind, that sounded a bit pompous, but Edward reminded himself of what he was willing to do to meet his responsibilities. Weighed against that, pomposity was the least of his sins. In any case, he was growing accustomed to the demands of his new life as the earl.

Answering when someone addressed him as Lord Chatham was another matter entirely. He still half expected to hear his father's voice responding from behind him.

When Frederica Tilbury ceased tormenting the piano, there was a blessed lull in the recital program. Edward's friend Sinclair leaned toward him and whispered, "Remind me again why we are here."

Sinclair had also been elevated to a title, but Edward rarely thought of him as Lord Ware. Sinclair was married to Edward's sister Caroline, which made him his brother-in-law as well as earl of a solid estate in the Lake District.

"Your favorite brother-in-law," Sinclair had often teased him.

As he was Edward's *only* brother-in-law, and destined to remain so, the distinction was much less grand than Sinclair made it sound. Besides, Edward always preferred to count Sinclair as his friend.

He'd discovered quickly that a peer of the realm had toadies by the hundreds, acquaintances by the dozens, supplemented by occasional allies in the House of Lords. However, a gentleman of title and property had few enough true friends that he was honor-bound to treasure them.

Besides, Sinclair was the only one who still called him Bredon. It was the courtesy title Edward had grown up with, the viscountcy associated with it a lesser possession of his father's. Edward had carried the name with him to Eton and he still thought of himself as Lord Bredon.

"We are here with a purpose," he whispered back to Sinclair. "To find the young lady whom I shall make my countess."

"Oh, good. I'd hate to think you were looking for an actual musician in this lot."

Actually, Edward was looking for more than a countess. He required an heiress.

Luckily, he didn't have to guess which debutante was a fortune with feet. A few weeks ago at White's, he'd stumbled upon a pamphlet entitled *A Register of Ladies of Means, or The Bachelor's Bible.* The current crop of marriageable ladies was listed within its dog-eared pages, complete with their ages, addresses, and expected dowries.

Edward wasn't diving into this endeavor blind. He didn't have to sleuth out an alliance that would meet the needs of the estate. Thanks to *The Bachelor's Bible*, he knew exactly which debutante he must pursue.

"Are you merely window shopping today?" Sinclair asked. "Or have you settled on a particular young lady?"

Edward nodded grimly. "Miss Martha Finch."

She was the daughter of an extremely well-heeled baron. According to *The Bachelor's Bible*, her hand came with the princely sum of eighty thousand pounds. Even that astounding sum wasn't enough to permanently right the listing Chatham ship, but it would plug the leak long enough for Edward to enact his reforms and rebuild the family wealth.

He was disgusted by the notion of a marriage based primarily on a business decision, but needs must. And he soothed his conscience by reminding himself that if he were truly the mercenary sort, he'd have set his cap for the Dowager Marchioness of Kent. The crotchety octogenarian's wealth was so immense, *The Bachelor's Bible* could only hazard a guess of *millions.*

However, the dowager was a conquest that required more self-denial than Edward possessed. In any case, in addition to a balanced ledger, he owed the Chatham estate another duty no amount of money would fulfill.

An heir.

The sooner he and his new countess produced one, the better for all concerned.

"You've chosen well, brother," Sinclair said. "From what I've heard, Miss Finch is the prize heifer in this Season's herd."

Edward shrugged.

"How did the two of you meet?"

"We haven't."

Sinclair's brows shot up in surprise. "You've seen her somewhere, at least."

Edward shook his head. "A defect which shall be remedied in a thrice. I believe she is next on the program."

"Yet you have already decided to put a countess's tiara on her head?" Sinclair sighed. "Bredon, I know you to be a man of conviction and deep feeling. This sudden decision to wed someone about whom you know nothing isn't like you at all."

"Perhaps it's not like Bredon. But it is like Lord Chatham. As you say, she is considered the catch of the Season. Miss Finch's hand comes with certain...inducements I cannot afford to ignore."

"I had no idea," Sinclair said. "If you are in need of funds, I—"

Edward cut him off. "No. I won't have it. A gentleman who settles one debt by acquiring another is no gentleman at all. In any case, the estate's financial difficulties are temporary."

"Nothing eighty thousand pounds won't cure, I take it," Sinclair said wryly.

"Evidently, you've seen *The Bachelor's Bible*, too."

"It is all anyone talks about at White's," Sinclair said. "Unfortunately, I made the mistake of telling Caroline about the pamphlet. It's a wonder you didn't hear her outrage over it from your study."

Sinclair and his sister lived on the same street, in the same row of terrace houses as Edward. Caro was given to strong opinions, but none of them had ever reached his study unless she carried them in with her when she popped round to visit.

"I take it my sister doesn't approve of men having as much information about their prospective spouses as women seem to?"

"No, she's worried for Freddie," Sinclair admitted. "Caro fears that if the size of Miss Tilbury's dowry becomes public knowledge, it will attract suitors with dubious motives. Oh! Present company excepted, of course. I didn't mean to imply you had bad intent simply because you plan to marry a woman whom you've never even seen, based solely on the generous curves of her dowry."

Edward snorted and crossed his arms over his chest. "Women marry for titles and wealth all the time. I consider *The Bachelor's Bible* turnabout fair play."

As soon as he wed Miss Finch, the earldom's difficulties would be well on the way to gone forever. His mother would continue to live in the opulence to which she was accustomed, and, to his mind, which she deserved. His younger brothers' paths would be smoothed both by their association with the Earl of Chatham and by the coin that would flow on their behalf from the estate.

With a modicum of luck, he'd sire an heir within the first year of his marriage. The "spare" would no doubt follow quickly.

Then Edward would have done his duty: receiving the trust of previous generations and preserving it for future ones. That's what his father had told him a title was really about. It was all that mattered.

"Still," Sinclair said, "I can't imagine contemplating marriage to a woman I didn't have at least a little affection for."

"That's because you were blessed with a love match. Not all of us are so kissed by Cupid." Besides, Edward had already lost his heart once. He'd never retrieved it. Even now, years later, he had no residual fondness left in him to give to another. A marriage of convenience would have to be just that. Convenient. But to appease his friend, he added, "I'm told many a successful marriage starts without affection, and later on, warm regard grows."

"So does mold."

"Ever the optimist, Sinclair."

"Warm regard, my backside." His friend spat the words out. "Are you listening to yourself? How can you be satisfied with such a paltry goal?"

Edward shushed him both because he didn't want to hear the words and because the next debutante to perform had just been introduced.

Miss Finch walked across the dais and took her seat at the pianoforte.

To say she was plain was too harsh. It was more that she was unremarkable. Average in height and figure, her hair neither blond nor yet quite brown, Miss Finch was an unobjectionable cipher.

"If she stood in the altogether before a beige wall and closed her eyes, she'd disappear entirely," Sinclair leaned to whisper.

Edward snorted and shot his friend a glare. However, the image Sinclair conjured up lingered. Miss Finch was easily the most forgettable lady in the room.

Then she began to play.

Miss Tilbury had mauled the piano. Miss Finch's fingers caressed it. Her lines were lyrical, if not especially powerful, and the lightness of her runs and trills was grace itself. The way she poured herself into her music spoke well for her character. Surely, she was of a person of great feeling and possessed of a noble soul.

Edward thought he could do far worse than to look forward to evenings filled with her delicate music after a quiet meal. It didn't matter that she was no great beauty. Such talent would last far longer than loveliness. For the first time since he'd decided she was the one he would court, Edward's gut unknotted. Her music soothed him and the uneasiness he felt faded a bit.

Perhaps marrying Miss Finch won't be so bad, after all.

Once the final note of her sonata faded, the audience sat in stillness for a few heartbeats, unwilling to disturb the afterglow of loveliness. Then hearty applause began and continued for far longer than the polite claps that had followed the other girls' performances.

"Brava!" someone shouted out. The acclamation seemed to surprise Miss Finch. Her cheeks colored becomingly.

Accomplished and modest. Not a bad combination.

After Miss Finch left the stage, Edward only had to squirm through a poetry reading by a young lady with a slight lisp and then the recital was mercifully over.

"I leave you to your fate," Sinclair said as they both stood. "Caro will expect a full report, and making a woman who's increasing wait for anything is never a good idea."

"Give her my love."

"Give it to her yourself. She's beyond weary of this confinement and complains that she never has any company—other than Freddie. Come to supper on Saturday."

"I will." Once his courtship of Miss Finch began in earnest, Edward would face a gauntlet of banquets and balls. It would do his heart good to have a quiet meal with his sister and her husband.

Sinclair had scarcely left when Edward turned, stepped into the aisle, and was nearly bowled over by a lady in a monstrously large bonnet. The headgear was festooned with enough feathers to cover an entire bird. He caught her in his arms before she could topple over from the force of their collision.

"Are you quite all right, madam?"

"I would be if a certain gentlemen would bother to glance about him before blocking the aisle." She tipped up her chin to meet his gaze, and the ridiculous bonnet seemed to disappear. All Edward could see were winged brows above soulful dark eyes, cheekbones that spoke of a beauty that would not fade, and of course, her mouth.

That mouth.

It was Anne. If someone had gut-punched him, he could not have been more surprised.

"Oh!" she said, as she pulled away from him. Her mouth widened in a false smile—he was too well acquainted with her real one to mistake this expression for it—and she extended a gloved hand. "Lord Chatham, I believe."

Woodenly, he took her hand and made a proper obeisance over it.

Manners are what one does when one isn't sure what to do, his mother had always told him. So, Edward was doing the mannerly thing, but part of him wanted to peel off Anne's kidskin glove and cover her naked fingers with kisses.

"You used to call me Edward," he said softly.

She tugged her hand from him. "And you once called me Anne, but Lady Howard will do now. After you left for your Grand Tour, I married—"

"Ah, yes, I know." The last thing he wished to hear about was her wedding. "I was in Hamburg when I heard the news."

"Then you were remarkably well informed on your travels."

He and his companion, Lord Rowley, had been lifting their steins in a beer garden that had been brewing in the same small alehouse since the 1500s when they were accosted by Mr. Reginald Dickey.

Dickey was a handsome, witty young man, and the son of the Duke of Hampton, a fact that he traded upon with regularity. However, his greatest misfortune was that he was an *illegitimate* son, but thanks to his father's open acknowledgment of him, Dickey wasn't shuffled off to obscurity the way most by-blows were. Instead, his father provided him with a gentleman's education and ample financial support. The duke frequently welcomed Dickey to the ducal palace, to the great consternation of the duchess, no doubt. Dickey was admitted to many of the great houses, probably to curry favor with his illustrious sire, but Dickey's wit was what kept him near the top of many worthy matrons' guest lists.

His penchant for gossip ensured that he never lacked for company. If there was bad news to be shared, he was determined to be the bearer of it. Knowing Edward had harbored a tendresse for Anne, Dickey gleefully reported that she had married Sir Erasmus Howard little more than a month after Edward had left England.

For the first time in his life, Edward had drunk himself into a stupor that night.

"My felicitations are belated, but I wish you and your husband every happiness." His mother would have been proud of him for being polite. The way his gut roiled, Edward feared he might be sick.

Anne cast him a sidelong glance. "Apparently, you're less well informed now that you are home. I was widowed some years ago."

Edward swallowed hard. It was difficult to offer condolences when he didn't feel the least sad about her husband's demise, but he was duty-bound to try. "I hope it wasn't...that is to say, I wish I'd been..."

"What? There to hold my hand in my grief? Please. Let us not sully the memory of what we were to each other with falsehoods now. You were no doubt in Rome or Paris or Prague when it happened, and wouldn't have wished to be elsewhere for worlds."

He couldn't say where he'd been, because he didn't know specifically when Sir Erasmus had gone to his reward. Once Edward learned Anne had wed so soon after he'd left England, he took pains not to hear any other news of her, lest he learn she'd given her husband an heir.

Or worse, died trying to.

But if he'd heard she had been widowed, nothing would have kept him on the Continent.

"Do not pity my single state," she said. "As it happens, widowhood agrees with me. I am my own mistress, in charge of my own affairs."

He hoped she meant financial affairs. He couldn't bear to imagine any other sort. "And you do not wish to remarry?"

"Why should I? It would only mean forfeiting my independence and allowing some man to make all my decisions for me. Thank you, no," she said with emphasis. "I am content to find happiness for myself."

She seemed sincere in her desire to be left alone, but as Edward looked down at her, the room seemed to fade around them. All he saw was Anne.

"I begged you to wait," he said softly.

Her dark eyes glistened up at him. "And I begged you to stay."

He shook his head ruefully and tried a smile on her. "It would appear neither of us is very good at begging."

She smiled back. A real one this time.

"No, nor are we likely to allow ourselves much practice at it. Once was enough to last my whole life long." She laid her fingertips briefly on his forearm. "I was sorry to hear of your father's passing. Lord Chatham was an esteemed gentleman."

An esteemed gentleman who didn't think she was cut from fine enough cloth to be his daughter-in-law. It was why the old earl had insisted with vehemence that Edward leave for his Grand Tour without waiting for the end of the Season, and specifically without proposing to Anne Spillwell.

"If your feelings for the young lady remain the same once you return, I shall not object," his father had promised.

Edward had never considered that Anne's feelings might be the ones that changed.

"I am surprised to see you here," she said. "As I recall, you are indifferent to music."

"It depends on who's playing."

"Fair enough." She tapped her cheek with her pointer finger.

Was that one of her glove signals? She'd tried to teach them to him once. By holding her gloves just so, she could communicate to him from across the room. *I am vexed*, or *Introduce me to your company* were as plain to him as if she'd said the words aloud. Provided he could remember the signals, of course. At the moment the only one that stuck in his memory was when she dropped both gloves. It was the signal that meant *I love you.*

Now her gloves remained firmly on her delicate hands.

"Am I right in assuming you have decided to enter the marriage market now that you have been elevated to your earldom?" she asked.

He'd always been an open book to her. There was no use denying it. "What if I have?"

"Then I should wonder which young lady has caught your eye."

Edward was barely aware of the almost involuntary flick of his gaze toward the base of the dais where Miss Finch was still being warmly congratulated on her performance.

"Oh, I see. Miss Finch, is it?"

"No, I—"

"Edward," she said sternly. "Remember what I said about falsehoods between us. You owe me a bit of candor, don't you think?"

"You're right." However severe her tone, it did him good to hear her call him Edward again. "On both counts."

"In that case, I should warn you that wooing Miss Finch will not be easy."

It certainly wouldn't be now that he knew Anne was no longer married. Still, he wasn't free to do as he pleased. Edward had responsibilities. He had to consider more than his own wishes. And Anne clearly didn't want him to pay her any address. In fact, she'd been quite vehement about remaining an unmarried lady.

"I trust that's not a comment on my worthiness as a suitor." Anne's warning aside, Edward didn't think it would be hard to win the hand of Miss Finch once he set his mind to it. It wasn't that he was too full of himself. He was simply under no illusions about his desirability on the marriage market. A peer of the realm, scion of a well-respected family, and, if he did say so himself, not at all a burden on feminine eyes.

"Oh, no, indeed," she said with a feline smirk. "Debutantes will likely swoon if Lord Chatham's mere shadow falls upon them. No, your difficulty will lie in convincing Miss Finch's sponsor. She fancies herself the girl's protector and will use every means at her disposal to keep her from being harmed."

"Harmed? You make me sound like the worst sort of cad," he protested. "And by your lights, this sponsor of hers must be a veritable she-dragon."

"Oh, she is," Anne said confidingly. "A bitter dowager, so they say, with a dismal view of men in general and ones who come courting in particular."

At that moment, Miss Finch joined them. "Did you hear, Lady Howard? I played well, didn't I?"

Anne gave her a quick hug. "You were brilliant, my dear. Now, allow me to introduce you to Lord Chatham. My lord, I have the honor to present Miss Martha Finch."

Wide-eyed, the girl bobbed in a deep curtsy. "Pleased to meet you, my lord."

"And I you." He returned her curtsy with a quick bow from the neck. The girl seemed much younger up close. Her cheeks were flushed and rosy, her nose sprinkled with a few freckles, and her eyes bright and innocent as a newborn fawn's.

She's such a child.

Edward would never see thirty again. While that didn't exactly make him ancient, he guessed Miss Finch was half his age. Edward knew it was common for titled gentlemen to take much younger wives, but, to his mind, this bordered on indecent.

In the awkward pause, he looked at Anne. Miss Finch didn't miss the glance.

"How do you and Lady Howard know each other, my lord?"

If she was that perceptive, perhaps Miss Finch wasn't as young as she appeared.

"Oh, Lord Chatham and I go back many years, don't we?" Anne said. "We're...very old friends."

He was feeling older by the minute.

"Good. I'm pleased Lady Howard knows you well," Miss Finch said. "Her opinion means a great deal to me."

"Very wise of you," he said with a slight nod.

"Well, it should, don't you think? After all, she is my sponsor. I rely upon her advice in all matters," Miss Finch said.

His gaze snapped to Anne. Her lips were spread in a broad smile, displaying her lovely white teeth.

A veritable she-dragon indeed.

Being a woman of independent means is not for the faint of heart, particularly when those means are not adequately matched to one's dreams.
—from the travel journal of Mrs. Hester Birdwhistle

Chapter 2

"Did I do well?" Martha demanded for the third time as Anne allowed the Finch footman to hand her into their waiting carriage. The girl was a dear child most of the time, but when it came to music, her perfectionism could be tedious. "Be honest. I rushed the arpeggio at the last, didn't I?"

"Your playing was fine," Anne assured her again. At least Martha's obsessing kept Anne from examining the way her insides still tingled after seeing Edward again.

Lord Chatham, she reminded herself sternly. It wouldn't do to allow herself to think of him in the familiar. So much had happened since she'd last seen him. So much time had passed. *Why, he must be over thirty now.*

He was no longer the young man she'd known, but Edward was still considered a gentleman in his prime. And she wasn't the same callow girl, though an unmarried woman of twenty-eight wasn't regarded as prime anything. Anne was a widow who wasn't actively seeking a husband. As such, she was an affront to the natural order of things, to the rule that decreed people must go through life as Noah's animals did.

Two by two.

"Fine? My playing was only fine?" Martha whined. "If that's not condemning me with faint praise, I don't know what is."

Anne sighed as the carriage rattled over the cobbled streets toward the fashionable Finch town house in Mayfair. "Compared to the other girls, you were a revelation. A veritable prodigy."

"But I don't want to be compared to the other girls. That's a very low bar indeed."

The girl didn't mean to be unkind, Anne told herself. Martha was simply the truthful sort and couldn't imagine prevaricating, even to spare another's feelings. It was one of the failings Anne had been trying to coax out of her. Truthfulness was admirable in small doses, but a little tact would go much further toward smoothing Martha's path in life.

"I'd much rather you compared me to the professional pianists you've heard," she said.

Anne sighed again. It had been a mistake to tell Martha about the wonderful concerts she'd attended, but when she first took the position as her sponsor, she'd needed a way to make the girl trust her and take her advice. They'd bonded almost instantly over their love of music.

Anne was glad she'd left out the fact that those concerts were in Venice, Barcelona, and Salzburg. Part of the charm of traveling independently was being able to please herself in the matter of entertainments. Sir Erasmus had never been one for the theater and had refused to take her abroad. So once he was gone, she'd taken herself, under an assumed name, of course.

Until her widow's jointure was cut in half by her stepson, Sir Percival.

Percy did not approve of her gallivanting ways. If she'd only return to Cornwall, he promised to reinstate her income in full—not that the entire amount was all that generous. Anne had to economize at every turn and find alternate means of supporting her wanderlust.

She certainly didn't relish living as simply as Percy would have her. His offer to increase her stipend included the caveat that she take up residence in the former gamekeeper's cottage on his Cornish estate. He promised to renovate it for her use, but it was hopelessly rustic. There was no chance of Anne becoming mistress of the dower house. Percy's grandmother was firmly ensconced in that elegant, if outdated home, and though it was expansive enough to have passed as a manor house on other estates, neither she nor Anne would find the space large enough for them to share.

The elder dowager had never approved of her son's second wife, and her opinion of Anne had not been improved by the way she'd gadded about since his death.

Anne's wandering ways were a well-kept secret, since Sir Erasmus's family took pains to keep it for form's sake. As far as London society knew, Anne had spent the last few years mourning in Cornwall instead of exploring the capitals of Europe.

When she finally popped up in London, Miss Finch's father met her at a poetry reading. He decided she was a respectable widow of exquisite taste and would be the perfect person to introduce his daughter to the right people. Martha's mother suffered from consumption and couldn't leave their country home for the insalubrious air of London. After engaging Anne's services as Martha's sponsor for the Season, Lord Finch returned to his wife, leaving his well-dowered daughter in Anne's care.

Once her charge was safely wed to a suitable gentleman, Anne would be paid a handsome fee. It would be enough to take her to the Americas for a few years, possibly even longer. She'd heard that Boston was becoming something of a city on the far side of the Atlantic, if one didn't mind rubbing elbows with the descendants of seditionists and Puritans.

"Come, Lady Howard. Tell me honestly. How did I do?" Miss Finch begged.

"You know you were brilliant. Your playing was not just technically perfect, it was heartfelt. Lyrical," Anne said as the carriage rolled to a stop before Lord Finch's town house. "In fact, if it wasn't indecent for a lady to play in public—"

"But isn't that just what I was doing this afternoon? What we all did?" Martha demanded.

"Not for money. There's the difference. A lady may play for her family and friends, but not for strangers. And certainly not for hire."

"But there were plenty of strangers this afternoon," Martha insisted as the pair of them alighted from the carriage and walked to the front door, which opened for them as they approached. One of the handsome footmen welcomed them back with a silent smile and took their wraps. Lord Finch's servants were the best sort—ubiquitous, willing, and very discreet.

"I knew very few of the ladies present and none of the gentlemen before today," Martha went on. "They were strangers to me and yet I played for them."

Once the girl latched onto an idea, she was like a dog with a bone. The pinch of a headache was beginning to form between Anne's brows. Martha was so full of questions. Anne knew the proper answers she should give her about the ways of the world.

The trouble was, she didn't believe in them for herself.

Still, Martha's parents were paying her handsomely to shepherd their daughter through her Season to a splendid match. Anne had hoped to spend the Season attending plays and gallery openings. After she became a widow, Anne had promised herself she wouldn't resort to the "done thing." Now something as plebian as serving as a permanent chaperone was what life required of her.

"A lady may not make a career of public performance," she said as she and Martha made their way to the parlor, where tea had already been laid out for them. "It's considered bad form."

"Why?"

Why indeed? Plenty of men achieved wide acclaim giving concerts throughout Britain. Martha's talent was easily equal to some of theirs. Were she a second son, it would be considered a perfectly acceptable method of making one's way in the world. Her gift was more than adequate.

Her gender wasn't.

"I don't know why," Anne said honestly. "I only know the rules for men and the rules for women are two entirely different things. It is decidedly unfair, but the world is thus. You may as well learn that lesson now."

"I don't see why I should." Martha settled onto the sofa and helped herself to a biscuit. "You haven't."

"Oh, yes, I have." Once she'd married the baronet, she'd learned quickly that while his bad behavior would be winked at, her conduct must remain above reproach. She ought not to express too much interest in the ideas of male authors, or even care to read in general. She must never go out in public to attend a lecture or a concert alone, but Sir Erasmus might keep any number of light-o'-loves with impunity.

It used to irritate her beyond bearing when she heard he'd taken his mistress to the opera. Not because he had a mistress, but because he'd never take *her.* If she'd actually cared for her husband, the situation would have been untenable. As it was, widowhood came as a welcome release. She had no idea how other women bore being treated as a mere appendage of a man, and not a very important one at that.

"The world may be unfair, but I don't think you've let that stop you from doing as you please, Lady Howard," Martha said with a sly expression. "I know who you really are, you know."

"What is that supposed to mean?"

Martha rolled her eyes. "You know perfectly well what it means, *Mrs. Birdwhistle.*"

"What?" A tingle of apprehension raked her spine.

"You needn't play coy with me. I *know*," Martha said. "You are Mrs. Hester Birdwhistle."

"But I can't be." Anne decided to brazen it out. If she couldn't cow a sixteen-year-old, she might as well retire to that gamekeeper's cottage and be done with it. "The lady is quite a bit older than I. Why, we attended one of her lectures on her travels only last week. You saw her with your own eyes."

Martha shook her head. "I saw someone, but she wasn't the real Mrs. Birdwhistle. You must pay her to give those lectures and sell your pamphlets. Is she an out-of-work actress, perhaps?"

Martha poured out some tea, laced it with milk and sugar just as Anne liked it, and offered her the cup. Anne took it so she'd have something to do with her hands. It wouldn't do to let Martha see them tremble.

"She does a fairly good job, by the way," Martha said. "But sometimes, she waffles when she doesn't know the answer to a question. You'd never do that."

Anne had removed her gloves and laid them across her lap before accepting the tea. Now she set down her cup and bunched the kidskin in a fist so tight her knuckles turned white. How could Martha have discovered her secret?

As if she'd heard Anne's thought, the girl said, "I saw the first draft of Mrs. Birdwhistle's next work on your vanity the other day."

"What were you doing poking about in my chamber, young lady?"

"Oh, no. You're not allowed to change the subject so easily. This is not about my behavior right now." Martha studied her through narrowed eyes. "If you are not the author, how did you happen to have an unpublished work by Mrs. Birdwhistle?"

Anne sank into the chair opposite the sofa. "She, ah...she asked me to give it a first reading before she sent it to her publisher."

"And she somehow wrote it in your hand?" Martha said with a grin. "Your capital *B*s have a particularly recognizable flourish."

Anne's lips tightened into a straight line. "Are you going to tell your parents about this ridiculous suspicion of yours?"

"Oh, it's much more than a suspicion, it's a fact. But heavens, no. Why should I tell my parents? They'd sack you at once if they knew I was being shuffled around London by a woman who travels the world unescorted. Who could blame them?"

"If that's how you feel, I wonder that you allow yourself to remain in the company of someone so..."

"Unconventional?" Martha supplied.

"I was going to say untruthful."

"Oh, I don't consider what you've done to be the least mendacious." Martha added another lump of sugar to her own tea and stirred it languidly. "I've watched you quite closely. You've taken pains not to lie directly. You've never actually said you spent the last few years in Cornwall. People merely assume you've been in seclusion."

"If you're right, and I'm not saying you are," Anne added quickly, "I didn't bother to correct them."

"If it's a sin, it's one of omission. I always think those are the easiest sort to forgive, don't you? Besides, it's their fault if they assume wrongly. And how kind of you to ignore the faults of others like that." Martha buried her nose in her cup for a quick sip. She emerged with a wicked grin. "I trust you'll ignore mine as well."

"Martha, this foolishness has to stop."

"It's not foolishness. I just want you to know that if I should wish to do something on my own, to go to a party or a private supper with artists and Bohemians and poets and free-thinkers, you must not only allow it, you must agree to cover my sins should the matter come to my parents' attention."

Anne set down her cup. She'd attended a few salons in Paris and been invigorated by sparkling conversations with artists and philosophers. However, it was a perverse truth that, after several bottles of wine, those events, which began with such lofty talk, tended to descend into lewd behavior, opium use, and total oblivion. Anne had always made it a point to leave as soon as the intellectually stimulating part of the evening wound down. It was one thing to frequent the demimonde in France under an assumed name. Anne would never attend such a gathering in London, because without a reputation, she'd have nothing.

And neither would a hapless debutante who wandered into one.

"No, Martha. I will not allow you to do that."

"But—"

"No buts. I won't take a chance with your safety or your good name. Your father may have more money than Croesus, but even he cannot buy back a tarnished reputation," Anne said with sternness. "If you feel the need to test me in this, I shall go straight way to your parents, and you shall find yourself back in Surrey before you can blink twice."

"If you do that, I'll tell them about Mrs. Birdwhistle," Martha threatened.

Anne stood. "You won't have to. I will have already told them your suspicions about me before I report your intention to behave badly. Do not think to bully me, Miss Finch. This is not my first Season and you are not nearly as clever as you suppose."

Tears gathered in the girl's pale gray eyes.

Anne came over to the sofa, sat down beside her, and put her arms around her. Martha began to sob. She might have a woman's body, but in many ways, she was still such a child. A headstrong child.

"There, now. Trust me, dear," Anne said. "I have your best interests at heart, you know."

"I know. For pity's sake, you just offered to destroy your own good name to save mine. But it's just...I'm not sure I wish to marry." Martha pulled a handkerchief from her sleeve and blew her nose.

"Of course, you do. All young girls dream of their wedding day."

"Did you?"

Anne nodded. But she certainly didn't dream her bridegroom would be Sir Erasmus.

Martha's tears dried up as quickly as they'd appeared. "Then why don't you wish to remarry? It's been long enough since your husband passed. You never talk about him, so I can't believe you mourn him still."

"Never assume you know what is in another's heart," Anne said. "Grief is a private matter. But you're right about one thing. Marriage is not for me anymore."

"Hmph! So even though it doesn't suit you, you believe I should marry."

"I do."

"Why?"

"Because the world is both grander and more tawdry than you can imagine, Martha." Not every woman was prepared to be responsible for her own life. Anne blamed the limited education her gender generally received. The most useful thing wellborn girls were taught to do was sew, a skill at which Anne had not excelled and thought a colossal bore, but it was at least a necessary accomplishment. Other than a smattering of conversational French, they studied no languages. No young lady of her acquaintance could converse with authority on scientific advancements or politics or philosophy. Anne was self-taught in those matters. She'd grasped an education for herself with both hands.

Worst of all, young women received no financial instruction, and Anne still struggled with handling her own funds. No one expected gentlewomen to be accountable for more than their pin money. The cook, who nominally consulted a lady of the house on weekly menus, was responsible for more household spending than her mistress.

"For most wellborn women, the best situation in the world is the protection of a good man," Anne told Martha. "And I intend to make certain you marry the finest of gentlemen."

Hopefully, one who won't break her heart, though that is an exceedingly tall order.

Martha cast her a sidelong glance. "Lord Chatham seems an amiable sort."

"Indeed, if one likes the type." Anne schooled her face into a passive mask because Martha's eyes were far sharper than she'd suspected. Even after all their time apart, there had been a definite spark between her and Edward that Martha might have recognized. The girl didn't need to know how seeing Edward—*Lord Chatham! I must think of him as Lord Chatham*—had upset Anne's sense of calm.

"The type? Oh, yes, I see what you mean," Martha said. "You're right. He is rather old, isn't he?"

"Lord Chatham isn't old."

"He's even older than you."

Anne scoffed. "Contrary to your opinion, I'm not exactly a toothless crone."

"No, but you act like one sometimes." Martha helped herself to another biscuit. Fortunately for her, she had the constitution of a hummingbird and could nibble on sweets all day without gaining an inch around her slim waist. "At balls, you spend your time with the other old ladies in the corner. Why don't you dance?"

"It wouldn't be appropriate."

"Because you're a widow?"

"No, it's been long enough since my husband died that no one would fault me for dancing." The swirl of silk, the touches and smiles, the heart-pounding sense of life coursing through her—Anne did miss it.

"Dancing would make you sad because it reminds you of Sir Erasmus?"

"Heavens, no." It would remind her of the night before Edward left. "I don't dance because I couldn't very well keep an eye on you if I was trying to keep some clumsy gentleman from treading on my toes."

"If I promise to be good as gold, will you promise you'll accept the next time you're asked to dance?"

"Martha—"

"Please?"

"Very well," Anne agreed. "If you promise to forget that nonsense about Mrs. Birdwhistle, I shall trip the light fantastic with the best of them at your next ball."

"Agreed. But Mrs. Birdwhistle is not nonsense. In fact, I'm rather pleased about your adventures." Then Martha put a finger to her lips and winked. "Quietly pleased."

When I feel this new life quickening inside me, I'm filled with joy. When I see my old life passing me by while I hide at home growing monstrously fat, I'm filled with despair. There truly is no happy medium for a lady who's increasing.
—from the diary of Caroline Lovell Sinclair, Lady Ware

Chapter 3

Caroline was grateful to be comfortably propped up with pillows and to have her husband, Lawrence, at her side. Usually, he'd have been giving her a foot rub, as he did at this time nearly every afternoon since she'd announced she was carrying his child, but as long as Miss Frederica Tilbury was present, such homely comforts would have to wait. Caroline was growing a bit dizzy watching her friend pace the parlor as she recounted the doings at her recital earlier that afternoon.

According to Freddie, her performance had been an absolute triumph. She hadn't missed a note. But Caroline was well acquainted with her friend's playing.

Oh, Freddie, dear, whacking each of them with the force of a miner's pick does not music make.

"Oh, Caro, I so wish you could have been there." Plopping down on one of the Sheridan chairs, Freddie finally ran out of both words and steam. She sighed in contentment as she helped herself to a cup of tea and took a sip. "Lady Daly said my playing was a wonder."

"The wonder of it was that her ears didn't bleed," Lawrence leaned toward Caroline to whisper.

"What was that?" Freddie asked as she set down her cup.

"Nothing." Caroline surreptitiously dug an elbow into her husband's ribs. "He was simply agreeing with you." Then while Freddie was mulling over her choices from the plate of biscuits, Caroline mouthed *Say something nice* to Lawrence.

Her husband grimaced but plowed manfully ahead. "Your playing... made everyone sigh."

While Freddie's attention was still on the refreshments, Caroline smacked her husband's chest with the back of her hand. He might be Lord Ware, a peer of the realm, and her lord and master before God and man, but when she'd fallen in love with him, he was simply Mr. Sinclair. If she held him in awe, it was on account of his sterling qualities, not because the world said she should. But aside from all that, the man had better not malign her dear friend if he wanted to remain in her good graces.

Even if his comment was truthful.

Freddie's playing does make everyone sigh...in relief when it's over.

"That's wonderful, dear," Caroline told her friend. "So the ladies present were fulsome in their compliments. Did any particular gentleman make a special effort to congratulate you on your performance?"

"As a matter of fact, I couldn't say there was any one particular gentleman."

"Oh," Caroline said, trying to hide her disappointment. This was Freddie's fourth Season. If she didn't find a husband this time, she might be permanently shelved while the Tilbury family trotted out her younger sister, who at eighteen was reportedly champing at the bit for her turn in Society.

Freddie smiled impishly at Caroline. "Actually, there were so many gentlemen waiting to speak with me, I lost count. Every unattached fellow at the recital fairly mobbed around me. Or I should say me and one other young lady. Miss Finch, I believe was her name. The others who performed were sadly ignored. Imagine that."

"Blame *The Bachelor's Bible*," Lawrence said under his breath.

Once again, Freddie seemed not to have heard him as she retrieved her cup and took another sip of tea. Caroline, however, sent her husband a pointed glare. When he'd first told her about the horrid pamphlet making the rounds at White's, and how Miss Frederica Tilbury's exceedingly generous dowry was marked with several asterisks, Caroline had been furious with the entire male half of the species. How dare they reduce her dear friend to nothing more than a number followed by a good many zeroes?

It was positively indecent.

Granted, Frederica needed whatever help *The Bachelor's Bible* could give her. But putting such an obvious monetary label on her hand would only bring out the worst sort of suitors.

"Oh!" Freddie said, as she set down her teacup on the low table again. She was normally quite adept at balancing the saucer on her knee, but she was still so excited, she was more fidgety than usual. "Lord Chatham was there."

"Teddy?" Caroline was the only person in the world who called Lord Chatham by her childhood pet name for him. She claimed the right as his favorite sister. The fact that she was Edward Lovell's only sister didn't diminish the privilege one jot. "He's never been one for music."

"Perhaps he had another reason for being there," Lawrence said cryptically.

Could her confirmed bachelor brother be looking for a wife? This was news Caroline could definitely use. Helping Teddy find just the right lady to make his countess would be an excellent diversion. Of course, the fact that Caroline had retired from public life on account of being with child would make it more difficult to arrange the perfect match for her brother, but she lived for a challenge.

"Well, it did seem that Lord Chatham and Lady Howard knew each other," Freddie said. "I was told they spoke for quite some time. Perhaps your brother was there to see her."

"I didn't know Lady Howard was in London. That's what comes of languishing at home all day." Caroline patted her belly and the next Earl of Ware gave her palm a kick.

"Who is this Lady Howard?" Lawrence asked.

"Anne Spillwell was her maiden name. When her father was knighted for service to the Crown, she came out and fairly took the ton by storm," Caroline said. "You and I were a few years behind her, Freddie. We were maybe thirteen or so when she made her début. But I remember all the adults around me talking about her when they didn't think I was listening. They'd have branded her a social climber except that she was so very natural and charming. And I must admit, she left quite an impression on me when I met her."

"If you were only a few years past playing with dolls, how did you meet her?" Lawrence said.

"Miss Spillwell was a frequent guest at Lovell House before Teddy and Lord Rowley left for the Continent."

"Oh, yes, I remember her now," Frederica said. "She was a real beauty—a diamond of the first water everyone said, even though at the time, Horatia said her family wouldn't be considered good ton for a couple more generations, at least. Why is that, I wonder?"

"Oh, you know how Horatia is," Caroline said, straightening her spine and continuing in her best imitation of their absent friend at her imperious best. "If one can't trace one's lineage back to William the Conqueror, one can't claim true aristocracy, and—"

"And now Horatia's married to a sea captain," Freddie finished for her. Their bosom friend, Horatia Englewood, like Freddie, had been through a number of seasons without a proposal. Then finally an offer for her hand had appeared. Captain Woodcock wasn't titled, but as a military man, he was still considered a gentleman, and therefore, an acceptable suitor. Especially for a young lady who'd had no other offers. But Horatia's children, should God grant the couple any, wouldn't be considered part of the ton at all.

So Horatia, who'd lived for gossip and societal intrigue, was now sailing toward the Orient, where her husband's ship would be stationed. She was living out Caroline's dream of traveling the world, whereas Caro's life had become the embodiment of Horatia's hopes—being a lady of title with an adoring, moneyed husband, mistress of a lovely town house and country estate, and to bring her happiness to fullness, a child on the way.

God, Caroline decided, as the unborn infant squirmed inside her, *has a singularly perverse sense of humor.*

"But back to my brother," she said. "I recall Teddy being terribly smitten with Miss Spillwell back then, and to all appearances, she returned his feelings. At least, I thought so at the time, but it seems I was mistaken."

"Mark the date," Lawrence said with a grin. "My wife was mistaken."

"Very droll, dear. Is that how you speak to the mother of your heir?" she said archly.

"Not a bit," he said in a contrite tone. "I only meant your being wrong is as rare as...as a unicorn sighting."

"That's better." Caroline scrunched up one of the tufted pillows that decorated the sofa and stuffed it behind her back. The little tyrant in her belly was dancing on her spine. Perhaps this was why expectant mothers stayed home. Out in public, there was never a pillow around when one needed it. "In any case, nothing came of Teddy and Miss Spillwell. He hared off on his Grand Tour—"

Lawrence broke in with, "And then I met him in Italy."

"And I'm ever so glad you did, dear. We'd never have met otherwise."

Caroline laid a palm on his cheek for a moment and he covered her hand with his own. It occurred to her that she and Freddie had been leaving Lawrence out of the conversation, but if he was going to be a father, he ought to become accustomed to it. A new mother couldn't fuss over her husband as much as a new wife could. At least, that's what her mother had told her.

"So the journey that brought me happiness when you and Teddy became friends may have cost my brother his." Caroline gently tugged her hand away from Lawrence. Perhaps later this afternoon, she'd give him a foot rub for a change. She might as well spoil him while she could. "At least, it would have, if my brother and Miss Spillwell had been as enamored of each other as I'd thought. Not long after Teddy left, she married Sir Erasmus Howard from Cornwall, of all the backwater places."

"She wasn't his wife long," Frederica informed her. "She's his widow now."

"Is she? Evidently, what happens in Cornwall rarely makes news in London."

"According to Lady Ackworth, Sir Erasmus died in '16, and, as it happens, he *was* in London when Death took him. Unexpectedly, Lady Ackworth said. Almost suspiciously," Freddie added. "You were probably too busy with other things that year to have taken notice."

"I suppose I was," Caroline said. "Young girls do seem fascinated by their own doings to the exclusion of all else."

"In addition, I overheard Lady Ackworth sharing something else about Lady Howard just today. And I don't need to tell you that if Lady Ackworth says a thing, we may trust its veracity," Freddie said. "In truth, it was the oddest thing. I don't know what to make of it."

Normally, Caroline eschewed gossip, but since her confinement, what else did she have to do? "What did she say?"

"That Lady Howard would have her hands full keeping the wolves from her little lamb."

"That is odd," Caroline agreed.

"Especially because everyone knows there haven't been wolves in England since the time of Cromwell," Frederica added. "And to my eye, Lady Howard didn't look the sort to keep livestock of any kind."

"Freddie, I suspect Lady Ackworth was speaking metaphorically," Caroline said gently. "Did she say anything else?"

"Only that Lady Howard would certainly earn her pay over Miss Finch."

"Ah," Lawrence said, rising to stretch his legs with a short trip to the window to peer out to the street. He likely wanted to escape from feminine nattering but wasn't sure how to do it without giving offense. "Would this be the eighty-thousand-pound Miss Finch?"

Or perhaps he doesn't care whom he offends!

Caroline knew immediately what he meant by eighty thousand. The girl's monstrous dowry was common knowledge thanks to that hateful pamphlet. Lady Ackworth's statement was plain enough now. *The Bachelor's Bible* had made Miss Finch as vulnerable as the weakling of the flock to the wolves of the ton. Caroline picked up the horribly embroidered pillow she'd labored over for weeks and threw it at her husband. "I'll thank you not to recite chapter and verse from *The Bachelor's Bible* in my house!"

"What in the world?" Frederica said, eyes wide with astonishment. Caro suspected her friend was ignorant of the existence of that awful pamphlet, so Freddie must have been shocked that she'd thrown a pillow at Lawrence. Caroline and her husband were usually such a close couple, their friends often joked that it was impossible to slip so much as a handkerchief between them.

"It's nothing, Freddie. Don't mind me." She shot an apologetic glance at her husband. "Ladies who are increasing are given to sudden odd notions."

"Truer words were never spoken." Lawrence crossed the room, caught up one of her hands, and pressed a kiss on her knuckles. "Remind me to make sure you're surrounded by nothing more lethal than pillows until you are delivered, my love."

Caroline's ire fizzled as quickly as it had kindled. Forgetting Freddie was even in the room, they leaned toward each other for a real kiss.

"Oh, wait! I understand, now," Frederica announced in triumph, unaware that she'd interrupted a private moment between her friends and just as oblivious when they sprang apart like a guilty pair of young lovers caught in an alcove behind the drapes. "I know exactly what Lady Ackworth meant. Lady Howard is Miss Finch's sponsor and chaperone, you see, so Miss Finch is the lamb. Lady Howard is responsible for her. When all the dandies line up to charm Miss Finch, they will have to earn Lady Howard's approval first."

"How clever of you to figure it out, Freddie."

Her friend beamed. Frederica was often described as extremely pleasant, but rarely as clever.

"Perhaps Lady Howard could use some assistance in culling the herd of bachelors clamoring for her charge's attention," Caroline said, leaning back into the couch.

"What are you thinking, my love?" Lawrence asked as he settled beside her once again.

Gingerly, Caroline thought. *I really ought not to throw pillows at the man.*

The babe shifted positions and now made her wonder how she could gracefully excuse herself for a quick trip to her chamber pot.

Honestly, there are so many reasons women "in confinement" willingly confine themselves.

"I believe we should host a dinner party," Caroline announced.

Lawrence raised a hand in caution. "But your condition—"

"Nothing too taxing—I promise. We'll make it a party of eight to ten. Twelve at the most. We'll invite Lady Howard and her protégé, Miss Finch."

"And me?" Frederica asked hopefully.

"Of course, you little goose," Caroline said fondly. "That goes without saying. Whom would you like us to invite to sit next to you, Freddie?"

"Oh, I shouldn't like to say. It's your party."

"Didn't any of the gentlemen who attended your recital stand out in your mind?"

"Only Reverend Lovell."

"Benjamin?"

Freddie nodded.

"Then call him by his name, dear," Caroline said. "After all, you've known my brother Ben since you were in leading strings."

Ben was the next eldest son behind Edward, and the true musician of the house of Lovell. He and his violin had filled countless family evenings with delightful melodies. Though Caroline found his playing divine, Ben didn't count himself talented enough to make music his occupation.

Neither did Edward. Oh, he found his brother's playing perfectly acceptable, but Edward thought Benjamin would soon tire of fiddling for his supper as a professional musician. He regarded it his duty as Lord Chatham to make sure his younger siblings found a respectable way to support themselves. So it was decided the Church was the best fit for the second of the five Lovell brothers.

After Ben finished his Oxford studies, Edward had seen his brother comfortably placed in a parish church within a half day's ride from London. Caroline never considered Ben as the particularly devout type, but his parishioners loved it when he pulled his violin from under the lectern after the benediction and played the postlude as he strode the aisle to the nave. When they queued up to shake his hand and depart in peace, there were always more positive comments on his music than his homily.

"You say Ben praised your music, Freddie?" Caroline asked, trying to conceal her surprise. Ben would know the difference between playing and pounding.

"Now that you mention it, no, not in so many words," Frederica admitted.

"Then what did he say?"

"That I should consider a different instrument."

"What instrument did Ben suggest?" Lawrence asked.

"The bagpipe."

Caroline choked back a laugh.

"Benjamin said he thought I'd be a natural." Freddie beamed, totally missing the insult.

"Very well, if you're sure you want him there, I suppose I can put Ben on the guest list," Caroline said.

If only so I can drag him by the ear into a corner and scold him for picking on my friend.

Normally, Ben was kindness itself to Freddie because their families were friends and they'd known each other all their lives. Caroline couldn't imagine what had gotten into him.

"I have already invited Bredon to supper on Saturday," Lawrence said, still not accustomed to calling Edward by his newer title.

"Saturday will be splendid," Caroline said. "I just need to round out the guest list."

"I believe Bredon may be interested in Miss Finch," Lawrence said.

Caroline arched a brow at him. Teddy must have said as much or Lawrence would never have offered that information.

"Is he?" Frederica said doubtfully. "I wouldn't have said so. They barely exchanged pleasantries. At least, that's what I heard. In fact, the earl spent a good deal more time talking with Lady Howard."

"Did he, indeed?" Caroline said.

"But if he's to have any chance of private speech with Miss Finch, you'll have to invite someone to keep the girl's chaperone occupied," Lawrence said.

"Oh, don't worry. I shall have it all sorted by the time our guests arrive. Never you fear, my love." Caroline smiled into her husband's dear face and mused that the old wives' tales were right. Men really didn't perceive things as well as women, not even when those things were directly under their noses. "Trust me. I already have someone in mind for Lady Howard."

Beware of Greeks bearing gifts, they say. 'Tis a pity Virgil didn't think to warn us of sisters as well.
—from the journal of Edward Lovell, Earl of Chatham and honorary Trojan

Chapter 4

"Teddy! There you are." As soon as Edward surrendered his coat and topper to Dudley, his sister's footman, he heard Caroline calling to him from the bottom step on the grand staircase. If he didn't know better, he'd swear she'd been waiting there for him to arrive, poised to make her own perfect entrance. Diamond pins sparkled in her hair, encircled her slender throat, and dripped from her ears, as befitted a countess. Dressed in a lovely green silk that did its best to disguise her delicate condition, Caroline swanned her way across the expansive foyer to greet him.

No, one can't say Caro swans *anywhere at present*, Edward thought. Her gait more closely resembled that of a duck, as befitted a lady in the latter weeks of her confinement. Still, his sister had never looked more radiant.

"Motherhood becomes you," he said as he kissed both her cheeks.

"Oh, you mean this pesky little melon I'm carting about?" She patted her belly. "This isn't motherhood. The real work, I'm told, will start once the tiny darling makes his appearance."

He tucked her hand into the crook of her arm and began escorting her toward the parlor, where he surmised Sinclair would be waiting. "Undoubtedly, you're right."

"Of course I am. Hold fast to that opinion, dear brother. It will serve you well."

Edward heard a number of voices coming from the parlor, a low nattering like a flock of geese. Someone must have told an amusing tale, for the whole party suddenly burst into peals of laughter.

"I thought this was to be a quiet family affair. I hope you haven't gone to too much trouble," he said. "A lady in your condition—"

"Should never be told she's gone to too much trouble," Caroline finished for him. "I'm fine, Teddy. A small dinner party requires very little effort on my part."

"Somehow, I doubt that. You were never one to do anything by halves."

"Honestly, the hardest part of this evening was finding a pair of shoes I could still squeeze into," she said with a laugh as they continued their stately walk toward the parlor. "All I did was write up a few invitations, and our wonderful staff did the rest."

"Speaking of your staff, I notice Dudley is back at his post as a footman. I take it he didn't work out well as Sinclair's valet."

Edward felt a twinge of guilt over Dudley. The handsome young man had been a less-than-adequate second footman at Lovell House. He fell asleep at his post near the door, broke serving dishes, and once he even dropped a spoon down the back of a lady's gown. And if not for the intervention of the family's excellent butler, Mr. Price, Dudley would have plunged his hand in after it! However, even after all that, because Dudley was Price's nephew, Edward had been loath to dismiss him.

So he'd fobbed Dudley off on Sinclair when his friend needed a valet and couldn't afford one. He salved his conscience by continuing to pay Dudley's wages, making it a perpetual wedding gift once Sinclair married his sister. Edward considered it an eminently practical expense and would never think of economizing by cutting it. The payments ensured against Dudley returning to service in *his* home.

"Actually, Dudley grew into the valet's position quite nicely. His demotion back to footman was at his request." Caroline dropped her voice to a whisper lest Dudley overhear them discussing him. "As valet, he worked closely with my lady's maid, Alice, which was fine as long as they were sweet on each other. It was less fine after he conceived a tendresse for our neighbor's scullery maid. But never fear, I have hope for Dudley and Alice yet."

"Ah, the perils of a belowstairs romance," Edward said. "I wonder that you should concern yourself with it."

"It's not as if I can go to the theater at present, brother. I must take my entertainment where it comes," Caroline said with a devious smile. "Why shouldn't I be interested in the lives and loves of those who serve me? Besides, tonight will be ever so much more entertaining than Alice and Dudley's ill-starred liaison."

"Why is that?"

"I shall have the pleasure of an orchestra seat for your romantic endeavors. Miss Finch is already here."

"Your husband tells you too much, I see." Edward didn't know whether to be more insulted that she should find his plan to court the young lady amusing, or that he had been lumped in the same category of diversion as Dudley and her lady's maid. "So I'm here to entertain you, am I? Alas! I left my hurdy-gurdy and monkey at home."

Caroline laughed musically. "Nothing so ridiculous, Teddy. I want to help. That's why I organized this party when Lawrence told me you've turned your eye toward the lady."

Edward pressed his lips together. Sinclair had never been one to carry tales, but he couldn't blame him. If she set her mind to it, Caro could wheedle state secrets from the most closemouthed diplomat and make him think baring his soul was his own idea.

"You've rushed your fences, sister. I'm only *considering* paying court to Miss Finch. Nothing has been decided," Edward said testily. "Kindly keep even that intelligence to yourself, if you please."

"Of course, Teddy. If word got out that the Earl of Chatham was seeking a wife, you'd be inundated with so many invitations, you'd scarce have time to think. However, because Lady Ackworth was in attendance at that recital, where you made it a point to speak to only one of the debutantes who performed..."

"Word of my interest in Miss Finch is already public knowledge, I gather," Edward said morosely.

"We may safely assume the ship of your wished-for secrecy has sailed," Caroline said. "But Lawrence and I are happy to help you proceed quietly in your conquest."

"Emphasis on quietly, please."

"Of course. Everything will turn out right. You'll see." She reached across her belly to lay a hand on his forearm, but despite her encouraging words, a frown creased her brow, and she sighed.

"Caro, are you ill?"

"No, dear brother," Caroline said breathlessly. "This is not illness. It's impending motherhood. I simply tire more easily."

He grasped her elbow and tried to steer her along. "Here, let me help you to a chair."

"No need. I can find my own way. Dudley has placed side chairs strategically throughout the house because, as he observed," Caroline did her best imitation of Dudley's untutored Cockney, "'M'lady has become like a rabbit, she has.'"

"How so?"

"Evidently, every time I stop, I sit." She gave him a wan smile. "But if you would do me a favor, Teddy, dear..."

"Anything." Seeing her paleness and obvious fatigue, Edward was powerless to deny her anything.

Sinclair must feel like this every minute of every day since he learned she was bearing.

"I believe a guest or two may have wandered into the solar before you came. I was just going to retrieve them myself as it's nearly time to go through to the dining room, but..." She sighed again and sank into a side chair Edward hadn't noticed was there. Dudley was earning his keep, after all. "If you wouldn't mind playing sheepdog."

"Say no more. I'll gather up the wandering lambs and we'll join you shortly."

"No need to rush. Lawrence insists I do everything at a snail's pace these days. I appreciate it when others slow to match me." Caroline waved him away. "Take your time. Supper will wait."

Edward had no trouble finding his way to the solar. Lawrence and Caroline's home was on the same row of terrace houses as his, so the interior plan was nearly identical. But while their home was furnished in the sleek classical lines that were fashionable now, his décor still bore the stamp of his mother's tastes and the fussiness of the previous generation.

A wife would likely fix that.

Edward often used a ledger sheet to make important decisions, tallying up pros and cons. He decided to put the fact that a wife would see to it that his home more accurately reflected his sensibilities in the pro column.

Particularly a wife who comes with eighty thousand pounds.

The monetary consideration also belonged in the column dedicated to Miss Finch's favor.

Then he batted the idea away as unworthy of him. Yes, his interest in the baron's daughter was predicated on her monstrous dowry, but he refused to entertain such mercenary thoughts for longer than it took for them to flit through his mind.

It was undignified. Belittling to all involved.

And unfortunately, true.

The arrangement Edward was considering wasn't unusual. Many gentlemen of his acquaintance had wed for financial reasons, and it had never struck him as particularly tawdry.

Merely practical.

He wondered if the situation would seem different if he went to the girl's father directly and made his case, gentleman to gentleman. Even in that scenario, he was offering himself and his title for mere money. Oh, yes, there was a girl involved, but because he didn't know her beyond nodding acquaintance, she scarcely signified in his decision. Eighty thousand was a princely sum, to be sure, but whether it was eighty or eight, he couldn't shake the feeling that he was selling himself cheaply.

There was a word for women who did that. He wondered if it ought not to apply to him as well.

A solution occurred to him as he walked through the music room on his way to the solar. If he could only bring himself to care for the girl, even a little, perhaps the exchange would seem less distasteful. Edward wouldn't have to conceive a grand passion for her. Mere fondness would likely ease his conscience.

How hard can that be?

The solar was situated near the back of the house on the ground floor. It faced south to gather as much warmth from the low-hanging winter sun as possible during the cold months. As summer was near, it was more important to keep too much heat out of the space than to coax it in, so the large windows were covered with heavy drapes. Potted ferns and several flowering plants gave the room a distinctively earthy scent that was quite pleasant. It reminded Edward of his country estate, which he loved so well. He missed Chatham Park every time he was required to leave it for Town.

At first, he didn't see anyone in the room, but then his nose twitched to a new scent. It was vanilla, with a hint of rosemary and a low note of cinnamon. The perfume was unusual, yet familiar somehow, though he couldn't place it exactly.

Whoever was wearing it was smelled good enough to eat.

The stone walls farthest from the windows served as a gallery for a number of family portraits. There in the dim lamplight, his eye was drawn to a slight movement. A woman was standing before a painting of his father, shifting her weight from one foot to the other, as if she were swaying to music only she could hear. Her dark hair was so heavy, the chignon gathered at her nape pulled her head back and tipped her chin up a bit.

It was Anne.

Lady Howard, he corrected himself. No good would come of thinking of her as his Anne. She'd made it quite plain that she was not the same girl he'd known.

"Good evening," Edward said as he crossed the room to stand beside her. She wasn't startled by the sound of his voice. It was almost as if she were expecting him.

Even though standing at her side meant he was close enough to realize she was the source of that delicious fragrance, it was safer there than across the room. If he stood beside her, he could focus his attention on the painting and not get lost in casting his gaze over her slender frame or marveling at her graceful bearing. She'd always reminded him of a prima ballerina—her weight balanced on the balls of her feet, leaning slightly forward, as if she might suddenly sprout wings and take flight.

"It's a good likeness of him," he said. "Don't you think?"

"I disagree." She stopped swaying and stood with perfect stillness, gazing at the portrait. "I'm not sure the artist has captured the previous Lord Chatham at all. Not the spirit of the gentleman, in any case."

She was always direct. It was one of the many things he'd loved about her.

Appreciated, he corrected himself again. *Not loved.*

He couldn't let himself dwell on the confusing emotions he'd felt for her all those years ago. And he definitely didn't need to be thinking about love and Anne Spillwell in the same—

Howard, he told himself with force. *She's Lady Howard now. You'd do well to remember it, you birdwit!*

"I recall your father as being...bigger, somehow," she went on.

Edward was grateful she was unaware of the silent argument he was having with himself. After all, he seemed to be losing.

"My father *was* larger than life," he agreed. It saddened Edward to think how much the old earl's illness had shrunken him at the last. "Life, however, has a way of catching up to all of us."

"Is that why you've decided to go courting, my lord?" she asked. "Because life has caught you up?"

This was dangerous ground. If he was as candid as she, he'd have to admit he was considering Miss Finch and his main interest in the girl was her dowry. Not only would it lower him in her eyes as the girl's chaperone, Anne would see how shallow he'd become, too.

Why did she have to turn up in London just now? Why did she have to be the Finch girl's sponsor? And why the devil does she have to smell so good?

Most women felt duty-bound to fill an awkward silence with meaningless chatter. Not Anne. Once she asked a question, she waited for an answer. However long it took.

"Regarding marriage, there comes a time in every gentleman's life when he must consider something other than himself and his own wishes."

There. That's better. It doesn't make me sound like a completely selfish toad. "Since I became Lord Chatham, I think of the needs of the estate in all that I undertake. The choice of a wife is no exception."

To his great consternation, and no small surprise, Anne laughed.

"Did I say something amusing?"

"For Heaven's sake, my lord, you make it sound as if you're trudging toward martyrdom, not matrimony."

He frowned down at her. "You've been married. Can you honestly recommend it?"

"For some, yes."

"For whom? I rarely see cases of unabashed marital bliss."

"If that is your subtle way of asking whether I was happy with Sir Erasmus, the answer is no."

The toadish bit inside him hopped up and down and cheered. Not that he was glad Anne had been unhappy. He wasn't as callous as that. But he was secretly grateful that she hadn't been happy with someone else.

Sweet Lord, I am the king of selfish toads.

"In my experience," she said, choosing her words with care, "marriage yields more benefits for the male half of a couple."

"Was your husband unkind to you?"

"Not always."

He bristled, fists clenched, because "not always" meant the lout had been cruel to her sometimes. Edward wished the man were still alive so he could have the pleasure of beating him half to death.

"Be easy, my lord, you've a vein bulging in your neck. You're like to pop the button on your collar," Anne said wryly. "In my late husband's defense, I should add that he wasn't aware when he was being unkind. He was simply being himself." Even though the corners of her sweet mouth still turned slightly up, her tiny smile was sad. "Marriage is but a small part of a gentleman's life, they say. For ladies, it is supposed to be all."

And was it all of your life? Did you love him? Why didn't you wait for my return?

If he let the first question out, the rest would tumble after it, as surely as an overstuffed wardrobe spilled its contents into a room when the latch was lifted.

"You seemed in a great hurry to marry," he said cautiously. Was it to punish him? If he could understand why she'd wed in such haste, perhaps it would quiet his soul a bit. "Especially because you couldn't have known Sir Erasmus long."

"What can I say? Women are trained from birth to regard marriage as their sole reason for living. The baronet proposed and I accepted and there's an end to it." A shadow passed behind her lovely dark eyes. "It seemed the right thing to do at the time."

"Was it?"

"I was ever so much younger then, and quite often the young are not nearly as clever as they think themselves." Then she seemed to cast off her momentary melancholy and smiled up at him.

Edward still recognized her repertoire of expressions. This was her brave smile. He wished he hadn't made her feel she had to raise that particular shield.

"I imagine Lady Ware is holding supper for us, isn't she?" Anne said.

"She is." Edward offered her his arm and was relieved when she just took it without any further fuss. "I'm told it doesn't do to keep a woman in a delicate condition waiting."

She let him lead her toward the doorway. Finally, they were doing something ordinary, something normal with each other. They were simply two old friends—that was how she had introduced him to Miss Finch, after all—going to supper together. Just talking with her had been exhausting because he was constantly weighing her words for hidden meanings, trying to read her expressions, and guarding his own tongue lest he say the wrong thing. Now they were just walking together.

The relief he felt was palpable.

However, if he thought Anne would let him skate away easily, he was mistaken. She stopped as they reached the solar's threshold.

"Lord Chatham, do not think for one moment that our previous association will influence me in the slightest concerning my current obligations."

He frowned in puzzlement.

"I will not allow anyone to hurt Miss Finch," she said, her jaw clenched. To be honest, he'd nearly forgotten about the girl. "I would never—"

"You would never mean to, Edward. I know your heart and it is a good one," she said softly, sounding like the girl he'd known. When she'd called him Edward, his chest grew strangely warm. Then her voice strengthened into the unwavering tones of a woman who knew her own mind and believed he should know it, too. "But intentions and outcomes are rarely the same thing. Be forewarned. Do not trifle with Miss Finch. Let your yea be yea and your nay be nay. Tell her the truth in all things, Lord Chatham. It's supposed to set one free, you know. Do the girl the courtesy of honesty. That is all I ask."

Then she abandoned Edward's arm and strode away to find the dining room on her own.

"The truth, she says," he muttered to himself. "I can just hear the proposal truth would have me offer. Miss Finch, would you do me the honor of joining your eighty-thousand-pound dowry to the House of Lovell? In exchange, you'll be honored as my countess and the mother of my future heir, but we have so little in common that calling this a true marriage would be the worst sort of farce. It is a business arrangement, neat and simple." The longer he allowed the pent-up words to tumble out of him, the louder he spoke. "I have no affection to give you. My heart is no longer mine. It was given into another's keeping and she has it still, though she's the impulsive sort, given to marry any fool who'd ask her, so she may well have misplaced it." He was shouting now, feeling as hot and disheveled on the outside as he did on the inside. "Oh, what total rot!"

With that, Edward stormed out of the solar, slamming the door behind him so hard, the panes in the windows rattled.

In a few heartbeats, someone stepped out from behind the largest of the potted palms.

It was Reginald Dickey, the bon vivant, the hanger-on, and easily Lady Ackworth's equal as a gossipmonger.

"You're right, Lord Chatham," he said with glee. "That particular truth will most assuredly *not* set you free."

Dinner parties are rather like ocean voyages. Some are graced by fair winds, smooth seas, and sunny skies. Others are marred by sudden squalls and are likely to run aground on a treacherous shoal. It is a wise dinner guest who keeps a weather eye on the glass to mark whether the quicksilver is rising or falling.

—Lady Howard, writing as Mrs. Hester Birdwhistle

Chapter 5

Anne discovered that Lady Ware was nothing if not thorough in her planning, even down to the seating arrangement of her guests. Lord Ware occupied the head of the table, of course. Miss Finch had been seated on his right. Anne was pleased at this mark of favor for the girl. There was an empty place to Martha's right.

No doubt Lady Ware has reserved that spot for Edward. At that close range, Cupid's dart can't fail to strike.

Anne tried to ignore the way heat crept up her neck at this thought, but she couldn't stop the spreading prickliness.

"Are you unwell, Lady Howard?" her hostess asked as they took their seats. "You seem flushed."

"No, I'm fine. It's just...it's an exceedingly warm evening for May."

For pity's sake! Edward Lovell is turning me into the worst sort of stereotype. Look at me, talking about the weather instead of owning how the man cuts up my peace.

Miss Tilbury was placed at Lord Ware's left hand, thankfully, nowhere near a piano. Next to her, Rev. Lovell took his seat. The young man was one of Lady Ware's other brothers, whom Anne vaguely remembered from years ago. Benjamin had been a bright boy with a musical bent. With his mischievous smile, she wasn't sure what sort of minister he'd make.

A card with Anne's name had been placed next to the vicar, and instead of taking the ornate chair at the foot of the table as was customary, Lady Ware had seated herself across from her. Anne was pleased that her hostess would still be close enough for conversation. She remembered Caroline Lovell from the time she and Edward had been courting, and looked forward to renewing their acquaintance. She was a few years older than the countess, but while it had made a difference when Anne knew her before, the gap between them seemed much less now.

The footman held her chair. By the time Anne had taken her seat, Edward appeared in the dining room doorway. She knew him to be a self-contained sort of man, never one to advertise his feelings, but at the moment his face was like a storm cloud.

No one else seemed to notice. Anne watched him master himself, schooling his features into his usual expression of half-bored graciousness. Even so, he fairly stalked into the room, moving toward the open seat next to Martha.

"No, brother dear," Lady Ware said, gesturing toward the seat she normally would have occupied at the table's foot. "I've given you a place of honor right here between Lady Howard and me. Handsomer than that, you couldn't wish."

"A thorn between roses, as it were," he said with self-deprecating charm.

"Oh, but we don't see you as a thorn, Teddy, do we, Lady Howard?"

"A weed, perhaps," Anne said, swallowing down the knot that had formed in her throat as she joined in her hostess's light banter. "Something a little bit prickly and difficult to eradicate, but certainly not a thorn."

Lady Ware laughed. Edward did not.

"Then who is sitting there?" He nodded toward the empty place between Lady Ware and Martha.

"I suspect that would be me," came a voice from behind him. Edward turned to face Reginald Dickey, who was leaning on the door jamb, one ankle hooked over the other. The man examined the nails on his right hand, buffed them on his lapel, and then grinned at the assembled dinner guests.

Edward smiled back at the newcomer.

At least, Dickey seems to think it's a smile.

Anne recognized that Edward was merely baring his teeth.

"Ah, Lord Chatham. It appears you were not expecting me. No matter. Neither was my father," Dickey said with a laugh, as he make his way around Edward and settled on the other side of his sister. The rest of the guests, with the exception of Edward, joined Dickey in good-natured chuckles. Part of Reginald Dickey's charm was that his humor was often directed at himself. And when it wasn't, his sarcastic barbs toward those who richly deserved them were so wickedly funny, even Lady Ackworth had been known to quip that every dinner party could benefit from the presence of a proper bastard.

Edward settled into the chair his sister had assigned him and scraped its feet on the gleaming hardwood as he pulled it closer to the table. Frustration seemed to radiate from him in roiling waves.

Anne wasn't sure whether it was because she'd upset him in the solar, or whether he was feeling thwarted in his pursuit of Martha here in the dining room. Sometimes, when she looked at him, she could see the soul of the man she'd loved shining through his eyes so clearly; it was as if the years and the choices that had separated them melted away. Then at other times, like now, he seemed an unreadable stranger.

Either way, just being in the same room with Edward Lovell made her feel as if her stays were too tight. It was hard to draw a deep breath.

Anne forced herself to focus on her place setting. The china was lovely, the silver sparkling, and the crystal as fragile as a butterfly wing. Lord and Lady Ware certainly knew how to entertain.

But not how to make their guests comfortable.

If Lady Ware had tried, she couldn't have given Anne more cause to be on pins. And not just over Edward. Anne appreciated Dickey's dry wit as much as the next person, but what could her hostess have been thinking when she'd seated him next to Martha Finch?

Dickey might be accepted by the ton, but Martha's parents certainly wouldn't accept him as a suitor for their daughter. A title was paramount in their minds. They expected her to become "Lady Someone" by the end of the year. It was all spelled out in the agreement Anne had signed when they'd engaged her services.

The butler filled all their wineglasses, and Lord Ware raised his in toast.

"To your health, my good friends, and may joy and laughter follow," he said. The gathering chimed in with "Hear, hear."

Eyeing Benjamin Lovell's dog collar, Dickey added, "Careful now 'bout too much laughter. A vicar's present. Will a sermon come after?"

This brought laughter from everyone.

Except Edward.

"I thought it might be fun if we got to know one another better by having a conversation with just one other dinner guest for the length of each course," Lady Ware said to the company at large. "For the soup and fish course, each lady will converse with the gentleman on her right. For the meat course, we will switch to the left."

"And after all that twisting back and forth, are we to stand on our heads, Lady Ware?" Dickey quipped.

"Perhaps," she said with a smile. "I shall let you know once the dessert arrives. Ah! Here comes Dudley with the tureen. Bon appétit!"

That meant Martha would be chatting with Reginald Dickey until the last drop of white soup and the final fillet of sole was gone. Then Anne's charge would converse with Lord Ware once the meat was served.

Perhaps that won't be too bad, Anne mused. The meat course would last far longer than the soup. She still hoped word that she had allowed Martha to dine with the illegitimate son of a duke—albeit an acknowledged, well-connected, ever-so-pleasant-to-be-around son of a duke—would not reach her parents' ears.

Once her soup bowl was filled and a poached sole stared its baleful eye up at her from the fish plate, she turned to Rev. Lovell to begin conversing as their hostess had dictated. Sly grin notwithstanding, Benjamin seemed the shy sort, but Anne had long since learned that the way to engage any man in conversation was to ask him about himself. He answered with surprising loquaciousness. She listened with half an ear to the vicar ramble on about his time at Oxford, while Edward and his sister held their own furiously whispered exchange.

Unfortunately, Anne could only catch one word in three of their conversation. However, she heard enough to glean that Edward was decidedly not pleased with the way the evening was progressing.

"So, after meeting with the parish committee," Ben was saying, "I decided to come to London and partake in the Season for my own safety."

"Pardon me, what? Your safety?" Clearly, trying to eavesdrop on Edward had made her miss something of great import in her conversation with the vicar.

"Perhaps I should say for my bachelorhood's safety," Rev. Lovell amended. "Don't mistake me, I am happy to serve my parish, but, in truth, a single vicar is in as much peril as a fox on hunting day. Every family in the shire with an unmarried daughter has been beating down my door."

"I had not thought it would matter to a congregation if their vicar wasn't wed," Anne said between spoonfuls of the well-seasoned soup. She detected a hint of nutmeg among the more savory spices, and made a mental note to ask Lady Ware for her cook's receipt. "I remember with great fondness the old gentleman who served my village church. He was a single fellow. His sister kept the manse for him and tended their garden. As I recall, she headed a number of the charity organizations, and ran the altar guild as well. Come to think on it, she did fulfill many of the duties of a vicar's wife. In any case, no one ever insisted he be married."

"The difference in our situations is that my sister would never run an altar guild," Rev. Lovell said, casting a fond glance across the table at Lady Ware. "Much less keep house for me."

A snort escaped Anne before she could stifle it as she tried to imagine Lady Ware on the business end of a broom and dustpan.

"And I believe you said your vicar was elderly," Rev. Lovell added.

"Oh, I see. Yes. I take your point." A young man of the cloth would be irresistible to matrons in the shire who hoped to find a settled situation for their daughters. "So does that mean you do not wish to wed at all?"

"Not necessarily. The Good Book says, 'Whoso findeth a wife findeth a good thing.'"

To Anne's amusement, the reverend actually blushed. She decided she really liked Edward's younger brother.

"I'm not in a position to argue with scripture," he went on. "I just don't want my future helpmeet decided upon by the parish committee."

"Understandable. Do you have a young lady in mind?"

He nodded, and his voice dropped to a whisper. "I don't wish to name her yet, but the young lady I hope to make my wife is participating in the London Season."

Anne didn't wish to dampen his spirits, but for most debutantes, life as a country parson's wife would seem terribly dull after the whirlwind of London. Not to mention that their families would probably be angling for a prospective son-in-law who possessed more of an income than a vicar's living would provide.

"I know what you're thinking," Ben said.

"Ah." She presented him with her brightest smile. It was usually enough to disguise any thought she might be entertaining, even the most wicked. "Are you a mentalist as well as a minister?"

"You're thinking a second son isn't much of a catch," he said.

"As you're a man of the cloth, I'll not dissemble," she admitted. "It crossed my mind, but I confess it as an unworthy thought. I'm sure you have sterling qualities."

"I'm Anglican, not Catholic. No confession needed here." He scraped up the last of his soup. "Though come to think on it, if I were a Catholic priest, no one would be trying to force me to marry."

"Well, I wish you joy in your romantic endeavors, Reverend."

"Please, call me Ben. So few do these days, I'm beginning to forget it's my name."

Anne decided she liked Edward's brother even more.

"And you must call me Anne. I believe you used to when..." She wasn't sure how to end her sentence. *When your brother was my sun, moon, and stars? When I was more smitten than wise? When I thought I understood men in general and your brother in particular?*

She was grateful when Ben rescued her with, "I do remember you, Anne. I was a bit young for it, but my parents allowed me to go with Bredon to a house party once where you were also a guest. You and I were paired in a three legged-race and we carried the day."

"Oh, yes. I'd almost forgotten. Didn't Edward and his partner end up going tail over teakettle into the lake during that same race?"

"They did." Ben laughed at the memory with her.

"Am I allowed in on the joke?" Edward asked.

"I don't believe it's time for us to switch partners yet, my lord," Anne said with coolness.

"Near enough," Edward said and signaled the footman to remove his soup bowl.

Anne wished she were wearing gloves. She'd bite the tips of them to give him the signal for *I wish to be rid of you.* But even if she'd had gloves, he'd never learned those signs well enough to make them a reliable means of communication. So she leaned toward him and lowered her voice to a whisper. "You are being rude."

His eyes widened in surprise.

"It's all right, Anne," Ben said. "The soup course is nearly over. I'll just see if I can talk with Freddie while the meat is being served."

Not only was he on a first-name basis with the young lady, Ben used a pet name for her. The vicar was full of surprises.

"Freddie?" Anne said, cocking her head at him.

"Miss Tilbury, I should have said. She and I are...old friends."

Something about the way Benjamin said "friends" made her inner lie catcher quiver, but he was a vicar. Surely he wouldn't prevaricate. She turned back to Edward.

He was alternately avoiding her gaze and glaring at Dickey.

"Well, my lord, you obviously wished to speak with me. What have you to say?"

Courtship is a ritual devised for and by women. The rules are as convoluted as a Gordian knot. A man would have settled matters in a much more direct fashion, like Alexander, cutting through the nonsense with one good slash.
—from the private journal of Edward Lovell, Lord Chatham

Chapter 6

What did he want to say to Anne? Words tumbled over one another on their way to his lips and formed a wall in his throat. He found himself unable to speak.

There was so much that needed saying. He wanted to explain things to her. He wanted her to explain things to him. His head hurt from trying to understand how events had gone so horribly wrong all those years ago.

But maybe the past didn't signify as much as the present. And presently, she seemed to regard him with suspicion.

Why was she so set on never marrying again?

Or maybe it wasn't Anne he should have it out with.

God was the one Edward really ought to talk to. After all, if a sparrow could not fall without His notice, how had God allowed the timing for him and Anne to go so hopelessly awry? Why would a loving deity bring Anne back into his life when, once again, he was not free to follow the dictates of his own heart? However, Edward decided he'd delay that conversation with the Almighty as long as he could. He suspected it would be less than cordial on his end.

A short hiatus in the dinner saved him from making a total ass of himself. The entire party waited quietly for the course change to be completed.

After the soup and fish were cleared away, the footmen removed all the place settings and replaced the white tablecloth with a green one for the next course. Great platters of roast beef, a rack of lamb, and a pork loin were presented along with several different vegetable accompaniments. Then the china, silver, and stemware were reset. Fresh wineglasses were filled with a red vintage for the meat course.

"Thank Heaven for the extended intermission in this gastronomical play," Dickey said, raising his glass in a mock toast. "My stomach needed the time to digest the first act."

The rest of the diners chuckled at this. Edward simply scowled. He'd never forgive Dickey for his obvious delight when he'd brought the news that Anne had wed.

Their plates were filled by the attentive footmen. Edward was pleased to see that Dudley acquitted himself fairly well. He didn't drop a single utensil.

Then once the servants stepped back to take their places of silent vigil, ready to spring into action should a diner need something, the dinner guests all turned to their new conversation partners for the meat course.

A single violinist strolled into the room and began to play.

It was thoughtful of Caro to arrange for music. It meant that his soft conversation with Anne would be less likely to be overheard.

"You interrupted my time with your brother in order to speak with me," Anne said. "Now it seems you have nothing to say."

He couldn't very well ask the questions that fairly scorched his tongue—not in so public a place—so he searched about for something innocuous to talk about. What was safe?

Caro had always told him the best topic when one didn't know what to say was...

"How...how did you find the weather in Cornwall?"

She stared at him for a few heartbeats. Anne must have known he was dissembling, but she was too well bred to call him out on it.

"Cornish weather is like most gentlemen of my acquaintance." She speared a chunk of beef with vehemence. "Changeable."

He deserved that. He should have known better than to try to stay safe with Anne.

After a few minutes of silence, she said, "I didn't mean to eavesdrop on parts of your conversation with Lady Ware, but I must admit you didn't seem pleased with your sister over something."

"It's all right if I'm out of countenance with my sister at the moment." He glanced at Caroline, who was having a spirited debate with Dickey, over something frivolous, no doubt, for they both seemed to be enjoying their banter. Dickey was being his clever, entertaining self, as usual. "Caro is not particularly pleased with me either."

"Did I hear you ask why she invited someone?" Anne said. "You didn't mean one of the other gentlemen, did you?"

"Ben? No, I've no problem with my brother being here. Besides, if you must know, I believe Frederica requested him." He hoped that tiny bit of gossip would steer her to a different topic.

"No, not Ben." Anne flicked her gaze toward the other male guest and rolled her expressive eyes. "I assume you are discomfited by the presence of Mr. Dickey."

Edward couldn't argue the point, so he took an oversized bite of pork to keep from having to answer.

"You shouldn't be. He's harmless, and in no way detracts from your pursuit of Miss Finch," Anne went on. "Dickey is an amusement and an excellent foil for you, actually. You have so many things to commend you."

"Like what?"

Anne smirked at him. "Are you really so starved for praise that you need me to enumerate the ways in which you are superior to Mr. Dickey? Very well. You've a grand title, land and houses, and—"

Edward made a noise that even to his own ears sounded suspiciously like a grunt.

"And no discernible sense of humor," she finished.

He frowned at her.

"If you don't want truth from me, perhaps we should eat in silence," she suggested. "It's supposed to be good for the digestion."

Edward didn't think poor digestion was responsible for the burning in his gut. "All right. I'll have the truth, if you please. Why are you doing this?"

She batted her eyes in feigned innocence. "I believe making conversation was your sister's idea."

"No, I mean why did you agree to take charge of Miss Finch?"

She balanced her knife and fork on the edge of her plate and folded her hands in her lap.

"I know it is beneath the notice of a gentleman of your station, but to those of us who live below your rarified level, ready coin is a thing much to be desired," she said in clipped tones. "I'm being well compensated for helping Miss Finch through her Season."

"Anne, if you are in need of—"

"You'd give me money, Edward?" she interrupted, arching an expressive brow at him.

If only she'd keep calling him Edward, he'd give her his heart's very blood. "Whatever you need, Anne. All you have to do is ask."

She gave a small, surprisingly ladylike snort. "Oh, I very much doubt that's all I'd have to do. Gentlemen who give women money always expect repayment, in one form or another."

"That's not what I was suggesting."

"Wasn't it?"

"I would never..." He couldn't finish the sentence because it wouldn't be true. He'd take Anne any way he could have her.

The idea hadn't occurred to him until that moment, but he suddenly realized if he married Miss Finch, he'd be well able to afford to keep Anne, too. Most gentlemen of his acquaintance kept a mistress, some of them for longer than they kept their wives. And with more devotion.

It was a way he and Anne could have a life together. Of sorts. He'd set her up in a snug home of her own, close enough to be convenient but far enough from Lovell House to be discreet. She'd never want for anything. He'd see to that. He'd be with her every moment he could spare.

Edward could picture them sharing cozy private suppers, long languid nights, and dewy-eyed mornings. It might not be ideal, but being with Anne would make it idyllic. Though he couldn't give her his name, she'd have his heart.

"Whatever you're thinking, stop it," she hissed.

"You've no idea what I'm thinking."

"Yes, I do." She met his gaze unflinchingly. "Because I'm thinking it as well. Plenty of women might jump at the thought of becoming your light-o'-love—"

"There'd be nothing light about it."

In a furious whisper, she went on as if he hadn't interrupted her, "But I am not one of them. I do not like what that sort of arrangement makes me."

"But you just admitted to thinking about it."

She bit her bottom lip. He wished he could do the same. The remembered taste of her slammed back to him with the force of a gale.

"Thinking and doing are two entirely different things," she said.

"Anne, I can protect—"

"You misunderstand me, my lord." No more Edward. By milording him, she'd raised a barrier between them. "Do not think I fear society's censure."

He shook his head. "You are a veritable lioness. I doubt you fear anything."

"You're wrong in that," she said. "I'm afraid of being powerless and at the mercy of another's whim."

"You would never be a whim."

"No, I won't. Because I shall never allow myself to become one. Never again," she said. "Besides, there are other ways of procuring the funds I require, ways which do not require selling my integrity."

"Such as?" Edward wished he could see a way to raise the money the estate needed without selling his.

"This, for one. Being the chaperone and advisor of a fine young lady is a worthy use of my time. A respectable use."

Anne reached for her goblet and took a sip. When she did, Edward's gaze was drawn to her white throat. He ached to place a string of kisses along her jaw and down that sweet, soft skin, but he forced himself to stop imagining what he wanted to do to Anne, and instead to attend to what she was saying.

"If I do well by Miss Finch, doubtless other families will want me to help their daughters," she finished.

"That doesn't sound like a very exciting life, always arranging for the happiness of others."

Anne shook her head. "Oh, I shan't take on a new girl every Season. Only when I have need of more funds. Between engagements, my life will have plenty of excitement."

"What will you do with yourself when you're not putting a debutante through her paces?"

She smiled a small, feline smile. "Every woman is entitled to a few secrets, my lord."

Edward wished he knew hers. At one time, he thought he did.

"You know, it occurs to me that we could help each other," she said. "If you are serious about pursuing Miss Finch, perhaps I would be willing to help steer her toward you."

"Why? You warned me off in the solar." Now she seemed in a great hurry to push him toward a wife. Didn't she care for him, even a little?

"Because..." Her eyes glittered for a moment and he thought she might be about to tear up. Then she mastered herself and went on, "Because you're a good man. You'd be a good husband. And I would have fulfilled my duty to the Finches."

"Anne." He slipped his hand under the table and reached for her left hand, which still rested on her lap. She wore no gloves at the dining table, so her fingers were bare. His thumb made small circles on the back of her hand. Her skin was even softer than he remembered.

"Don't," she said, but made no move to tug her hand away. If anything, it seemed she lifted it into the soft strokes his thumb was delivering. Her hand trembled. "Please."

She feared being powerless, she'd said, and that's how he'd made her feel.

Edward had rarely experienced shame. Young lords were not raised to regard their desires as shameful, but he felt it now. It flowed over him in all its hot misery.

He released her hand.

Caro clapped hers together. "Time for the dessert course, and, while the board is reset, it is time for us to reorder ourselves, as well. Ladies, you may remain seated. Gentlemen, stand, if you please."

Edward and the other men rose to their feet while Dudley and the other footman quickly removed the goblets, china, and silver. Then they folded up the green tablecloth and left the gleaming mahogany table bare. Fresh linen napkins, dessert-sized plates, spoons, and aperitif glasses were set all around before the footmen disappeared to retrieve whatever sinfully delicious trifles the Ware cook had conceived for them.

Edward hadn't tasted much of his meal, but he was sure that was his fault, not his sister's kitchen staff.

"Now, gentlemen, kindly shift to the seat previously occupied by the gentleman to your left," Caroline said. "So, Lord Chatham, you will take Mr. Dickey's place, and so on."

"Hold a moment. Surely I'm not to displace Lord Ware," Dickey said. "A man like me sitting in an earl's place of honor? If that won't curl the *ton's* toes, I don't know what will. Perhaps we should leave his lordship where he is and I'll boot the good reverend from his seat. He won't mind. His lot is used to turning the other cheek."

To punctuate his remarks, Dickey smacked his own bum, and the others chuckled. Nervously, this time. Edward glowered at the man for dancing so close to lewdness in mixed company.

Before Caroline could object, Dickey did as he'd suggested and took the seat between Frederica and Anne. Ben, always amiable, gave way to him and moved to the chair at the foot of the table that Edward had just vacated.

"Well, that will be fine, I suppose," Caroline said.

Edward narrowed his eyes at Dickey. *That slyboots has managed to wiggle his way next to Anne to spite me.*

But Edward didn't want to be the cause of any unpleasantness at his sister's party. Sinclair had told him with regularity that it was not good to vex a woman who was increasing.

As the only girl in a houseful of boys, Caroline frequently got her way. Privately, Edward thought Caro was milking this confinement for all it was worth.

"Let me think," Caro said. "For the last course, the ladies conversed with the gentlemen on their left. Shall we go right this time? Oh! I see a problem with that. Lord Ware and Miss Tilbury have already shared a course. Freddie, dear, be a lamb and trade places with me."

"Of course." Then once Frederica sat in Caroline's seat, she said, "But Rev. Lovell and I have already shared a course, as well."

"Oh, but you won't mind another will you, dear? Ben, I'm counting on you to entertain my friend," Caroline said in a tone that brooked no refusal. As she settled into the place next to her husband, she and Dickey exchanged a quick smile.

It occurred to Edward that a conspiracy might be afoot. The two of them had colluded to maneuver Frederica and Ben into spending more time together. If it was true, his favorite sister had also been part of putting the ton's "proper bastard" next to Anne.

Edward was now positioned on Miss Finch's right and would be her partner for the rest of the meal. For the life of him, he couldn't think of anything to say to the girl.

He was saved by the arrival of the desserts—iced orange slices, blancmange à *la vanille*, and a nougat almond cake. The dainties smelled like heaven on a plate and were almost too pretty to eat.

Miss Finch, however, fell upon hers as if she had been starved in the woods for a week. Then she requested a second slice of cake before Edward had finished his first. If she kept going at this rate, the girl might be mistaken for a Rubens model before she was thirty.

Edward cleared his throat.

"Have no fear, Lord Chatham," she said, as though he'd spoken his uncharitable thought aloud. "However much we eat, the women in my family do not run to fat."

"How...fortunate for you."

"Actually, my lord, I was thinking you might consider it fortunate for you."

Bone of my bones, and flesh of my flesh, indeed. Adam was an idiot.
When God presented him with Eve, he ought to have politely declined.
—from the journal of Edward Lovell, Lord Chatham

Chapter 7

"It makes no difference to me should you wish to eat a dozen cakes," Edward said. First, Anne had tempted him by turning his thoughts to adultery. Then Miss Finch made him imagine her with a sugar cake in each hand, ballooning into portly middle age. Truly, he was surrounded by women who invaded his mind and inserted thoughts that were wholly inappropriate for dinner in polite company. "I would never presume to comment upon how much a lady eats."

"Perhaps not," she said with a shrug of her narrow shoulders. "I simply wanted to set your mind at ease."

"My mind is..." *Surprisingly empty at the moment.* "Suffice it to say I wasn't at all concerned about your eating habits."

"Oh! That is good to know," Miss Finch said between bites. "Mr. Dickey expressed the opinion that I ought to eat like the bird for which my family was named. But he's wrong because birds eat quite a lot actually, pound for pound a good deal more than people do."

"Mr. Dickey is frequently mistaken. He doesn't seem to realize God gave us two ears and but one tongue," Edward said. "There's an inherent lesson there."

"Yes, but a tongue has two uses—speech and taste, so perhaps one might count that member twice."

He glanced at Anne—lovely, unreachable, completely kissable Anne. Miss Finch should count the tongue three times. Edward could think of at least one other use for his.

"I can't think of a second use for my ears," Miss Finch said.

Obviously, no one has ever nibbled on them. Again, Edward's gaze strayed back to Anne before he forced it to return to the pleasant, but unremarkable, face of Miss Finch.

He was trying to find something to like about the girl, but so far, she wasn't giving him much to work with.

"I suppose," she mused, waving her fork in the air, "if the Finches were a poor family, the fact that we seem not to be able to carry excess weight would be considered a curse. But because my father, Lord Finch, is more than comfortably situated, I've always been able to eat my fill. The fact that I can indulge in the appetite of a horse while maintaining the frame of a gazelle is a blessing."

Or perhaps it's a tapeworm, he thought. But all he said was, "Quite."

Any other response would make matters worse and surely prolong this particularly odd topic. Edward didn't care what else they discussed as long as it wasn't Miss Finch's gustatory practices. Anything would be an improvement.

"That is not to say that despite our slenderness, we Finches aren't a prolific lot," Miss Finch said between bites of orange. "My mother gave birth to eight healthy babes, six of them sons, and has buried no children. My parents count themselves lucky in that regard." She cast a glance at him. "How many children do you hope to have, my lord?"

Edward nearly choked on his bite of cake. He was wrong. This topic was definitely worse. "I suppose I hope for however many children the Lord grants me."

"Hmph. That's rather more pious than one might expect from an earl," Miss Finch said. "I don't know the particulars required to produce children, you understand. It's astounding how the world conspires to keep young ladies in ignorance about such matters. Even Lady Howard says so, though she refuses to educate me in this subject as well. However, I'm quite certain a husband has more to do with how many children a wife has than the Lord does."

From discussing overeating to wondering aloud how children were conceived, Miss Finch obviously had no intention of sticking with approved topics of conversation. Edward was beginning to see why her parents had hired Anne. The girl definitely needed a keeper.

"Lady Howard is someone you can trust," he said, hoping to steer the conversation in a safer direction. "You'll do well to heed her advice in all matters."

"Do you say that because you think she'll advise me to accept your proposal?" She grinned at him, like a tabby before a mouse hole.

"I do not recall having offered one."

"If you don't, you may be the only eligible bachelor in London who doesn't," Miss Finch said. "I say this not because I'm conceited. Exactly the opposite. I have no illusions about my lack of beauty. In fact, the only thing that commends me, besides my dowry and my skill at the pianoforte, is my honesty. However, as Mr. Dickey has informed me, I seem to be the, let me see...how did he put it? It was so very clever...oh, yes! I'm the favored filly in this Season's steeplechase."

"That's a rather common way of saying it." Edward shot a glare toward the offending Dickey that ought to have rendered him a smoldering pile of ash. It wasn't because of his comment to Miss Finch. Dickey was saying something to Anne that made her laugh.

When's the last time you did that, you clodpate? He couldn't remember. Anne might have laughed *at* him a time or two, but not because he'd said anything clever on purpose. He'd yet to see her give him a genuine smile since she'd reentered his life.

Miss Finch popped the last orange slice into her mouth. "As Mr. Dickey would be quick to point out, he *is* common, so he's likely to say common things. What else may we expect?"

"You would do well not to heed Mr. Dickey."

"I'd do well here. I'd do well there." The girl rolled her pale eyes. She had plenty of lashes, but they were so blond as to be almost invisible. "Honestly, Lord Chatham, don't you ever want to *not* do well?"

"With astonishing regularity." He forced himself not to look at Anne.

To his surprise, the girl laughed.

The devil of it was, once again, he wasn't even trying.

When did I become such a buffoon?

To Edward's great relief, Caroline announced that the ladies would adjourn to the music room for cordials. "The gentlemen will join us after they've had their port."

"Oh, dear," Dickey opined. "Here I was hoping I might join you as well, but if it's to be gentlemen only..."

"That includes you, Mr. Dickey," Caroline assured him with a grin. "We're counting on you to lead us in rhyming riddles."

"Oh, good. I thought one up just today that will suit our present company better than jam and cakes."

"Excellent. Ladies, shall we go through?"

* * * *

With Martha at her side, Anne followed Lady Ware and her friend Miss Tilbury to the well-appointed Ware music room. In addition to a splendid Broadwood & Sons square piano tucked into one corner, there were several music stands and a number of chairs that could be arranged for an impromptu concert. Opposite the pianoforte, a full-sized pedal harp stood on a small dais.

"What a lovely harp," Anne said to her hostess. "Do you play?"

"No, as my husband and brothers could tell you, there's nothing the least angelic about me," Lady Ware answered as she perched on one of the chairs, "but I keep hoping one of my guests will be able to play it someday."

"Someday is today, Lady Ware," Martha piped up, and then settled on the seat next to their hostess. "Lady Howard told me she plays."

Anne shot her protégé a frown. She'd only mentioned the harp in passing when she was trying to establish a rapport with the girl. Clearly, whatever Martha knew, she felt obliged to share with the world. Anne would have to guard her tongue more carefully around the girl lest something more important than harp playing slip out.

Lady Ware leaned forward, an expectant smile on her face. "Is this true?"

"If it is, how lovely," Miss Tilbury chimed in. "Perhaps we can play a piano and harp duet. Tell me, do you know 'Robin Adair'? It's a cracking good air with a bit of a Scottish lilt."

Anne could only imagine how Miss Tilbury's pounding of the keys would demolish anything with a lilt. "My repertoire was more classical than popular, and I haven't played for years. In truth, my fingers haven't touched the strings since my Season."

Once she'd married him, Sir Erasmus refused to move her instrument to his Cornish estate. His wife, he told her, would be more useful plucking chickens than harp strings. He was a firm believer in maintaining a deep connection with the land that was the main source of his family's wealth. Which meant the baronet worked alongside his tenants during harvest time and kept a small farmstead of livestock and a huge vegetable garden specifically for the needs of the manor house as well. He never actually required Anne to pluck chickens, but when he took away her harp, he took her last link to beauty, the romance that had infused her London Season, and a tangible reminder of her feelings for Edward.

Anne always suspected Sir Erasmus knew that.

"So you play the harp," Lady Ware said admiringly, obviously not heeding Anne's denial. "I had not recalled that about you."

"Obviously, your mother didn't drag you out to one of my interminable recitals."

"Won't you play for us?" her hostess urged. "Please."

"I honestly don't think I remember how," Anne said.

"You may not," Miss Finch said. "But I'll wager your fingers do. Truly, sometimes I haven't the foggiest notion of where a piece is going, but somehow, my hands know and it all comes out right. Do give it a try, won't you?"

Once, Anne's life had been filled with beauty and the expectation of exquisite joy. She'd been young and an acknowledged beauty and had discovered the aching breathlessness of first love. Nothing embodied this heady time in her past so much as the music of her harp.

Anne needed no more coaxing. She settled herself so the fine instrument fit between her knees, and then tipped it back to let the frame rest lightly on her shoulder.

It felt right. When she positioned her hands near the strings, she discovered Martha was correct. Her fingers seemed to move of their own accord. Unerringly, they found the haunting Boccherini tune that had been the main melody winding through Anne's younger life. Her hands remembered.

And she did, too. As she closed her eyes and let the music take her, she allowed herself to remember everything.

* * * *

She stood in the midst of the moonlit garden, hugging herself to keep from bursting out of her skin for pure joy. The tiny walled space behind her family's town house was overgrown with vine-hung arbors and tall hedges. It was private enough that no one was likely to see her even if anyone in the house should be awake at this hour to glance out the windows.

The moon, that shimmering coquette, slipped shyly from behind one bank of clouds to the next. When the shining disc stopped playing the flirt and shone down on her in full glory, Anne raised her slender arms in the silver light. In that moment, she understood why the ancients had worshiped the moon.

The distant orb kissed her with a kindly light. It smiled down on her, sharing her joy.

Edward had asked her to meet him there.

She'd let her hair down and combed it out before she had slipped silently into the garden. The night that had seemed crisp earlier now turned balmy. Anne gathered her hair and held it up in a long tail so the night wind could breathe on her nape.

She closed her eyes and imagined it was Edward's warm breath teasing the curls along her hairline. Just thinking it made her shiver, but not with cold.

What was keeping him?

The evening had been perfect. Edward had been entranced by her harp playing. In fact, the way their gazes locked when she finished, it was as though they were the only people in the room and she'd played just for him.

Then when the dancing began, he'd partnered with her for more sets than was proper. They were scandalizing the matrons of the ton, but she wouldn't exchange those breathless waltzes for the approval of all the Lady Ackworths in the world.

Edward had dined beside her at supper. She couldn't remember exactly what they'd talked about, mostly clever nothings, she supposed, but there hadn't been any awkward silences. Indeed, all Season long they'd seemed to finish each other's sentences. She knew Edward's heart. She knew what he'd say about something before he said it.

More than once during the evening, the base of her spine had tingled for no reason. When she'd lifted her head, she would discover that he was watching her.

It was like a touch, that warm gaze of his. She felt it all over.

People whispered that their match was a misalliance of the first order. He was heir to the Earl of Chatham, she the daughter of a newly made baronet. Her father might have earned the gratitude of the Prince Regent, but he was rewarded with little other than a new "Sir" before his name. Anne's dowry was miniscule indeed when weighed against the tiara of a countess. Everyone said there hadn't been a more off-balanced pairing in recent memory.

Edward told her he didn't care. He only wanted her.

What was that tune that had been playing when he pulled her into an alcove and begged her to meet him later in the garden? Something by Boccherini...

She hummed a few bars of it and then began to dance, moving to the music that continued only in her mind. Sinuous and slow, she circled the splashing fountain, turning gracefully on her toes, arching her back so her face was bathed in liquid silver.

Then the tempo of the music in her mind changed and the dance became a frenzy of twirls and undulations no dance master had ever taught her. She ached as she had never ached before. She wanted...desperate, wicked things, she was sure, but she wanted them nonetheless.

Without knowing exactly what it was she longed for.

Anne thought she might die of wanting. Her father's gardeners would find her body in the morning amid the lavender and rosemary, and wonder how she'd come to die with such longing stamped on her young face.

Then her dance stopped suddenly as she collapsed in a dizzy heap. There was a rustle behind the gorse bush near the garden gate. She stayed perfectly still, scarcely daring to breathe.

Then Edward stepped from the shadows.

Anne raised her head to meet his gaze. A flash of knowing sparked between them. He'd been watching her the whole time.

She had danced for him. Not the moon.

He strode toward her, and she rose to meet him. But when he was an arm's length from her, she raised a hand to stop him. This was too dangerous. Too forbidden.

She wanted him anyway.

"Do you love me, Edward?" she asked.

"God help me, yes," he whispered back. "I do."

She smiled and stepped into his arms, molding herself against him. Even though she'd been the one dancing, his skin was covered with a fine sheen of perspiration. The scent of the garden clung to him. He smelled of musk and earth and green growing things, or maybe she did. It was hard to tell where one of them ended and the other began.

Edward found her mouth and joined his breath to hers in a kiss tinged with desperation. Her soul broke free and flowed out of her body to mingle with his. They were so tangled up together, it was a bond too complete to sever without damage to both of them.

Without knowing how it happened, she found herself kneeling on the fragrant grass with him. He worshiped her with his mouth, reveling in the small sounds of helpless pleasure that escaped her when he sucked and nipped at her neck and earlobes.

And when he parted her gown and moved lower...

Anne didn't stop him. She didn't care that it wasn't right. She didn't care that she risked all. This was what she wanted.

She lost herself in him. He'd heard the rhythm of her secret music, moving in time with that silent melody. He knew exactly what she needed.

She took all of him as he emptied his love into her, all his hopes, his desires, all he was. Anne gave herself to him in return with no thought for what might come of this night.

Afterward, they lay twined together without speaking. The stars wheeled overhead and the smiling moon blessed them.

* * * *

Anne was startled by the applause. While she was playing the harp, she'd been back in that garden. It was a terrible jolt to find herself in Lady Ware's music room with so many people looking at her with enthusiasm and pleasure stamped on their faces. At some point the gentlemen must have joined them, for Lord Ware, Rev. Lovell, and Mr. Dickey were all clapping and calling for an encore alongside the ladies.

Only Edward stood silent, hands by his sides, near the door.

Ready to leave. Again.

The moon was never a goddess. It was only a cold, lifeless rock. She forced herself to remember that, but her body began to remind her how it was to lie in Edward's arms, what it felt like when he called her "Beloved," and how it hurt when he left. The memories made her ache, but not a pleasantly needy ache. She was hollowed out. Used up.

I will never worship the moon again, she promised herself.

There are seasons in a woman's life when familiar stars grow cold. Those are the times to seek a new sky.
—Lady Howard writing as Mrs. Hester Birdwhistle

Chapter 8

"Do play another, Lady Howard. Please," Martha urged.

"No, I don't remember any more." Anne didn't dare remember. Not with Edward in the same room, breathing the same air. She'd been incredibly stupid on that moonlit night. She owned that now, but she still felt that undeniable pull toward him. When the man was near, she more readily forgave her younger self her folly.

Or at least, understood it better.

"Well, perhaps it's for the best if you don't play any longer," Dickey said. "Tempting us with angelic music is hard on us mere mortals. Such beauty is more than any man can bear. Don't you think, Lord Chatham?"

Edward's gaze never left her. "For once, Mr. Dickey, you and I are in complete agreement."

"Perhaps we should alert the *Times*. Such rare accord between the likes of his lordship and myself is not like to come again," Dickey quipped.

"What shall we do now?" Miss Tilbury asked. "Shall I play the pianoforte?"

"No," Lady Ware and Reverend Lovell said with force and in unison. Then Anne's hostess went on in a softer tone, "I thought we'd play some parlor games now that the gentlemen have joined us, Freddie dear. I believe Mr. Dickey is prepared to be our games master."

Games, Anne thought as she tried to ignore Edward's hot gaze on her. *As if I haven't had enough of those in my life.*

"Indeed, I am ready to lead you all in frivolity, Lady Ware." Dickey sketched an elaborate bow. "Thank you again, Lady Howard, for that ethereal music. As the French are wont to say, 'From the sublime to the ridiculous there is but a step.'" He spread his hands before himself and shrugged. "And here I am at the very bottom of the stairs."

Most of the company chuckled at Dickey's gentle poke at himself. Anne smiled politely. Edward shoved his hands in his pockets and studied the tips of his shoes.

It's as if he can't bear to be here. He doesn't want to join in. He won't pay court to Martha. He insults me at supper with the suggestion that he'd offer me carte blanche.

Anne wished the idea hadn't tempted her so.

Edward should just go ahead and leave. It's what he does best.

"So here is my rhyming riddle to tickle your brainpans," Mr. Dickey said. "I beg to put before you a conundrum whose answer is a word of two parts."

Dickey folded his hands, like a schoolboy giving a recitation, and said, "My first is a preposition. My second a composition. My whole is... an acquisition."

"Oh, dear," Freddie said. "I'm wretched at these sorts of things. May we have another clue?"

"Only that the word is especially fitting for this gathering, for it is something that is topmost on a number of minds."

"To?" Martha suggested.

"Don't you mean 'to whom'?" Freddie asked. "To whom is this word topmost?"

"No, I mean *to*," Martha repeated. "He said the first is a preposition. My guess is 'to.'"

"A valiant effort, Miss Finch, but incorrect," Dickey said. "Do give it a try, Miss Tilbury."

"With?"

"Wrong again. Reverend Lovell, you're a man of words. Never met a vicar who wasn't. Care to hazard a guess at the first part?"

"In?"

When Dickey shook his head, a number of other prepositions were called. *Out, at, near, by, over,* and *under* were all offered and rejected, until Anne said, "For?"

Dickey tapped the side of his nose. "That's the preposition. Now, for the composition."

"Novel," someone said.

Dickey shook his head.

"Poem."

"No."

"Limerick?"

"Inventive, but no."

"Is it letter?"

"Remember when I said the answer was uniquely suited to the present company?" Dickey prompted.

"What composition have we failed to mention? Oh! I know. Lady Howard played a *musical* composition." Lady Ware said. "Sonata?"

"No, but you're on the right track."

"Nocturne," Rev. Lovell suggested.

"You're being too specific."

"Melody?" Martha guessed.

"No, no, no. I never dreamed it would be this difficult," Dickey said with a grin. "Wait until I try my truly diabolical riddles on you!"

"Tune," Edward said, finally speaking up.

Dickey bowed gravely in his direction. "Indeed, my lord. You have it."

"Tune. For tune. Fortune," Miss Tilbury put them all together. "But why would fortune be topmost in mind at this gathering?"

Oh, dear. She is indeed a lost lamb.

"It's something all men seek," Lady Ware explained.

"Not all," Rev. Lovell said.

"Most," Edward amended, narrowing his eyes at Dickey. "Some by more trickery than others."

"They say fortune favors the bold," Dickey said. "But it's been my experience that fortune favors those whose very birth gives them prior claim to it."

For the first time that evening, Dickey's quip about his status as a bastard was more depressing than droll. No one laughed.

"Perhaps we *should* have more music," Lady Ware said to break the silence. "Freddie, why don't you give us a tune?"

"Notice we did not ask you for a *fortune*, Miss Tilbury," Dickey said, his tone overly bright, "but undoubtedly someone will before the Season is over."

The party chuckled at that, a bit nervously this time, Anne thought.

As Miss Tilbury began adjusting her seat at the pianoforte, Edward crossed the room to his sister.

"Caro, I regret I must depart."

"So soon?"

From her seat across the room, Anne saw Lord Ware mouth *Take me with you* to Edward. Lady Ware gave her husband a stern look and he leaned back in his chair as Miss Tilbury executed a series of scales with the ruthless efficiency of an automaton. Anne sympathized with Lord Ware, but clearly only the first rat would be allowed to leave this sinking ship.

"I have a previous appointment which I only now recalled. It must be kept. Don't get up, Sinclair," Edward said to Lord Ware and then leaned in to kiss his sister on the cheek. "I'll see myself out."

Then he took the few steps to where Martha was sitting with her arms crossed over her chest. Edward gave her a proper bow and a few murmured words of farewell. He shook hands with Benjamin and avoided Mr. Dickey altogether.

Then as Miss Tilbury switched from scales to arpeggios that made the mahogany case of the piano rattle, Edward came to stand before Anne.

"Good night, Lady Howard."

"Good night, my lord."

Suddenly, he didn't seem inclined to leave.

As Miss Tilbury launched into a bombastic rendition of "The Minstrel Boy," Anne leaned forward to whisper, "That is the first song in Thomas Moore's Irish cycle. If you do not make good your escape before the end of the first song, you will be obliged to remain for the entire set."

He still made no move to go. "Come with me."

Didn't he realize how ridiculous that was? How could he even suggest it?

Drat the man, it's as though he knows how much the thought tempts me. And not just to escape Miss Tilbury's assault on the keys.

Against all sense, Anne still longed to be with Edward Lovell.

Anywhere. Any time, and devil take the hindermost.

"Good-bye, Lord Chatham." To encourage him to leave, she offered him her hand. *If he'll just make a proper obeisance over it and go.* Anne could bear any amount of wretched piano playing. She couldn't bear Edward Lovell and the temptation to make a fool of herself with him again.

But she'd forgotten there were times when Edward refused to do what was proper.

"Au revoir." Not good-bye or even good night. *Until I see you again.*

Then he bent and kissed her hand. Not properly on the knuckles. He turned it palm up and pressed his lips to the pulse point at her wrist.

A lover's kiss.

Then he straightened and made for the door.

Once again, he'd left her bewildered. She didn't know how to feel. Or how to stop feeling. Embarrassed at the low ache between her legs. Angry that he could still make her feel it with nothing more than his mouth on her wrist.

She closed her eyes and tried to think of something—anything—besides Edward Lovell. She imagined her next journey, the one to the Americas. It was said to be a raw place. Not quite civilized. A new land would give her new thoughts.

Of course, depending upon the time of year, the North Atlantic was said to be a difficult crossing, full of great swells and dangerous icebergs that could stove in a ship's side.

It couldn't be any more treacherous than trying to negotiate a London Season when Lord Chatham was in Town.

Anne was actually grateful for Miss Tilbury's horrendous piano playing and the fact that the song cycle she'd chosen to inflict upon them was a ponderously long one.

Surely she would master the urge to flee from Lady Ware's home and try to find the man by the time the musical nightmare was over.

Small lies are the social lubricant that makes polite discourse possible. Big ones, however, make life impossible.
    —from the journal of Edward Lovell, Lord Chatham

Chapter 9

Edward didn't turn in to his stately residence when he came to its wrought-iron gate. He kept walking, trying to clear his mind. Indeed, he felt he could walk to the cliffs of Dover without an ounce more clarity, either in his thinking or in his plans.

He didn't head for a pub. If he'd wanted to drink, he'd have gone home and told Price to bring him that fifty-year-old bottle of single malt scotch he'd been saving. The oblivion it offered was tempting but he didn't think it would help. He wasn't hungry, even though he'd not done justice to the meal served at his sister's home. What he craved wasn't food.

He was a jumble of frustrations.

He needed to move, to wear himself out. He welcomed the cold slap of night on his cheeks. It almost took away the numbness in his chest.

After walking for the better part of an hour, Edward realized his best pair of shoes was not really conducive to a late-night ramble. A blister festered on his left heel. When he happened upon a churchyard with a bench set among the headstones, he turned aside. There in the dim cemetery, he removed his shoe and stocking to survey the damage.

The church was located on a curiously winding side street without benefit of the public lighting which was becoming more common in finer parts of the city. He couldn't see much of his blister, as the gas lamps hung by householders across the street barely penetrated the tall hedges. But he could feel it, swollen and aching. At least the pain in his heel made him stop obsessing about the way his chest constricted.

Edward drew a deep breath. A slight breeze ruffled the yew tree at the far end of the cemetery, its new needles whispering in a language he couldn't comprehend. An owl hooted. If Edward were the superstitious sort, he'd be apprehensive about being there, surrounded by the moldering bones of the dead.

But he was, above all things, a rational man. Why else would he be so committed to following the dictates of his head instead of his heart?

However, rational or not, Edward started when he heard a couple of men's voices from behind him. He turned to see a pair of middle-aged fellows, one bearing a lamp and the other a pickax and shovel, entering the cemetery from the church's side door. Feeling mildly embarrassed at the way he'd jumped, he realized that it was only the sexton and a gravedigger.

"When did the funeral furnisher say as they need the new hole?" the brawnier of the two asked.

"Tomorrow morning, so look sharp, John Fernsby," the smaller one ordered. The little terrier of a man fancied himself in charge of the mastiff with the shovel. "And mind you make those corners good and square."

"It'd go a mite faster if I weren't the only one what was doin' the digging," Fernsby grumbled.

"Who died?" Edward asked.

Now it was the sexton and gravedigger's turn to jump.

"Who's there?" The sexton lifted his lantern and squinted in Edward's direction. "I say, show yourself."

Edward stepped into the yellow pool of lamplight. "I am Lord Chatham," he said as grandly as he could with one shoe on and one shoe off.

The pair of them nearly fell over each other bowing and scraping. Evidently, they didn't often receive midnight visits from the aristocracy.

"Your lordship asked about the dearly departed. May it ease your mind, my lord, that the dead man is far beneath your touch. No one someone of your greatness might know," the sexton said, laying on the flattery in broad strokes. "It's only the baker in the next street but one what's passed away."

"Undoubtedly, he will be missed," Edward said.

"His hot cross buns will be, an' that's God's truth," the gravedigger said as he turned another shovel of sod.

"An' it not be impertinent of me," the sexton said, "might I inquire as to why your lordship is here?"

"Because I was walking along and developed a blister." Edward lifted one foot to show the man he was unshod.

"Oh! If it please you, my lord, let me tend to that. I've a plaster or two in my chest. If you'd care to follow me..." The sexton headed toward the side door to the stone church.

Edward didn't follow the man. He'd been an indifferent churchman all his life. He had, however, reached what he felt was a gentleman's agreement with the Almighty. Edward supported his local parish lavishly. He made the odd appearance on high holy days. But as long as God left him alone, Edward returned the favor.

Lately, though, Edward felt the Lord had not lived up to His part of the bargain. Between the shaky Chatham finances and Anne popping back into his life without an honorable way for them to be together, Edward was feeling more than a little "smited" by the trials and tribulations being visited upon him.

However, he wasn't ready to confront his Maker about these injustices just yet. He was counting on the Almighty to relent and show a sense of fair play, without Edward having to point out the inequities of his situation. Being inside a church might tempt him to accuse God of something he'd later regret.

"The night is pleasant enough," Edward said. "I'll wait here while you fetch your emoluments."

"Very good, your lordship," the sexton said and scurried away to do his bidding.

"You know, your mightiness," the gravedigger said, "you ain't the only high-toned person in this churchyard on the moment."

"Oh?"

"We got ourselves a lord mayor of London somewheres in here. O' course, his stone is pretty old. Not much more than dimples left on the limestone, but the sexton can point it out to you if you've a mind to see it."

The digger leaned on his shovel and pulled a disreputable-looking handkerchief from his pocket, which he used to blow his nose, wipe his face, and slick back his hair. In that order.

"And then there's Lady Blackwood," the man went on. "She takes up most of the southwest corner, her and her brood. Birthed eleven children and two stillborns, she did. Didn't none of 'em exactly thrive, you understand, which is why we got 'em all bunched together over there for all eternity. Comforting, ain't it?"

"Hmm." Comforting wasn't the first word that sprang to mind. He wondered how much longer it would take sexton to fetch his plasters.

"And I dug graves for 'em all. Well, not the old lord mayor, o' course. Reckon that was my grandfather's grandfather what did for him," the man admitted as he continued to dig. "I s'pose the finest gent what I ever helped plant meself was a few years back. Sir Erasmus Howard."

"Sir Erasmus?"

"Aye. Handsomely paid for that grave, I was, too. Twice the usual on account of it being high summer and us needin' to get him in the ground on the quick. Let me tell you, his good lady didn't stint on the particulars when it came time for her to don the widow's weeds. Sent her gentleman off good and proper, she did."

"Where is his grave?" Edward asked, morbidly curious about the final resting place of the man who had called Anne his wife.

"Fairly close to the church, where all as can afford it likes to be buried." The man pointed with a crooked finger that had undoubtedly been broken and badly reset once or twice. "Third row, second stone."

The sexton came out of the church, poultice and plaster in hand, to find Edward standing over the baronet's grave.

"Ah, you'll have found Sir Erasmus, may he rest in peace. Did you know him, my lord?"

"No. Only of him."

"Ah, well. Sometimes what we know of someone may not be all there is to it, eh? Come and make yourself comfortable, my lord, while I tend to your blister."

It occurred to Edward as he settled back on the bench and allowed the sexton to dress his blister that the junior churchman was looking to move up in the world and hoped the Earl of Chatham might give him a hand. "What did you mean? About me not knowing all there was to know about Sir Erasmus?"

"Only that there were whispers after he died."

"What sort of whispers?"

"If you'd known the gentleman, or were a particular friend of his, I'd not trouble you with them, because I confess, they fair curled my hair when I first heard them." The fact that the sexton was bald as an egg didn't lessen the sense of importance he seemed to attach to the gossip he was about to pass on. "There are those who speculated that the baronet's death was not...natural."

"In what way?"

"Well, Sir Erasmus had no known illness. He suffered no injury. His father lived to a ripe old age and by all accounts his mother is still with us, so folks expected he, too, ought to have lived more years than man's allotted three score and ten."

"What did his physician say at the time?"

"You mean Dr. Morton?" the sexton said. "Oh, he'd not talk about it. At least, not to me. But I have heard, second- and thirdhand, you understand, that he suspected Sir Erasmus had been helped along on his way to his reward."

"How?"

The sexton leaned forward to whisper, "Poison, they do say."

"Who would do such a thing?" Edward said indignantly. It was insufferable that anyone should dare attack a member of the ton with so underhanded a weapon as poison. He forgot for a moment that if Anne had to have a husband, he should be more than glad that it was a dead husband. "Did anyone question his cook?"

"The cook, he says. It's always the help as gets blamed for such things," the gravedigger groused. "Answer me this. Why would his cook do for him, I asks you? Like as not the gentleman's death put her and all his other servants out of their positions."

That made sense. No one who was in Sir Erasmus's employ stood to benefit from his death. "What of the baronet's heir?"

"Oh, his son was in Cornwall at the time of his passing, so they say," the sexton said.

Edward decided he'd better watch what he said in the man's presence or "they" would soon know the particulars of this conversation as well. But his curiosity was too roused to let the subject go without a couple more questions. "Whom did this Dr. Morton suspect of poisoning Howard?"

"Well, it's doubtful we'll ever know for sure who could've done it. Very circumspect, is Dr. Morton. To my knowledge, he never did name names. He'd only say as poison was a woman's weapon."

Edward tugged on his sock and shoe and rose to his feet. "As soon as I find him, he'll speak plainly to me."

"Oh, that he'll not," the gravedigger said.

"Why not?"

"Because Dr. Morton rests over by that yew tree near the back churchyard gate." The digger hitched a thumb over his shoulder in that direction. "Planted him there myself only last March."

The sexton shot his underling a poisoned dart of a glare and positioned himself between Edward and the gravedigger. "The good doctor picked the plot his own self when he realized the fever that finally carried him off would be mortal. Now, my lord, is there any other way we might be of assistance? Anything at all?"

"No, thank you. That will do. I shall write a letter to your vicar informing him how helpful you have been."

"Oh, there's no need for someone as important as yourself to trouble about the likes of me."

"Don't ye mean the likes of us?" the digger grumbled without stopping the rhythm he'd established with his shovel.

Ignoring his counterpart, the sexton went on, "I myself have often hoped I might serve our heavenly Lord in a country parish...oh! and the earthly lord as supports the church at the same time. As a curate, of course. I've no great learning, but I could help shepherd a small country flock because I interest myself in the lives of people."

"And their deaths and everything in between," said the digger.

"Now that you mention it," Edward said as he tugged on his sock and eased the shoe on over the sexton's clumsily applied plaster, "a friend of mine, Lord Kirkland, is looking for a curate to serve the church he had built on his station."

"Oh, my lord! How marvelous. How miraculous. How...what exactly is a *station*?"

"A great farmstead, far bigger than any you've ever dreamed of, I should imagine." Edward stood, testing his weight on the injured foot and deciding he might make it home without removing the shoe again, but only if he could hail a hansom within a block or two. "Of course, Lord Kirkland's station is in New South Wales."

"Oh." The man's narrow shoulders slumped.

"I'll mention your desire to serve a rural parish in my next correspondence with him. What did you say your name was?"

"Me, um...Fernsby. John Fernsby."

The gravedigger stopped working and pulled a face at his coworker. Edward recalled that the sexton had called the digger by that name.

"You do that, my lord," the real Fernsby said. "I expect John Fernsby could be as good a curate in New South Wales as he might be anywhere else. Might even be willing to dig a grave or two should there be a need. Good evening to ye, Lord Chatham."

Epictetus teaches us that wealth consists not in having great possessions, but in having few wants. But that worthy ancient was a Stoic, which means he believed he had no control over the events in his life. If I, as an English lord, may assert my will over my servants and tenant farmers, indeed, over any subject of the Crown whom I outrank in precedence, but have not control over my own Fate, I am the most miserable of creatures.
—from the journal of Edward Lovell, Lord Chatham

Chapter 10

"Mr. Higgindorfer is here, my lord," Price said as he ushered the gentleman into Edward's study without further preamble. Then the butler, ever discreet, pulled the door closed as he left.

Edward was expecting Higgindorfer, though he wasn't looking forward to the meeting. A few weeks ago, he'd asked the Lovell family's man of business to research and present investment opportunities which were more speculative in nature than he usually suggested. Edward assumed higher risk equaled higher reward. Higgindorfer was doggedly efficient, but not terribly imaginative. Edward feared his recommendations would be too conservative to stop the estate's decline.

Lucius Higgindorfer had always reminded Edward of an aged tortoise. Loose skin hung in rings about his thin neck, and he seemed to have no lips at all, just a mouth that was generally set in a hard, straight line. The old gent had served the house of Lovell in a trusted capacity for as long as Edward could remember. He'd advised and outlived the two previous earls. Like the tortoise he resembled, he might even outlast Edward.

Age, conservatism, and his unfortunate likeness to a tortoise aside, Higgindorfer's business acumen was undeniable. The only times the

Chatham fortune took a dip were when his prudent suggestions weren't followed by Edward's predecessors.

"My lord." His voice was so gravelly, the tone almost made his greeting sound like a curse. The man placed a ponderous ledger book on the edge of Edward's desk and took a seat without being invited to do so. Such was his importance to the Lovell family. Edward took no offense.

Besides, he must be over eighty. He's earned the right to a seat in my study.

"Good day, Higgindorfer."

"You won't think so after you see this report." The old man's expression was habitually that of one who had just swallowed a rancid bit of herring, but Edward thought he looked even more sour than usual.

"I consider myself duly warned," Edward said. "What are the damages this quarter?"

"Legion, my lord. Despite the economies we instituted when last we met, the past quarter saw very little improvement in our situation."

Edward was comforted rather than affronted by Higgindorfer's use of "we" and "our." It was evidence of the old gentleman's commitment to the House of Lovell, and his willingness to accept responsibility whether things went well or poorly.

"Drastic measures may be required," he warned.

"Such as?"

"My lord, I have uncovered an opportunity which, if all goes to plan, should more than expiate the estate's current debt within the next nine months. After that, it will lay a foundation for a profitable future for generations to come."

Edward swallowed back his surprise. Higgindorfer must have stumbled upon a veritable gem mine of an investment. But if the opportunity held such promise, why did the man look as if Edward would have to surrender his firstborn in exchange for it?

"What is this investment?"

"It is a ship—the *Ana Fernanda*, to be precise."

Higgindorfer had always counseled against shipping in the past. Edward swallowed hard. That he would suggest buying interest in a ship now spoke volumes for the desperate nature of the Chatham financial situation. "The *Ana Fernanda*, you say. Spanish registry?"

Higgindorfer shook his head.

"Portuguese?"

"Not exactly."

"Then what?"

"The ship is Brazilian, my lord."

"That's a bit far afield, isn't it?" Edward said with a frown. "And haven't you always said shipping is a risky business? As I recall, you discouraged my father from investing in a whaler."

"And in that instance, I was proven right." Higgindorfer's head bobbed up and down, further strengthening his likeness to a tortoise. "That particular ship was lost in a Pacific typhoon. But suppose the ship had returned to Bristol with all hands and its hold full of oil and ambergris. Further suppose that your father had overruled me and invested in that scenario. In that happy phantasm, why, all would be well with the House of Lovell and we would not be having this conversation. But alas, I was right, and your father the earl did well to heed my warnings."

Edward suspected the man's convoluted story was his way of hinting that the current earl of Chatham had better heed Higgindorfer now. "How is this ship different from the whaler?"

"For one thing, the *Ana Fernanda* sails only in the Atlantic and in the more placid southerly latitudes, far from the North Atlantic squalls," Higgindorfer said. "The risk of loss is far less than a whaler. You may confidently expect a tripling, possibly a quadrupling, of your investment in less than a year."

"What aren't you telling me?"

"Have no doubt, Lord Chatham. This venture will be lucrative. Very." Higgindorfer grasped the armrests of his chair so hard that his knuckles went white. "However, I fear you may be put off by the cargo, my lord. The *Ana Fernanda* carries slaves from the coast of Africa to South America, where the trade is still legal."

"Put off?" Edward rose to tower over the man, hands fisted. Heat surged up his neck. If Higgindorfer were younger, Edward would happily knock him into next week for such a wretched suggestion. "You mistake me, sir, if you believe I could ever be a party to such an enterprise. In truth, I would rather go about with my backside bare than earn so much as a farthing in the slave trade."

The old man sighed.

"Frankly, I'm surprised at you, Higgindorfer. And more than a little appalled."

For the first time since the man of business had entered the study, the hint of a smile lifted his mouth. "But I am not surprised at you, my lord. You have responded as I'd hoped. I did not relish sullying the House of Lovell with an association to such human misery."

"And yet you presented the investment to me?"

"I was compelled to do so," Higgindorfer said. "When one looks only at the numbers, the *Ana Fernanda* is a sound financial venture, and in the end, I owe you the final say."

"Then consider this final. No. Never." Edward lowered himself slowly back into his chair. His heart ceased hammering and settled back to a normal rhythm. "We must find another way to turn our situation around that doesn't involve trafficking in despair."

"I confess myself to be at a loss, my lord."

"What about the estate's unentailed properties? The mill in Essex, the ironworks in Wales, and...fiend seize it! What is that other one?"

"The dolomite quarry near the Scottish border," Higgindorfer supplied. "Yes, my lord. All of them are valuable assets which might be sold to alleviate our present woes, but they are the most profitable of the estate's holdings. Selling them means an immediate infusion of ready coin, but a perpetual loss of the income they should generate well into the future. What shall we do if the family's fortune declines further and we have nothing left to sell? Will you be prepared to petition the House of Lords to break up your estate lands so you can sell them off a parcel at a time?"

Edward suppressed a shudder. Losing the land was the course of last resort. It would mean he'd failed utterly. He drummed his fingers on the desk. Was Miss Finch truly his only option for saving his family from a steep decline?

He hoped not.

"We shall follow the Lovell family motto: *Tempus omnia monstrat.* Time shows all things. The right course will present itself."

"Let us pray it presents itself soon, my lord." Higgindorfer rapped his knuckles on the ominous ledger volume and made for the door. "You have shown yourself to be the gentleman I hoped you'd become. I hope with equal fervor that you will not become a prophet."

"How is that?"

"If the direction of the estate's finances does not change, you may well find yourself without a covering for your noble backside. Good day, your lordship."

What a ray of sunshine. Too bad the blasted old man is always right.

"Hold a moment, Higgindorfer. I have another matter for you to investigate."

"What might that be, my lord?"

"I require the name of the funeral furnisher who made the final arrangements for Sir Erasmus Howard." The firm who'd undertaken the gentleman's burial would surely know more than rumormongers about what had actually caused his death.

"When and where did the gentleman die?" It was a measure of Higgindorfer's extreme discretion that he did not pepper him with additional questions.

"I'm not sure when, but Sir Erasmus is buried in St. Thomas-by-the-Way churchyard here in London, so I would assume he succumbed while he was in Town."

"I shall have the information within a day or two." Higgindorfer frowned. "My lord, the House of Lovell has always used Creavey and Horvath for funerals. If you were dissatisfied with their service in the matter of your father's arrangements, you should have said and—"

"No, it's not that. Creavey and Horvath will continue to plant dearly departed Lovells for the foreseeable future. I simply need to know the name of the firm that took care of Sir Erasmus. My reasons are...personal." Since his midnight meeting in the graveyard, he couldn't shake the niggling doubts about how Anne's husband had met his end. Because the rumors pointed to a female poisoner, Anne was the most likely suspect. If a magistrate were to become interested in the matter, it might be a short walk from innuendo to indictment, especially when Anne had eschewed the protection of her stepson. In fact, if the rumor that Sir Erasmus had been poisoned reached the ears of the current baronet, he might legally cut off all her support. But once Edward discovered the truth of the matter, he could protect her from wagging tongues. Or something worse. "If you cannot assist me—"

"No, no, Lord Chatham. I have an associate at the *Times* who will surely be able to ferret out the name of the funeral furnisher in question. As I have several clients, he will have no idea who is requesting the information. You may rely upon me in this matter," the old man said as he headed for the door. "Send word if you require clarification on anything within the ledgers. As ever, I am at your disposal, my lord. Good day."

Edward glanced at the offensive volume, and then upward to the gilded ceiling. He began to wonder if the estate's woes were the Almighty's not-so-subtle way of forcing him to rethink his policy of mutual indifference with the deity.

Perhaps a prayer or two would not come amiss.

But Edward didn't have time to start a conversation with his Maker just then. No sooner had Mr. Higgindorfer left than Mr. Price rapped on the door, requesting admittance.

"The post has come, my lord." Price set a salver stacked with mail on the edge of Edward's desk.

Most are probably bills, Edward thought morosely.

"One item came by special courier," Price said. "He awaits a reply."

Edward sighed. "Which one?"

Mr. Price lifted the first item on the pile, an elegantly gilded notice, done up with a silver bow. "It is from Lady Ackworth."

Edward groaned, suspecting what the missive contained, but he dutifully tore open the neatly folded invitation. Every spring, as predictable as new blooms, the gossipy hostess threw an ostentatious ball, the better to scout out all the budding romances, the misbehaviors, and the enmities that had grown among the ton during the previous year. A fortnight hence, Edward would be required to make an appearance at this ball.

As short an appearance as I can manage without angering the old witch.

"Send my acceptance to Lady Ackworth, Price. Attendance is mandatory if one does not wish to spend the next year with a target on one's back."

The butler cleared his throat. "Begging your pardon, my lord, but the courier was told to wait for a *written* reply."

"Very well. Return in a few minutes and he shall have it." Muttering a few choice words questioning Lady Ackworth's lineage, Edward trimmed a quill and penned a carefully crafted acceptance.

When Price returned to collect it, the butler said, "Shall I send for your tailor so you can have a new suit made for the occasion?"

"Why? It's just Lady Ackworth's yearly ball."

"I would not have broached the subject, except that you have not had a new suit of clothing made since the summer you returned from your Grand Tour, my lord. As you know, I'm not the sort who wishes to carry tales, but..." Price fidgeted with his already oh-so-correctly-straight necktie. "But her ladyship's courier...well, perhaps I've already said too much."

"Or not enough. Out with it, Price," Edward said. "Let's have it."

"The courier let slip that her ladyship is expecting a member of the royal family in attendance. Perhaps several of them."

Surely not the king himself, Edward thought. But Lady Ackworth might have enticed a high-ranking person in King George IV's inner circle to attend, perhaps his younger brother, William, the Duke of Clarence. If so, it would behoove Edward to do his best imitation of Beau Brummell and dress with the same elegance.

"In that case, you'd better send for the tailor."

Price beamed. "At once, my lord."

In truth, Edward was indifferent to what he wore most of the time. Wearing the same suit for several Seasons was an easy way to economize.

Hadn't he just told Higgindorfer he was prepared to go bare rather than go against his principles?

But the idea of Edward ordering a new suit seemed to please Price out of all knowing.

It occurred to Edward that those who served him were not blind. They were aware of the economies he'd introduced. Because their livelihoods depended upon him, the fact that he was willing to skimp on himself must have disturbed them. There was no greater misfortune for someone in service than for the family to whom they'd committed so many years to suddenly become insolvent.

Edward could just imagine what a stir his new suit would create among the staff. Word of his updated wardrobe would circulate through the belowstairs folk like quicksilver. From Price all the way down to his bootblack boy, Lovell House would rejoice over their lord's shiny new buttons and starched white collar.

They would find reassurance of the safety of their positions in the outward trappings of their lord's station. They had fretted for nothing, they'd tell each other. Lord Chatham's austerity measures were a passing whim, not a bony-fingered harbinger of more draconian belt tightening in the future. Surely his lordship was over it now. Cook would be able to buy more sugar. They'd have beeswax candles once again instead of the tallow they'd been using on his lordship's orders. The times of plenty were returning to the House of Lovell.

Edward owed a living to more than his younger brothers. He owed one to all those who served his family. Sometimes, the weight was so prodigious, he couldn't help but bow his head.

And as long as he'd assumed the position...

"Lord, I don't presume to ask Your blessing on the House of Lovell for myself. There are others far more deserving of Your favor, and many of them are in my employ. So I ask for those who depend upon me. Show me the right path, so that they will continue to be provided with the means of life. You will find me appreciative. Amen."

There. That should be sufficient to reopen a dialogue with the Almighty. Of course, the Lord might need a little more pertinent information.

Edward bowed his head once more.

"And if, in Your boundless wisdom, Lord, Your providential plan for the Chatham estate does not include my having to marry Miss Finch, You will have my profoundest gratitude."

Children are a blessing, they say. Perhaps when they are young and can do nothing but coo. However, once they begin to speak, beware, for when they reach the ripe old age of ten and six, one cannot get them to stop speaking.
—from *Why a Life of Personal Adventure is Preferable to Motherhood* by Mrs. Hester Birdwhistle

Chapter 11

"Oh, this little hat is just the most cunning thing." Martha adjusted the red velvet capote and admired herself in the milliner's mirror. "Don't you think so, Anne?"

"Lady Howard," Anne corrected under her breath, as she took the caplet from Martha and returned it to the milliner. With her dark hair and eyes, Ann would have looked splendid in the scarlet cap, but Martha's delicate coloring faded even more in contrast to its jewel tones. "Something with less flash and more in keeping with the young lady's complexion, if you please, Mrs. Winterbottom. A hat should complement the wearer, not announce to the world that its own velvety self has arrived."

"But of course, Lady Howard. I believe I may have just the thing in the back room. One moment, please." Round little Mrs. Winterbottom scurried away as quickly as her neatly booted feet could carry her, which given her girth wasn't all that fast. But she gave it her best effort. The tradeswoman had been Anne's milliner for years and didn't want to disappoint her.

"So, the hat needs to match me," Martha said with a sigh. "A guinea says she comes back with a hat dull enough for a scullery maid."

"First, you do yourself a disservice with that remark. I won't distinguish it with further comment except to say that you are far more attractive than you credit yourself. Secondly, where on earth did you learn to speak as if you were a habitual gambler?" Anne ticked off her protégé's sins on her gloved fingers. "And lastly, you *must* remember to call me Lady Howard unless we are at home by ourselves. We agreed not to call each other familiar in public. It simply isn't done."

Martha rolled her eyes and dropped a mock curtsy. "Yes, m'lady."

"Honestly, if you also wish to have a 'Lady' before your name by the time this Season is done, you need to remember how to conduct yourself."

"In the grand scheme of things," Martha said, as she fingered a bonnet made of pleated green silk, "calling you by your Christian name seems a small sin indeed."

"Perhaps it does, but only because you insist on using language that might be heard in the most disreputable of gaming hells. *A guinea says*, indeed!"

"How do you know how they talk in gaming hells?" Martha asked. "Have you been to one? Oh, I do hope so!"

"No," Anne said with firmness. *At least not in England.* "And I trust I will not hear you offering a wager in your conversation again."

"You won't. I'm sorry, Lady Howard," Martha singsonged. Her tone proved she was not.

"I was going to wait until we returned home, but because Mrs. Winterbottom seems to be taking her time finding that hat, now is as good a time as any to address your behavior at the Science Academy lecture today," Anne said. Once she began correcting Martha's missteps, it was difficult to stop.

The girl snorted.

"I'm serious," Anne said with sternness. "You should not shout 'What a pack of faradiddles!' and stalk out of a lecture simply because you disagree with the speaker. To say that you made yourself conspicuous is to put it mildly."

"I thought you told me we attend those things so that I may catch the notice of the ton."

"Well, you certainly accomplished that, but trust me, it was not in the way you wish to be noticed. You behaved with unladylike shrillness."

Martha waved her hand dismissively, as if Anne's scolding was no more bother than a cloud of midges. "I couldn't keep still any longer. The gentleman was an idiot."

"Granted," Anne admitted. Poor judgment about how she'd conducted herself aside, if she'd found the lecturer's premise ridiculous, Martha was probably more intelligent than Anne had suspected. "But one does not make a spectacle of oneself simply to prove a point."

"Please." Martha rolled her eyes. "Mr. Appletree claimed he could determine a person's character simply by feeling the bumps on his subject's head. Phrenology is the most ludicrous scientific idea to come along since people believed the sun circled the earth."

"I don't disagree," Anne said, "but you really shouldn't have made such a scene."

"Would you have rather I remained in my first-row seat and laughed aloud at him through the rest of his presentation?" Martha asked. "Because I confess that idea had real appeal."

"No." The girl was being purposely obtuse. For the umpteenth time, Anne wondered if Lady Finch was truly as ill as Lord Finch said, or if she and her husband simply wanted to escape Martha for the Season. "That's not the correct way to deal with someone with whom you disagree either."

Martha picked up yet another unflattering hat—this one in a violent shade of orange—and tried it on. "Perhaps I should have meekly volunteered to allow him to measure my cranium with his silly calipers. Then we could have listened to him wax eloquent about how I have a propensity for constructiveness or secretiveness or alimentiveness—"

"You do lean toward alimentiveness."

"Do I? I only remembered that word because I don't know what it means." Martha tied the pumpkin-colored ribbons on the millinery monstrosity under her chin. Her skin tone instantly seemed several shades more sallow. Anne immediately untied the bow so she could remove the offending hat.

"Alimentiveness means you like to eat."

"Oh! Still, even after Mr. Appletree measured my skull, he would have no doubt told me the exact opposite. All his pronouncements were nothing more than guesses based on other observable attributes of his subject. It takes no set of calipers to realize a matron with frown lines has a choleric temper."

Anne forced her own frustrated expression to relax. She hoped to realize a significant payment from her position as Martha's sponsor, not a set of frown lines.

"One thing is certain, you'll never know what Mr. Appletree might have deduced about your character by his methods now," Anne said. "In fact, I very much suspect we will be refused entrance to lectures at the academy of sciences. Or if we're allowed in at all, we'll be shown to seats at the rear of the hall, whence you might storm out without disrupting the proceedings."

Martha's head drooped, and if she were anyone else, Anne would have thought her contrite. However, she'd spent enough time in the girl's company to know she rarely regretted anything she said or did.

"What ought I to have done, then?" Martha asked with every appearance of meekness.

"You should have listened politely," Anne said, "and then, if you had objections to his theory, waited to speak to him afterward."

"Oh! Yes, during the question and answer period he promised. You're right." Martha's pale eyes were bright with mischief. "I'd have had the entire hall in stitches while I skewered him with my salient points of logic."

Anne shook her head. "Public ridicule rarely convinces others to change their minds. You'd have done better had you spoken with him one on one, calmly and rationally."

"Hmph." Martha walked over to admire a display of feathers that might be used to adorn a bonnet. "Using that method, were you able to change Lord Chatham's mind, then?"

"What are you talking about?"

"The night of Lady Ware's dinner party." She picked up a pheasant tail feather and ran its length over her palm. "You and he seemed to be having a pretty serious tête-à-tête while you were conversation partners. Even Mr. Dickey thought so."

"Did he?" Thanks to the strolling violinist during the meal, Anne doubted her conversation with Edward was overheard, but Reginald Dickey was notoriously sharp-eyed. "What did Mr. Dickey say?"

"Only that it looked as if Lord Chatham was neglecting a fine joint of beef because he'd much rather be eating you alive."

Anne's breath hissed in over her teeth.

"What did he mean by that?" Martha asked, all innocence.

"Nothing that need concern you." Anne bit her lip for a moment. She believed it unfair to keep young ladies in total ignorance about the things which passed between a man and his wife, but this was not the place to educate Martha about them. "I insist you avoid Mr. Dickey in the future."

"Why?" Martha cocked her head. "He's easily the most amusing person I've met all Season, even if I don't understand what he's talking about some of the time."

Such things really should be left to the girl's mother. Anne shoved away any thought of sharing carnal information with her charge, even if the knowledge might help Martha understand why Anne wanted her to give Mr. Dickey a wide berth. "I'm glad you don't understand Mr. Dickey."

"You shouldn't be glad of my ignorance," Martha argued. "I'm dying to know what he meant by that remark about you and Lord Chatham. Besides, aren't you always decrying the sorry state of education among ladies?"

"Which is why I make sure you attend lectures designed to improve your mind." At this point, Anne was ready to use anything to turn the subject of conversation in another direction. The less said about her and Edward, the better.

"Today's speaker hardly makes a case for improving my mind."

Anne sighed, thankful the girl had taken the conversational bait. "You're right. Mr. Appletree gave a weak presentation, wholly unsupported by evidence."

"Finally! You and I are in accord once again." Martha's smile seemed genuine for a heartbeat, but then it turned sly. "So, did you and Lord Chatham also find accord?"

Honestly, the girl is like a dog with a bone. "Lord Chatham and I were not in disagreement."

"Good, because according to Mr. Dickey, his lordship will be in attendance at Lady Ackworth's ball."

Anne and Martha's invitation had arrived a few days ago, and since then, Martha hadn't been out of her sight. Reginald Dickey had not crossed their path as they went about their daily outings. In fact, Anne hadn't seen him since the dinner at Lady Ware's home. "When did you speak to Mr. Dickey about the ball?"

"I didn't. He sent round a note yesterday."

"What?" Anne was supposed to monitor the girl's mail. It was a condition of her employment upon which Martha's parents had insisted. She wouldn't open a missive without her charge present, but she took note of those with whom Martha regularly corresponded. Mr. Dickey was not on that list. "Do you mean to tell me you allowed Mr. Dickey to write to you without talking with me about it first?"

"I didn't allow anything." Martha batted her eyes and pulled a face. "I can hardly control when someone else decides to write to me."

"I suppose not. And you may be excused on account of your inexperience, but Mr. Dickey may not." By writing to her, he was de facto paying court to the girl. Many a courtship had been accomplished through well-written letters. Martha's parents would never approve of their daughter encouraging a man like Reginald Dickey. "He knows, even if you don't, that it was improper of him to write to you without permission from either your parents or me."

Martha grinned. "Mr. Dickey says permission is overrated. Forgiveness after the fact is always more fun."

"He would." *And forgiveness is not always given*, Anne thought but didn't say. She wanted her relationship with Martha to be that of a trusted advisor, not a guard dog, so she needed to temper her urge to scold. "Still, you might have waited to open the letter—"

"Letters. He's sent more than one."

"Heavens! How long has this ink and foolscap romance been going on?"

"Since Lady Ware's dinner party. He sends round a short note almost every day," Martha said.

"And how is it I've never seen these notes?"

"He arranged for the first one to be tucked in with the milk delivery," Martha said. "Sometimes it comes from the greengrocer or the baker."

"And who in your parents' employ is complicit in delivering the notes to you?"

"Oh, no. I'll not give up any of my confederates. That wouldn't be fair."

Anne supposed not, and likely the household staff relished being part of a scheme that pleased the younger lady of the house. Anne sighed. Keeping track of Martha made her feel old, and she despised the feeling.

"But you're wrong about Mr. Dickey. The letters are not at all romantic," Martha said. "He simply wants to be my friend. He makes me laugh."

"He'd like to make you do a lot more, I'll wager," Anne muttered.

"Now who's talking as if she just came from a gaming hell?"

"Martha, if he writes you again, you must allow me to see the letter."

"Oh, no. If I do that, you'll send it back to him unopened."

"With a scathing missive of my own," Anne said with force. "You may believe this an innocent lark, but he knows better. It is totally unacceptable for a gentleman to correspond with you in secret."

"Honestly, I can nearly see steam coming from your ears. If you have a disagreement with the man," Martha said, sweetly as the cat who ate the cream, "why don't you speak with him calmly and rationally instead of making a scene?"

"Oh, no, young lady, this is not about me," Anne said in clipped tones. "It's about you not seeing danger when it's right before your eyes."

"Oh, pish! I seriously doubt a letter or two can be dangerous."

In the wrong hands, they could be ruinous. "Have you written back to him?"

"No," Martha admitted.

Heaven be praised! The girl has a bit of sense. "That is very good news. I wish you'd sent the first letter from Mr. Dickey back unopened, but at least you acted sensibly by not responding."

"Oh, I'm responding all right," Martha admitted. "But I don't dare write him back because anything I say might sound ridiculous. He's ever so much cleverer than I."

"But he's not more prudent. You, my dear, have been the sensible one in this instance."

"Have you any idea how boring being sensible sounds?"

Anne did, actually. When she wrote as Mrs. Birdwhistle, she regularly advised throwing the sensible course of action out the window in favor of an adventurous one. However, as Lady Howard, it was becoming more and more difficult to live up to her alter ego's unconventional conventions.

But while a widow might bend the rules a bit, it was downright dangerous for a young girl like Martha to toss the accepted standards away. Even the appearance of a scandal with Reginald Dickey could ruin her utterly.

"Martha, when we get home, I must insist that you bring Mr. Dickey's letters, and I mean all of them, to me."

"Perhaps I've forgotten where they are."

"In that case, I shall escort you home to your parents and wash my hands of you forthwith."

Martha sighed long and loudly. "Do you never tire of playing that card?"

"Not as long as it trumps everything else. One way or another, I'll have those letters, my dear."

Martha's rounded shoulders slumped even further. "Very well. But please don't destroy them. They really are amusing. No matter how many times I reread them, they still make me laugh."

"All right. I won't destroy them," Anne promised. "And I'll even help you write a response to them."

A broad smile spread over Martha's face, making her almost pretty in a freckled pup sort of way. She clasped hands with Anne. "Oh, thank you, thank you, thank you!"

"Don't thank me yet. Your letter will ask him to refrain from writing to you again."

Martha's shoulders slumped back down.

"Trust me, dear. I only have your best interests at heart."

"And I have yours." Martha arched a pale brow at her. "You promised me you'll dance the next time you're asked. Will you?"

"Yes."

"What if it's Lord Chatham who asks you?"

"I will accept no matter who invites me to dance, because when I promise, I keep my word," Anne fired back. If she acted as if she'd make an exception for Edward, it would signal that her feelings for him were anything but indifferent. Martha was already too quick to pick up on cues that she and Edward had a past. Anne didn't want to give her any more to ponder.

"It just seemed odd that he left early that evening at Lord and Lady Ware's," Martha said.

"If you'd been able, wouldn't you have made good your escape once Miss Tilbury began playing?"

"Point taken," Martha admitted. "Only even as Lord Chatham was bidding everyone good night, he took an inordinate amount of time parting from you."

"You claim you couldn't help that Mr. Dickey wrote to you," Anne said. "I also cannot be held to account for an earl's lingering farewell."

Martha smiled, a triumphant one that bared far too much of her gums to be attractive. "Agreed. Neither of us can be held responsible for the behavior of the gentlemen in our lives."

Anne mentally kicked herself. She'd let the girl manipulate her into minimizing the problem of Mr. Dickey. And elevate Anne's problem with Edward by naming him a "gentleman in her life."

Lord Chatham! she scolded herself for at least the twentieth time. *I must think of him as the earl, not as my Edward.*

Anne prided herself on being strong minded. She had the mental discipline to stop thinking of the man he had been.

But did she have the physical discipline not to melt if the man he was now asked her to dance?

Some might suspect that a habitual traveler is fleeing from something distasteful in their normal life. The truth is there are plenty of inconvenient, dare I say distasteful, moments on any journey. However, I prefer to think of my adventures as flights toward things that are difficult to find in my normal life—a sense of wonder, enlightenment, and, even in the midst of inconvenience, that most elusive of all discoveries, self-knowledge.
—Lady Howard writing as Mrs. Hester Birdwhistle

Chapter 12

Anne could still fit into the ball gown in which she'd debuted, but never thought she'd have occasion to wear it again until Lady Ackworth's invitation arrived. The watered silk was a pale, almost icy, blue, a color which became her quite well, but the cut of the gown was several Seasons out of fashion. Its style was far too simple. An unadorned bodice and capped sleeves topped a sleek column of shimmering fabric that reached nearly to the floor, allowing just the slightest glimpse of her matching slippers.

But the ton was mad for rows of flounces and furbelows now, so the blue silk's sleek lines seemed hopelessly outmoded. Martha had argued that if Anne refused to let her pay for a new gown for her, she at least ought to permit Martha to use some of her clothing allowance to refurbish the old one.

"People will think my parents are being terribly miserly with you," Martha had said.

"The sensible ones won't. Wearing my old gown doesn't trouble me at all. Don't give it another thought," Anne had countered. "Besides, no one will notice how I'm dressed. I'll likely be, as you said, hugging the wall with the other matrons."

Martha had arched a brow and found a way to partially circumvent Anne's wishes. The girl asked Mrs. Winterbottom to design a clever three-strap headband, the type that adorned so many statues of Greek goddesses, in the same shade of blue as Anne's gown.

The effect was charming, Anne had to admit, but she didn't want to be charming at Lady Ackworth's ball. In fact, if it would have been appropriate, she'd have chosen to dress in something on the dowdier side and hide beneath her ridiculous feathered bonnet.

That course would be safer if Edward were there.

However, Martha had whined and prodded, and in the end, Anne was as well turned out, if not as fashionably, as her protégé on the night of the ball.

As they surrendered their wraps and followed Lady Ackworth's butler to the wide doorway where their arrival would be announced to the assembly, Anne ran an approving eye over the young lady under her care.

Martha was wearing a gown in an unusual shade of green. It wasn't a color most women could wear, but the light sage seemed specifically designed for Martha, bringing forth previously unnoticed golden undertones in the girl's skin. Her headdress was a combination of the same green and a fine cream color, accented with golden spangles that caught the light of the Ackworth chandeliers and the eyes of every onlooker. Martha's entrance turned plenty of heads.

Miss Finch was suddenly interesting for more than her skill at the keyboard and her monstrous dowry. She was unique. And surprisingly lovely.

Martha has grown into herself.

The girl moved with assurance, and when the butler intoned, "Lady Howard and Miss Martha Finch," she smiled at the other guests and dropped a dignified curtsy.

Anne couldn't have been prouder. On their previous outings, Martha had been awkward or distracted or downright unpleasant. Now she was grace itself, and Anne credited her tutelage for Martha's improved comportment.

Except that my ultimate task has just been made more difficult.

When youth, accomplishment, and attractiveness were combined with a princely dowry, there would be no shortage of suitors beating a path to Miss Finch's door. Many of them wholly *un*suitable.

As if to prove her fears well founded, Reginald Dickey presented himself before them almost immediately.

"Good evening, Lady Howard. Miss Finch." Dickey bent in a deep and exceedingly proper bow. "How lovely to see you both."

Martha bobbed a curtsy in response, but Anne just blinked at him in surprise. He'd surely received Martha's letter asking him to cease writing to her. By pushing himself toward her in public, he was ignoring her dictates completely. In times like this, Anne wished she possessed the fortitude to deliver a cut direct, that most fierce of public punishments for a breach of etiquette.

However, if she blatantly ignored Dickey, it would signal to the ton that something dire had happened. As yet, only she, Martha, and Dickey knew of the clandestine letters. If Anne cut him, Dickey wouldn't care. He laughed off Polite Society's attempts to make him adhere to its rules with regularity. A snub would rebound and only be damaging to Martha.

And he knows it, drat the man.

"Mr. Dickey." Anne gave him the shallowest curtsy she dared. "If you'll excuse us, please. Come, Miss Finch. There is someone to whom I wish to introduce you."

Anne had no one specific in mind, but it was the best way she could think to extricate them from Mr. Dickey. At that moment, the quartet in the far corner began playing, and the dance master called for couples to form up for a cotillion.

"Ah, the dancing has begun," Mr. Dickey said with a grin.

"So it has," Martha said with a nervous giggle.

"Then let the games begin as well. Will you do me the honor of the first dance," he said quite correctly, before turning to Anne and finishing with, "Lady Howard?"

Anne was ready with an acceptable excuse for Martha to decline a dance. It had occurred to her that they had not yet visited the ladies' retiring room to freshen their appearance after their carriage ride to Lady Ackworth's home. "Actually, I believe Martha has—" But she realized that Mr. Dickey had not invited Martha to dance. "Pardon me, what? I must have misheard you."

"Lady Howard, will you do me the honor of the first dance?" Dickey repeated, his eyes full of mischief.

"But—" Anne stopped herself. She couldn't plead the need to find the retiring room now. She had promised Martha she'd dance if she was asked. By anyone.

Never in a million years would she have dreamed it would be Reginald Dickey.

Anne curtsied again and gave the approved answer, albeit in clipped tones. "The honor is mine."

From the corner of her eye, she could see that instead of Martha being upset that her supposed "friend" had asked Anne to dance rather than her, the girl was beaming.

Somehow, the two of them arranged this.

Anne had no idea how they'd managed it. She'd effectively barred written communication once she'd learned about the letters. But as she allowed Mr. Dickey to lead her to the dance floor, she was certain that the two of them were conspirators in this ambush.

"Very clever," she said under her breath.

"Thank you. I try."

"It wasn't a compliment," Anne said as they joined hands and circled with the other three couples. The dance called for the eight participants to change direction several times while employing the balancé step. Anne was grateful because it meant Mr. Dickey could not continue their conversation while they tripped about with the other dancers.

That changed when the rigadon section of the cotillion began. She and Dickey were obliged to clasp right hands and swing around each other separately from the group.

"Ah, Lady Howard, you wound me," Dickey said softly enough for only her to hear. "Tell me how have I have offended you, and I shall endeavor to make amends."

Anne pressed her lips together for four counts, but then the words burst out in a furious whisper. "I know what you're doing, you know."

"The most stylish cotillion on the dance floor? Thank you, my lady. I do make a point of keeping in practice," he said with an ingratiating smile. "A gentleman should always be ready to partner a lady to good advantage."

"Yes, a *gentleman* should."

"Then you think because I'm no gentleman, I seek an unfair advantage," Dickey said as he took her other hand as well for a series of partner turns which required them to face each other.

Anne forced a pleasant expression on her face, but it was an effort. "I did not say that you are not a gentleman."

Though, in point of fact, you're not.

"Ah, but you are thinking it so loudly I could hear it even over that rather squeaky first violin."

Clearly, she was not succeeding in presenting a pleasant face to the man. "More dancing, less conversation, if you please."

"As you wish, my lady," he said grandly. "I am a veritable genie in a bottle. Your wish is my command."

"Then it is my wish that you not worry Miss Finch."

Merciful heaven, will this dance never end?

"I would never worry Miss Finch," Dickey protested. "Unless, of course, you mean as a dog might worry a bone, for I do confess she's a delectable young lady, and even a more scrupulous man than I might be tempted to take a bite."

"Mr. Dickey!"

Anne was saved from making a scene by a change in the dance which allowed her to escape him momentarily. All four ladies of the octet performed a sprightly moulinet, first to the right, then the left, giving right hands to one other as they crossed, and their left when they returned to their partners' sides.

"I do apologize," Mr. Dickey said once Anne danced back to him and they began another round of rigadon. "Force of habit. When one relies upon one's witticisms for inclusion in society, it is difficult to turn them off, even when one wishes to be serious. As I do now." His expression turned uncharacteristically sober. "I have no bad intent toward Miss Finch."

"You'll forgive me if I doubt you, sir."

"I understand it, but cannot forgive. You do wrong me in this. Truly. I mean your little lamb no harm." His expression turned sly again. "Lady, by yonder blessed moon, I swear—"

"Ugh! Spare me your mangled Shakespeare, I beg you, Mr. Dickey. Miss Finch is not your Juliet and you're certainly no Romeo."

"No, that role belongs to more august fellows. Like Lord Chatham."

Anne tried not to stiffen at the thought, but she felt sure her discomfort would travel through their dance hold and Dickey would deduce how she felt.

However, though Dickey was dancing with Anne, he seemed preoccupied with Martha. "I suppose you think Chatham is worthy to address Miss Finch, to write her, to court her."

It hurt her heart to think of Edward turning his attention toward Martha. Or anyone. But she couldn't admit that to Mr. Dickey.

"I have been charged with determining the suitability of Miss Finch's admirers," she admitted, wishing she could in good conscience find a reason *not* to recommend Edward.

"Ah! And you've taken that role upon yourself with gusto."

"As I should," Anne said testily. "Her parents are depending upon me to make sure Martha makes a good match."

"And what is your definition of a good match, pray?"

"You'll only use what I say to mock me."

"No, indeed, my lady. Trust me. I am not trying to offend, nor am I milking the cow to take away the calf," he said, referencing the easiest way to separate a bovine from her young.

"Well, what lady doesn't live to hear herself compared to a cow," Anne said.

"I ask your pardon. I didn't express myself well. I am glad Miss Finch has your guidance and protection. And I sincerely want to know your thoughts. Truly."

Surprisingly enough, Anne sensed no guile in him. But she was unable to respond just then because the dance called for the gentlemen to leave their partners to perform their moulinet figures.

Once he returned to join hands with Anne and begin a series of turns, he said, "As Sir Thomas More said, 'It often happeth, that the very face sheweth the mind walking a pilgrimage, in such wise that other folk suddenly say to them, a penny for *your* thought.' Are you ready to share your thoughts regarding what constitutes a good match, despite my having no penny to offer on the moment?"

Reginald Dickey was apparently very well read. His quote showed off the education his father the duke had provided for his ill-begotten son.

"Very well," Anne said. "A good match means the parties are of equal standing, have a similar circle of associates, complement each other in every way, and bring honor to both houses with their union."

"Rubbish."

"I beg your pardon."

"You gave me the ton's answer. It's what Miss Finch's parents want for her," Dickey said, as he began to lead her in the promenade which would eventually end the cotillion. "But what about you, Lady Howard? What do you want in a match?"

"I am not seeking a husband."

"I didn't say a marriage. I said a match. Someone whose soul fits yours," Dickey said. "Don't you long for someone to know you? And contrary to what you're thinking, I'm not making a joke about knowing someone in the biblical way."

The man must be a mentalist. She had suspected he was positioning himself to deliver an off-color jab at the scriptures. Instead, he was in earnest, so she decided to answer him earnestly.

"Yes, I suppose that is the desire of every heart, to know and be known," Anne admitted.

"And with the knowing, to be accepted," Dickey added.

Anne nodded. She'd once thought she had that deep knowing with Edward, but as it turned out, she didn't know him at all.

"When I started writing to Miss Finch, I confess that at first, I did it to be provocative. But after a few days of baring little bits of my soul to her, I discovered that my motivation had changed. I wanted her to know me,"

Dickey said with every appearance of candor. "Not as the duke's by-blow. Not as the clown I play for the ton's amusement. But simply...as myself."

"Why, Mr. Dickey..." Anne said as they completed the final figures. "I had no idea you felt that way."

"No one does," he said. "That's the point. There are very few to whom we may bare even a small piece of our true selves. The perfect match is the one we make when we risk showing all our innermost parts to another. And that darling other doesn't run away screaming."

The last note died away, and the assembly applauded the dancers' efforts, if not particularly their skill.

"Thank you for the dance, Lady Howard," Dickey said as he offered Anne his arm to lead her from the dance floor.

"The pleasure was mine, Mr. Dickey."

Anne didn't say it simply because it was the done thing. It was actually true. There was much more to Reginald Dickey than she'd suspected.

No one could have been more surprised by that than she.

Houses, titles, lands. Honors, pride of place, the trappings of wealth. To such things all men aspire. By an accident of birth and not, I confess, by my own merit, I attained them.

Yet I am forced to wonder, do I really possess these things, or do these things own me?

—from the journal of the increasingly frustrated Earl of Chatham

Chapter 13

Edward always preferred to arrive long after the other guests at any event hosted by Lady Ackworth. He had to endure less time under the gossip's sharp scrutiny. A late arrival meant he escaped mingling with the press of the other guests for a whole interminable evening. He avoided being harangued by those looking to curry his favor, and spent less time as the target of determined debutantes and their even more determined mamas.

But this evening he alighted from the Chatham carriage at Lady Ackworth's front door just as the clock tower chimed nine. He was right on time.

The ton might decide the Earl of Chatham arrived in a timely fashion because he was seeking a countess. But Edward knew he couldn't help being on time. Anne was supposed to be there.

After he was announced, he was mobbed by Lady Pickering and Lady Hapsted, both of whom had daughters they were frantic to introduce to him. Because the fact that he was seeking a wife was probably common knowledge now, these ladies evidently believed the race belonged not only to the swiftest but to the boldest. The point was further driven home when, after he disentangled himself from the first gaggle of hopefuls, he was accosted by Lady Burns, a Scottish baroness who was the proud mother of twin girls, both of whom had hair the color of a carrot and eyes like two cornflowers.

Edward was only allowed to escape after he made a vague promise to dance with each of the Scottish lasses at some point during the evening. Feeling very much like a fox harried by hounds, he made his way to the punch bowl. It was strategically located in the far corner. From this position, he could survey the room like a general preparing to marshal his forces and go forth into battle. Or, if events warranted a retreat, he could make a hasty exit out the double doors that led to the garden and risk splitting the seams of his breeches by hopping the back fence.

He was seriously tempted.

But Edward knew he should be moving forward with his plan to woo Miss Finch, especially after his sobering meeting with Mr. Higgindorfer about the state of his earldom's finances. He'd considered his situation from every angle for days, and it was the only reasonable course of action.

But then he'd catch a whiff of vanilla in some dish his cook had sent up, and all he'd be able to think of was Anne's sweet perfume. Or he'd wake in the dead of night, still half in a dream state, only to see her fleeing with her hair unbound away from him. It filled him with such despair, he wouldn't find sleep again.

But he had to move past his feelings. They were a luxury he could not afford. He had to steel himself to do what was required. He had to—

He suddenly caught sight of Anne. She was dancing. He watched her move through the figures of a cotillion with three other ladies. She was as graceful as a swan amid a flock of pigeon-toed ducks.

A surge of warmth flooded his chest. He'd always loved watching Anne dance. For a few moments he allowed himself to remember that silent waltz she'd performed in the moonlight when she didn't know he was watching. She was as wild and as lovely as a faery. Just the memory of her supple arms stretched to the sky, her face silvered by moonlight, her delectable form...Edward found himself crowding his new trousers.

Then Anne left the chain of lovely steps that the ladies in the cotillion performed together, and she danced back to her partner.

Reginald Dickey.

The backs of his eyes burned as if hot coals were being heaped upon his head.

"Good evening, Lord Chatham," piped an irritatingly cheerful voice at his elbow. He looked down to discover that Miss Finch had appeared suddenly at his side. It was an effort to turn his attention away from Anne and her blasted partner long enough to bow in response to Miss Finch's hiccup of a curtsy, but Edward somehow managed it. "I see you successfully passed through the gauntlet."

"I beg your pardon?"

"The other young ladies and their mothers. I feared for you, my lord. Lady Pickering and the rest can be most insistent, but I see you managed to escape unscathed," Miss Finch said with a contented sight. "I'm ever so glad Lady Howard doesn't force me on people."

Why should she when Miss Finch did that quite well on her own?

"I hope you don't think it too forward of me to greet you first, Lord Chatham," Miss Finch went on, undeterred by the way his gaze wandered back to the dance floor. "But because we have already been introduced, I believe it's quite proper that we should speak. After all, we passed an entire evening together at your sister's home, so I assumed you wouldn't mind if I initiated our conversation. Isn't that right, Lord Chatham?"

He'd stopped listening to her drone on because Anne had clasped hands with that waste of skin Reginald Dickey. But when Miss Finch said his name, Edward's attention was yanked back to her. He hadn't heard her entire question, but he assumed an affirmative response was the safest course.

"Yes, Miss Finch, by all means."

When she smiled smugly at him, he hoped she hadn't been forward enough to have proposed to him while he wasn't attending, because it would mean he'd just accepted.

"Not all means, my lord. I wouldn't try to force you into asking me to dance, for instance." She pulled out a lacy sage green fan and waved it before herself. "Isn't it warm in here? Might I trouble you for a glass of punch?"

He was too surprised to respond. Any of the other young ladies in the race to become his countess would have fainted dead away rather than ask a peer of the realm to fetch a drink. But Miss Finch was not a pattern sort of girl. In fact, she defied Edward's efforts to decide what sort of person she was actually.

Miss Finch was bright enough, he supposed, or at least she seemed to be. No one could play the piano with as much artistry as she without a modicum of intelligence, but Miss Finch had a habit of saying such strange things.

"My lord?"

"What?" He'd been distracted by the dancers again. As his gaze followed Anne around the room, he'd almost forgotten Miss Finch was there.

"The punch?" she repeated. "I suppose I could get a glass myself, but I've been told gentlemen like doing such things for ladies. Am I incorrect in that assumption?"

"Yes. I mean, no. I do beg your pardon. I was...woolgathering for some reason."

"Oh, I could tell you the reason," Miss Finch said, her lips curved in a sly smile, "but I doubt you'd care to hear it."

Edward was suddenly grateful for any excuse to escape this very odd young lady. "I should be glad to fetch you a cup of punch. I'll only be a moment."

He filled a glass for her and took his time returning with it. His gaze kept darting back to the dance floor, where Anne was now holding both that infernal man's hands. Edward snorted in frustration as he handed the punch to Miss Finch.

She thanked him prettily and took a sip. "Why does it trouble you so for Lady Howard to dance with Mr. Dickey?"

His gaze snapped to her bland face. Why would she say such a thing? "I can assure you, I am not troubled by the likes of Reginald Dickey."

"Is that because you think him so far beneath you?"

"No." Edward tried not to keep score in that way, though in order of precedence, he was much farther up the chain than the bastard son of a duke. He couldn't very well tell the girl that Dickey had delivered the worst news Edward had ever received in his entire life, and the man had done it with unabashed glee. Now he couldn't help feeling that Dickey had asked Anne to dance simply to rub salt in the wound.

"But you don't like Mr. Dickey much," Miss Finch guessed. "I find that hard to understand. He's so amusing—everyone else likes him immensely."

"I do not require being amused," Edward said, wishing he didn't sound like some old curmudgeon, but Miss Finch seemed so very young, he couldn't help being aware of the yawning gulf that separated their experiences. How could he ever steel his will enough to propose to her? "I am not required to like Mr. Dickey. However, we are all God's creatures, so I try to be tolerant of all men."

Even Reginald Dickey, drat the scoundrel! He's looking at Anne with much too earnest an expression for a casual dance partner.

"Hmm..." Martha tapped her front teeth with the tip of her fan. Edward wondered if it was a signal, yet another secret code he was supposed to understand, like Anne's glove language. If so, the only thing Miss Finch's gesture communicated to him was that her teeth were rather too big for the rest of her.

"Then if you're not upset with Mr. Dickey, that scowl of yours must mean you are out of charity with Lady Howard."

"What? No. Lady Howard is...I'm not...Would you like more punch?"

"I haven't finished what you gave me yet, but I'm gratified by your attentiveness, my lord." She lifted her cup and drained it in several large gulps. "Most refreshing. Now I would like some more, please."

Edward obliged, feeling a bit like a footman. At that moment, he'd willingly trade places with one if it meant he could disappear to the belowstairs portion of Lady Ackworth's home and not have to see Anne in another man's arms. Even if it was just in a dance hold.

"Thank you, Lord Chatham," Miss Finch said, as she accepted a second cup of punch from him. "I, for one, am delighted to see Lady Howard dancing. Do you know this is the first time she's done so since the death of her husband?"

"No, I didn't."

"Don't attribute any great depth of devotion to the fact," Miss Finch warned. "I rather think her marriage can't have been a love match."

Edward leaned toward her, suddenly interested in what the girl had to say. He'd never considered that she might be a good source of information about Anne's life while he was on the Continent if he were subtle enough to pose the right questions. "Why do you say Lady Howard's marriage was loveless?"

"I didn't say it was loveless. She did marry him, after all. Who knows if she grew to like him sometimes?" Miss Finch said. "But she never speaks about Sir Erasmus now. However, on one occasion of which I'm aware, she did visit his grave."

"Did she?"

"Yes, but her visit didn't require much of a journey. He's buried here in London instead of on his estate in Cornwall. Isn't that odd? He lived most of his life within sight of the ruins of Tintagel, but now he'll spend eternity in the shadow of St. Paul's."

Once again, Miss Finch proved herself not the average debutante. None of the other hopefuls would be discussing gravesites with a gentleman they hoped to impress.

She doesn't hope to impress me.

The realization hit Edward with the force of a blow. And lifted his spirits considerably. He even decided he liked Miss Finch a bit better for it.

"But the strange thing about that visit to Sir Erasmus's grave," Miss Finch went on, "was that Lady Howard brought enough flowers for two plots."

"Two? Who rested in the other?"

Miss Finch shook her head. "I don't know. There was no stone. Just a clump of yellow Lent lilies to mark the grave. When I asked her, she said she just thought the plot looked lonely, but that wasn't it. She's very good at hiding her feelings, but not that good. She knew very well who was there, and that person meant something to her."

"Who do you think it was?" Who would Anne be remembering with flowers? Her parents were still alive in York as far as Edward knew.

"I'm not sure, but her excuse that the spot looked lonely was exceedingly thin," Miss Finch said. "*Every* grave looks lonely, don't you think?"

"I think graves are far too serious a subject for a ball."

"Very well. What shall we talk about?" Miss Finch asked, and then proceeded to answer her own question. "I know. You may ask me for the next dance. I believe the cotillion is almost done. I hope the next one is a quadrille. If so, you needn't fear that I'll tread on your toes. I'm quite well versed in that dance."

Perhaps she's not such an unusual debutante after all. Miss Finch is just craftier than the rest.

Edward could see no other option. He bowed. "May I have the honor of the next dance, Miss Finch?"

"The honor is mine," she said with a giggle.

"Have I done something to amuse you?"

"No, my lord. At least, not on purpose. It's just the absurdity of the prescribed wording used to request a dance," she explained. "What's so honorable about it? It's only a dance. I find the whole thing mildly ridiculous."

At the moment, Edward did, too. But the cotillion came to an end, and after a smattering of applause, the strings started up again. Edward offered his arm to Miss Finch and led her onto the dance floor while Dickey squired Anne off.

Anne didn't meet his gaze, but the weasel she was with had the temerity to give him a snide grin.

Edward wished that Dickey was a gentleman of consequence to whom he could issue a genuine challenge. However, once he and Miss Finch formed up with the other dancers, thoughts of the irritating Reginald Dickey fled when he recognized the gentleman across from him.

It was Viscount Schaumberg of Bremen. The burly German had the physique of a brick layer and the grace of a farm hand, but Gottlieb Schaumberg was the cousin of Princess Caroline of Brunswick, the uncrowned queen of King George IV. It was no secret that the king had despised his wife. When she'd died last year, claiming from her death bed that she'd been poisoned, some in her family agreed with that assessment.

Edward wondered if Viscount Schaumberg was one of them. And if that was why he was in England now.

When I agreed to become Miss Finch's sponsor, I suspected the task of helping this unique young lady make a suitable match would be Herculean. However, I greatly fear I have done my job too well.
—Lady Howard, writing as herself

Chapter 14

As soon as Mr. Dickey took leave of Anne, she found a chair by the wall with the other matrons and surveyed the room, looking for Martha. Given the girl's propensity for eating every chance she got, Anne glanced first in the direction of the table that held light refreshments, but surprisingly enough, Martha wasn't there.

Lady Pickering, who was seated beside her, made a hmph-ing noise and drew her skirts closer so that not a stitch of her ensemble touched Anne's.

Anne decided to ignore her snub and continued to look for Martha.

Lady Pickering cleared her throat wetly.

Anne turned to her. "Do you have something you wish to say to me, Lady Pickering?"

"Because you feel compelled to force it out of me, yes, I do," the woman said, fairly quivering with suppressed outrage. "I hope you are proud of yourself, Lady Howard."

"In general, yes, I am." Anne blinked in surprise, wondering how she could have offended the lady merely by sitting down beside her. "To what specifically do you refer?"

"Pay her no mind." Lady Hapsted had to lean forward to speak to Anne because she was perched on the other side of Lady Pickering. "She's merely upset because his lordship requested his first dance of your Miss Finch instead of her Eleanor."

"Oh!" Anne hadn't thought to check the dance floor for her protégé, but sure enough, there she was, lightly tripping along beside Edward. Martha wasn't the finest dancer on the floor, but she wasn't disgracing herself either. "Well, so he has."

Lord Chatham was definitely wearing his station this evening. His dark suit of superfine fabric was cut in the first stare of fashion. Diamonds winked at his cuffs and down his shirtfront. His shoes were so brightly polished, Anne suspected she'd be able to see her reflection in them. But even without all that sartorial splendor, tall, broad-shouldered Edward was far and away the most handsome man in the place.

Especially without all that. Anne's chest constricted and she forced herself to draw a deep breath.

"As if you're surprised that Miss Finch should be granted the honor of the first dance with his lordship when it's clearly your doing," Lady Pickering said. "It seems to me you and Lord Chatham spent a good deal of time in each other's company the year you came out. You know the earl quite well."

"It is no sin to know someone."

"But to use that knowledge in an underhanded way to cut out more deserving young ladies...well!"

"I had nothing to do with Lord Chatham's choice of dance partners," Anne said testily. "And Miss Finch is no less deserving than your daughter. Besides, I consider it his lordship's great good fortune to be dancing with Miss Finch, not the other way around."

Anne thought nothing of the kind, but she wouldn't let Lady Pickering denigrate Martha by intimating she was too inconsequential to deserve Edward's notice.

Lady Pickering lifted her lorgnette and peered at Anne through the thick lenses, clearly taking her measure and finding her wanting. Anne stifled a giggle at the way the device magnified the lady's eyes and made her look rather like an out-of-sorts bluebottle fly.

"Yes, indeed, everyone said you were the Original of your Season, though I could never see it myself," Lady Pickering went on. "And I was proven right in the end, when you had to settle for a mere baronet. Not to speak ill of the dead, but Sir Erasmus was quite a comedown after the visions of a countess's tiara that must have danced in your head."

Anne was too shocked to respond to this diatribe. Clearly, to Lady Pickering the Season was a blood sport.

"And yet, it is obvious to anyone with eyes that *your* past experience with the earl has given the Finch girl an advantage," Lady Pickering said with a sneer.

"Oh, pish!" Lady Hapsted said, swatting her friend with her folded-up fan. "You're only upset because Lord Chatham overlooked your Eleanor."

"Well, he's not dancing with your Leticia either. And Lord Chatham did *not* overlook our daughters. He was ambushed by Miss Finch. I saw her approach his lordship and force him into conversation with her." Then for emphasis, Lady Pickering added, "With my own eyes."

"You couldn't very well have done it with anyone else's eyes," Anne muttered. Lady Pickering seemed not to have heard her, for she went right on.

"Frankly, Lady Howard, you'd do well to keep a tighter rein on that protégé of yours. She pushed herself forward quite shamelessly. The girl is as bold as brass, I tell you. Why, Lord Chatham, fine gentleman that he is, was *obligated* to ask her to dance. Honestly, I've a mind to write to Lady Finch to warn her of your deficiencies as a guardian for her daughter."

"Please do that, Lady Pickering," Anne said as she stood. "And be sure to include the fact that you're concerned that Miss Finch is enjoying the company of the most eligible bachelor in London while he ignores your darling daughter Eleanor. No doubt, my services will be dispensed with at once."

She dipped a quick curtsy to Lady Hapsted, who had been much kinder than the other matron. "I'm sure his lordship will dance with your daughter at some point this evening."

"Do you think so?" Lady Hapsted's smile spread from one droopy cheek to the other. "Leticia will be so pleased."

"What about my Eleanor?" Lady Pickering demanded.

Anne turned and left before she said something rude about her Eleanor. At least the woman's unpleasantness had taken Anne's mind off the fact that Edward was dancing with Martha. She knew she should be happy for the girl, but her gut roiled all the same.

Anne wound her way through the press of people, barely noticing who else was there. Her insides were tangled in a jittery knot. She told herself it was because of the unpleasantness she'd endured at the hands of Lady Pickering, but that wasn't the real reason she felt sick.

Sick at heart, sick in mind, sick in her soul.

Edward was dancing, but it wasn't with her.

He'd kissed her wrist the last time she saw him and the mere brush of his lips had been enough to make her nearly unravel. Yet here at Lady Ackworth's ball, he was dancing with a debutante.

Anne was unmarried. Available for wooing. True, it would be unusual for an earl to take a widow to wife, but he and Anne had a history. They had—

Anne couldn't let herself dwell on what they'd had. She was in a public place. Some of the people around her wished her well, but, as Lady Pickering had so deftly proved, some of them decidedly didn't. She couldn't allow herself to feel any of the messy, unruly emotions that Edward stirred up. Her face showed too plainly what was going on inside her.

And the only thought screaming through her brain was that Edward still seemed determined to court Martha.

It hurt so badly, even breathing was an effort.

Woodenly, she moved from one clump of guests to another, presenting a false smile and nodding in greeting as she passed. Her cheeks ached, but she dared not let the mask drop for a second. She was so conscious of how she must appear to others, it scarcely registered to her who the others were.

As a result, she didn't even recognize her own stepson until she was almost upon him.

"Ah! There you are. We've been looking for you," Sir Percival said as he sketched a haphazard bow. He'd been a dissolute youth who'd grown into a dissolute man. Despite his excellently tailored suit, his belly could not be contained by any manly girdle. His nose and cheeks were mottled red, the sure sign of a dedicated tippler.

"Sir Percy, what are you doing here?" Anne asked in surprise. Cornwall was a long way from London.

"We were invited," he said, puffing out his chest in a stance that reminded Anne so starkly of his father it was almost like seeing her husband's ghost. "You remember my wife, Sofia." He gestured to the tall, sturdy woman at his side. "Her cousin, Viscount Schaumberg, is here. Lady Ackworth invited a number of people who are related to the royal family, so of course, we were included."

Trust Lady Ackworth to overplay her hand. She had spread the rumor that there would be royals present at her ball to increase attendance. However, relatives of the unloved dead wife of King George IV hardly signified as relations of the royal family any longer. In fact, tension still ran high between the House of Hanover and the House of Brunswick. And Sofia was merely the cousin of a cousin of the late lamented Princess Caroline.

"Of course, I remember you, Sofia." Anne dipped in a curtsy.

The woman bobbed shallowly in return. "I would appreciate if you would address me properly. Call me Lady Howard."

In fact, there were three women who could use that name, as Percival's irascible grandmother was still alive as well.

"While we are in London, you must go by the *Dowager* Lady Howard to avoid confusion," Percival's wife said with a sniff.

"Now, now, we likely won't be seeing each other that much because we'll be traveling in different circles." Percival patted his wife's hand in a conciliatory fashion.

Sofia had never been friendly to Anne, but now her expression was downright hostile.

"How long will you be in Town?" Anne asked. London was a big city, one of the grandest on earth, and yet it suddenly seemed far too small.

"That remains to be seen," Percy said mysteriously.

He always did have a flair for the dramatic.

Anne hadn't seen her stepson or his exceedingly unpleasant wife since around the time Sir Erasmus died. The couple had come to London for an awkward visit during which Anne's husband spent most of his time berating his son. Percival had always been an inveterate gambler and general layabout, so the criticism was warranted. After a particularly virulent dressing down, Percy and his wife had left for Cornwall. That had been about a fortnight before Sir Erasmus was suddenly stricken ill and died. Anne had sent word to Cornwall immediately, but Percival claimed there wasn't enough time for him to make it back for the funeral.

She almost didn't blame him after the way he and his father had parted.

But he managed to attend the reading of the will a week after that, Anne thought sourly. "What brings you back to London now?"

"It has been communicated to us that the king wishes to make amends with the House of Brunswick for his shameful treatment of Princess Caroline. He plans to start by playing host to her cousins," Percival explained. "That is why Viscount Schaumberg is here."

"And why I am here," Sofia added. "If we send back a favorable word to my parents and cousins in Brunswick, perhaps the royal families will not feel themselves quite so divided."

"Plus our daughter Harriet is fifteen. She'll come out next year," Percival said. "It seems wise to make a few connections in London before her Season."

And when better to impress a new acquaintance than when one is being feted as a royal cousin?

"Besides, we are not like Lord and Lady Finch. I heard that the baron and his wife *hired* someone to sponsor their daughter," Sofia said, her lip curled in distaste. "Can you imagine?"

"Yes, I can. I am Miss Finch's sponsor."

Sofia gasped in obviously feigned surprise. "But it's so very irregular. After all, most mothers prefer to guide their daughters through this delicate time themselves instead of entrusting the matter to a stranger." She pulled out her fan and waved it languidly before her. "Still, there is no accounting for taste, is there?"

"No, there certainly isn't," Anne said, eyeing her stepson pointedly, but realizing he was too dense to recognize that she was silently criticizing his choice in a wife. "Is that the only reason you're in Town?"

"Not exactly." The baronet and his wife exchanged a glance. "Is there someplace where we might speak privately?"

That had an ominous sound, but Anne kept her tone light. "I'm sure we might be able to pop into an unused parlor or out into the garden. It's a lovely night."

"No, not the garden," the younger Lady Howard protested. "Lady Ackworth's is full of night blooming narcissus. The smell disagrees with me."

Anne suspected most things did.

"Then let us go in search of a quiet spot somewhere in the house," Anne said as she led the way out of the large room that had been given over to dancing.

There was a small parlor off the foyer which was unoccupied, but Lady Ackworth obviously meant for her guests to make use of it because a pair of lamps had been left burning on either side of the cold fireplace to light the space. As they entered, the drawn curtains swayed a bit. Anne decided someone must have left a window ajar.

With any luck the scent of night blooming narcissus will waft its way in here shortly.

"Very well." Anne turned to face her stepson. "What did you wish to tell me?"

The Cornish Lady Howard gave her husband a nudge. Percy cleared his throat. "It has come to our attention that my father left you a jointure."

"Yes, but this is not news to you. You were present at the reading of his last will and testament." She thought it quite thoughtful of Sir Erasmus to have bequeathed a small lump sum to her.

"Well, what we didn't know at the time was that because he stipulated that you receive the jointure, it was intended to be in lieu of a dower portion."

"What?" Anne was already splitting the dower's share of the estate with her dead husband's mother. The amount shrank each year under Percival's unsteady hand until it was barely enough to meet her needs, let alone feed her wanderlust.

"That's right. You are entitled to either the jointure or a dower share, but not both," Sofia said with vehemence. "The lawyer said so."

"And as you have already taken possession of the jointure—"

"We don't owe you so much as a farthing," Sofia interrupted her husband. "You have received your last payment from us."

"Sofia." Percy raised a hand and glared at his wife. Surprisingly, Sofia took a step back. Anne wondered if her stepson was as harsh with his fists as his father had been with his tongue. "If you'd only come home when I asked you to and taken up residence in the cottage—"

"The *gameskeeper's* cottage." Anne's sharpest recollection of the tumbledown place was the rank gameskeeper himself. The man had smelled like a goat, and his essence permeated every inch of his dwelling.

"Yes, well, if you had acceded to my wishes," Percy said, "we might never have sought out an attorney and discovered that we have been paying you moneys you were not owed."

"We ought to demand repayment," Sofia chimed in, and this time Percival did not reprimand her.

Anne's vision tunneled and her knees buckled. Fortunately, she had been standing close enough to the sofa to sink onto it instead of the floor.

"No, no, we won't do that. You may keep what we've given you in past years," Percival said. "We are not heartless."

Anne suspected Percy was more concerned about his reputation than caring for her plight. The ton would have plenty to say about a gentleman trying to wring money from a widow.

"But you should know that what you have is what you have," Percival said. "You will not be receiving anything more."

The lump sum she'd received upon Sir Erasmus's death was only slightly larger than her yearly stipend had been. Each year, she tried to make her dower share from Percy stretch to cover her expenses, but she was usually forced to take out part of the jointure as well.

The amount she had left was frighteningly small. There would be no more Howard money forthcoming. Anne didn't make that much on the Mrs. Birdwhistle pamphlets after she deducted the cost of paying the actress to impersonate her. And the lion's share of the remuneration she expected from Lord Finch hinged on whether or not Martha made a good match.

For the first time in her life, Anne didn't know what to do.

"I shouldn't worry were I you," Sofia said in an oily tone. "You're so very clever. If you can't persuade another gullible family to let you sponsor their daughter next year, perhaps you might find a position as a governess. Or maybe a paid companion."

A governess? They were the most tragic of creatures. Usually well-born and educated but unable for one reason or another to have a family of her own, a governess was neither fish nor fowl. She wasn't considered a servant, so she didn't enjoy the camaraderie of the belowstairs folk. Neither was she counted as part of the family she served. A governess was doomed to dine alone in her rooms unless a rarity occurred and the number of guests was lopsided so that an extra lady was needed at table. Then there were the children to contend with. They might be holy terrors or little angels, and she might come to love them either way, but they would never be hers.

The life of a paid companion was not without its pitfalls either. There was a chance her employer would be kindly, but she was more likely to be the crusty, unpleasant sort whom no one wished to spend time with unless they were being compensated for the dreadful experience.

I've fallen into the ninth circle of hell.

But Anne forced herself not to crumple before her stepson and his wife. She stood and lifted her chin. "Thank you for bringing this matter to my attention. Do not trouble yourselves on my account. I shall be fine."

She kept repeating *I shall be fine* over and over in her mind while Percival and his wife made their exit. Then once the door closed, she sank onto the couch again. Deliberately, this time. She trembled like an autumn leaf, but she was determined to maintain her composure.

Her throat was a tight knot, but she would not sob. It was what Percy and that hateful Sofia wanted.

However, her tear ducts did not respond to her efforts to control them. All alone, Ann wept. But her tears flowed in silence, as if she were a lost child who feared any sound would call forth the terrors that lurked just beyond her sight.

Were I to die tonight and meet St. Peter at the Golden Gate, I would confess to one besetting sin. Envy. I am jealous of every man who has ever looked at Anne, who ever listened to her play the harp, who ever spoke with her. But I am most envious of any man who is free to make her his own, for, God help me, the Earl of Chatham does not enjoy that sort of liberty.
—from the journal of Edward Lovell, Lord Chatham

Chapter 15

Edward had given up finding Anne among the press of people in the ballroom. He'd even slipped out for a quick look around the garden, but no one had wandered out to stroll the graveled paths through the spring blossoms. Then he started through the other rooms on the ground floor of the house.

He began to wonder if Anne had left Lady Ackworth's home completely, but then realized she'd never abandon Miss Finch. As long as that young lady was still on the dance floor, Anne had to be there somewhere. He finally discovered her in a small parlor off the foyer. There she was, seated on the sofa that faced the cold fireplace, her back to him.

"Anne?"

She shot to her feet but didn't turn to face him. Instead, she ducked her head as if to hide in plain sight like a rabbit that freezes when a hound is near. She didn't speak.

"Dearest, what's wrong?" The endearment slipped out before he knew it was on his tongue. "Are you ill?"

Anne shook her head, straightened her shoulders, and turned around to meet his gaze. She was wearing her brave smile again, but her nose was slightly pink, her eyes overly bright. She'd been crying.

Edward hurried to her side, but when he drew close, she straight-armed him and retreated to the far side of the room as if he carried the plague.

"No, no, it's nothing." Her voice broke as she swiped at her cheeks.

"It doesn't sound like nothing."

"I'm fine. Leave me, I beg you."

"I will not. You're obviously upset." Edward's arms ached to hold her, to take away whatever had disturbed her. "I passed Sir Percival and his wife in the hall. Has he done something to disturb you?"

"Percy told me—" She stopped herself. "It's a Howard family matter. I don't wish to discuss it."

It rankled his soul to hear her name herself a member of the Howard family, but it was unfortunately true. He wished with all his heart that he'd defied his father years ago and eloped with her when he'd had the chance. She'd be a Lovell now. His to cherish and defend. "If you won't tell me what's wrong, how can I help you?"

"You can't. No one can. Go back to the ball." She wouldn't meet his gaze. "I'm certain there are any number of debutantes who are dying to dance with you, Lord Chatham."

There was that wall again. It rose up between them each time she called him by his full title instead of Bredon or Edward. Oh! how he wished she'd use Edward. Anne sounded angry now, still shaking a bit, but no longer teary-eyed.

Good. I'll take an angry Anne over a weeping one any day.

The music of the strings wafted in through the crack in the door behind him. It was a sadly sweet tune in three-quarter time. He recognized it from someplace.

"I know that tune."

"It's a Boccherini waltz," Anne said. "The first one we ever danced together."

He suddenly realized it was also the same melody Anne had played on his sister's harp the other evening. She must be as full of memories of those golden days and silver nights as he. Oh, that aching, breathless time, those stolen moments, the yearning...he'd wanted her with every fiber of his body.

Sweet Lord, how I want this woman still.

"Dance with me."

She swiped her lower lip with her little pink tongue. "That is not the proper way to ask for a dance."

And that's not a no.

"I don't feel the least proper toward you, Anne. And I'm not asking."

Edward closed the distance between them and put his hand on her waist. Her breath hissed in over her teeth at his touch, but she didn't stop him as he drew her nearer. That hint of vanilla in the perfume she wore wrapped itself around his brain. He longed to seek out all the places where she applied that scent, to bury his head in the sweet spot between her shoulder and neck, between her breasts...

Anne was as supple as he remembered as she leaned into him. She still trembled a bit, but she didn't seem angry any longer.

He captured her hand and drew it to his lips to plant a soft kiss on her knuckles. Then he sheltered it in his as they began moving together in a small box step in time with the distant music. With each measure, Edward pulled her closer until her body was flush against his.

She was all that was soft and willing and woman. His whole body thrummed with need and frustration.

"The waltz is my favorite dance," she whispered. "We still do it well together."

"We do." Edward wasn't thinking about how well their bodies remembered the waltz. He was too lost in memories of the other dance they'd discovered together. The ancient one that needed no other music than the beating of their hearts.

"But it's only my favorite when I dance it with you," Anne whispered.

Did that mean she hadn't loved her husband? That she'd found no pleasure with the baronet? He hoped she had not. He hated himself for being such a toad, but that selfish part of him still hoped he'd been the only one to give bliss to Anne.

She'd stopped shaking now, and moved herself against him.

He bent and pressed his lips to the pulse point on her neck. She made a soft moan. He wanted to pleasure her. To feel her give herself over to him. To live again while he died a little in her arms...

"Edward, please. We shouldn't—"

He covered her mouth with his to quiet her, kissing her into silence and delicious oblivion. Somewhere in the back of his mind, he was aware that the door was still slightly ajar. Anyone could come upon them at any moment in this compromising situation.

He almost hoped someone would.

It would settle the matter in one stroke. Even though she wasn't a blushing debutante, being caught with him like this would damage her reputation beyond repair. He'd have to do the honorable thing and marry Anne to avoid subjecting her to public scandal. It wasn't the best way to make this woman his own, but he'd take it.

Edward had tried to choose Chatham over her. He'd tried with all his might to do the honorable thing. The just thing.

But his heart was too bound up with the woman in his arms.

If only there were a way to fulfill the needs of the estate along with his own needs, he'd die a happy man. But the earldom didn't signify in the slightest at the moment.

All that mattered was his Anne.

"Edward, you're not playing fair," she murmured when he finally released her mouth. "You make me..." She palmed his cheeks. "I want to..." Her eyes went all soft and dewy, the whites showing beneath her lovely dark irises. "You can't expect me to..." Her mouth turned down into as much of a frown as she was capable of. "I don't think I like you right now."

He liked her plenty. Loved her, even. Aching need overwhelmed him.

Then to his surprise, she reached up and pulled his head down, demanding that he kiss her again. She drew all the breath from his lungs in a surprised rush.

He gasped when she released his lips. "I thought you didn't like me."

"I don't. I don't like you very much." She tugged him closer and his mouth descended on hers for another bruising kiss.

Her words might not welcome him, but her mouth certainly did. When her lips parted, his tongue swept in to claim her dark moistness.

He figured he probably tasted of that weak-willed punch, but Anne's mouth was as sweet as he remembered, her lips as soft. He was freshly shaved, but her skin was like butter compared to his sandpaper. He feared he'd scratch her. Her breath feathered across his cheek.

She wiggled a bit in his arms and he wondered if she wanted to pull away. If he was determined to keep her, his strength would make the contest woefully lopsided.

But he didn't want her like that. He wanted her willing.

He eased his hold on her and she relaxed into him, melting against his body.

Then she began to kiss him back in the playful, lusty way he remembered, chasing his tongue and nipping at his bottom lip. Her fingers curled around his lapel and pulled him closer. He groaned into her mouth.

His hands left her waist and found her breasts, stroking them through the thin silk. Longing sang in his veins and pooled between his legs.

It had been so long.

Now he was the one who was shaking. With need. Still kissing, they moved together, the waltz turning into a stylized dance of lust, toward the credenza in the corner.

Edward reached around her and shoved aside all the doilies and figurines and decorative dust-catchers. They tumbled to the floor, pounding one after the other in a crashing rumble. With the music and the constant din of conversation, no one in the ballroom would notice the clatter of their breaking. And even if someone did, Edward didn't care.

He lifted Anne and set her down on the sturdy piece of furniture that was blessedly the right height for what he had in mind.

"Careful," she warned breathlessly, "you'll bring the world down on us."

"The world is already down on us. Ask me if I care." He bent and reached under her skirts, running his palms up her legs all the way up her thighs.

Her breathing hitched, but she sat perfectly still. "Do you care, Edward?"

"Only for you."

He stroked her then. Anne grasped his shoulders and let her head rest against him as he caressed her. She whimpered his name. Touching her was like touching a shrine, an unreachable piece of perfection. He profaned her, he knew, but he couldn't stop himself. He was near that place of unraveling madness.

Someone knocked on the door.

Edward ignored the sound.

It creaked open.

No, he didn't hear that. It was his imagination. Anne, who was biting her lower lip to keep from crying out, gave no sign of having heard a thing.

"Lord Chatham," came a gravelly voice from behind him.

Edward froze. He hadn't imagined that.

Anne's grip on his shoulders tightened.

The someone who'd entered the parlor cleared his throat. Loudly. "My lord."

The intrusion was all too real. They'd been discovered. Edward pulled her skirts back down. He and Anne had been caught in a delicately awkward situation. He would *have* to marry her now. Euphoria flooded his chest.

Edward was tempted to kiss whoever had interrupted them right on the mouth.

Then he turned, hiding Anne behind his body, and discovered the interloper was Mr. Higgindorfer, his fusty old man of business.

Just my luck. Found out by the soul of discretion.

My father used to tell me, "If you have to slink about, lie, or avoid being seen while you're doing something, you probably ought not to be doing it." But what if the slinking, lying, and avoiding is to protect the someone you're doing it with?

—from the journal of Edward Lovell, the mildly embarrassed Earl of Chatham

Chapter 16

Lucius Higgindorfer's loyalty to the House of Lovell rivaled his allegiance to the Crown. Edward could have been engaged in a naked orgy with a whole troop of opera dancers and Higgindorfer would have taken the secret to his grave. Anne's reputation was safe with him.

"My lord, I need to speak with you."

"Now?"

"Yes, my lord. I would not presume to intrude upon you did I not deem the matter of the utmost importance." Higgindorfer marched over to the cold fireplace and studied the highly flattering portrait of Lady Ackworth installed above the mantel. "I shall concern myself with this unrecognizable portrait of your hostess while the young lady takes her leave. She may rest assured I have no notion of, nor interest in, her identity."

Anne had already hopped down from the credenza. Edward wanted to reassure her that everything would be all right, that somehow, he'd fix things. He'd never allow her to be shamed, and whatever Sir Percival had done to distress her, he'd fix that, too. But once Higgindorfer began staring up at Lady Ackworth, Anne skittered out of the room before Edward could say a word.

"How did you find me?" he demanded of the old man.

"Mr. Price informed me that you were a guest at Lady Ackworth's ball, though I must say, I did not expect to find you thusly employed, my lord."

"You forget yourself, sir." Edward drew himself up to his full height and glared sternly at the old man. "I value your opinion only on financial matters. Keep all other advice or censure to yourself."

"Quite right, my lord. I ask your pardon, but in my defense, I've known you since you were born. Sometimes one forgets you are no longer a youth in need of moral guidance." The old man's grating tone belied his words. Given half the chance, Higgindorfer would give Edward a dressing down to rival his father at his imperious worst. "I came tonight hoping to find his lordship in the company of a well-dowered young lady whose fortune might benefit the estate. However, I'm guessing the woman who captured your attention is neither of those things."

"She is a lady and that is enough," Edward said crossly. "And if you have anything further to say on the matter, be warned that your association with the House of Lovell will be in peril."

"Ah! Just so. To business then," Higgindorfer said. "I have discovered the information you require about the funeral furnisher for Sir Erasmus Howard."

"And it couldn't wait until tomorrow?" Edward raked his fingers through his hair in irritation.

"No, my lord. The intelligence is distressing enough that I felt compelled to pass it on to you immediately." Higgindorfer left his place by the fire and toddled over to one of the wing chairs that flanked it. He started to sit, but then stopped himself. "With your permission, Lord Chatham. These old legs aren't as young as they used to be."

Frustrated, Edward gestured for him to sit and began to pace, hoping to exhaust his still roused body.

Once Higgindorfer settled himself, he began to speak. All he lacked was a snifter of brandy and a cigar, and he'd have been taken for a raconteur holding court with his story. "The funeral furnisher for Sir Erasmus Howard was Chenowith and Sons, an old and well-respected firm. Time out of mind, they have served the best of families. But since the funeral of Sir Erasmus, they have gone out of business, which struck me as rather mysterious given that the company has operated here in London, passing from father to son, since the Great Fire."

Intrigued despite his annoyance with the old man, Edward stopped pacing. "What happened to them?"

"I'm glad you asked. Because it seemed odd, I instructed my agent to inquire further without your express order to expand the investigation,"

Higgindorfer said, jutting his jaw forward like a turtle emerging from its shell. "I trust I acted in accordance with your wishes, my lord."

"Yes, yes, you did well." Edward had to admit the old man had a sixth sense about the needs of his clients, but he also needed to hear that he was right with annoying regularity. "Go on."

"In any case, shortly after Sir Erasmus's death, they closed up shop and moved to Cornwall. To the village of Tintagel, my agent says."

As soon as Edward learned that Anne had married Sir Erasmus Howard, he'd made it his business to know about the baronet's holding. Tintagel was the village nearest Sir Erasmus's estate.

"It's hard to imagine that Chenowith and Son's business was failing here in London," Edward said. "The market may be up or down, but death is a sure bet in any economy."

"Aye, my lord, you've the right of it. So I expanded the scope of your inquiry yet again. According to my agent, who is entirely trustworthy, I assure you, Chenowith and Sons received a mysterious windfall of funds right around the time of the baronet's death. Within a week, they were gone."

"Curious," Edward said. "But surely they wouldn't have taken all their contractors with them."

A funeral furnisher was merely the director of the sad event. He hired out the actual work to others, from designing and producing the mourning gifts to be distributed to the departed's family and friends, to the disposition of the body and arrangements for the final resting place. A funeral furnisher was rather like a conductor, who waved his arms before an orchestra while the actual musicians made the music.

"Indeed, my lord, Chenowith and Sons did not relocate their underlings. My agent was able to ferret out the pair of crones who washed and dressed the body of Sir Erasmus for burial." Mr. Higgindorfer cleared his throat noisily. "Let me tell you, my lord, those women told quite a tale."

But evidently you can't without me prying it from you. "Out with it, man."

"According to the last people to see him intimately, Sir Erasmus's skin was discolored in several places. But nothing that anyone would have seen if he were fully clothed, you understand, so no alarm was raised by mourners at his viewing," Mr. Higgindorfer said with a sigh. "But the sad fact is there is no dignity in death. The women who bathed his body for the final time reported dark and mottled patches on his skin. 'Like raindrops on a dusty road' was how they described it."

"And why didn't they tell anyone this at the time?"

"My lord, the women were regular contractors for Chenowith and Sons. Discretion is paramount in the business of death," Mr. Higgindorfer said. "They were expected to be close-lipped about their work, and rightly so."

"But surely—"

"Surely, the women didn't want to disrupt a source of steady income," Higgindorfer said.

"Because Sir Erasmus's death was unexpected, anything unusual ought to have been mentioned. I can understand why they might have feared for their livelihood, but they were without excuse once the company closed," Edward said. "They could have come forward to report what they'd seen to the authorities after Chenowith and Sons left Town."

"My lord, women who wash the bodies of the dead for a living are not ladies of consequence. No one would believe them after the man had been moldering in the ground for a week. If no one asks, they assume no one wants to know." Higgindorfer spread his hands before him, palms up, in a full torso shrug. "And until now, no one asked."

"To what do you attribute the skin discolorations?" Edward hoped it wasn't the French Pox. That ailment sometimes presented a telltale rash. He could happily wish Sir Erasmus thrice damned if the baronet had been unfaithful to Anne and had brought the cursed disease home to her.

"Poison, my lord," Higgindorfer said.

Relief washed over him. Anne was safe.

"Specifically arsenic, according to my agent," Higgindorfer went on. "It is odorless, tasteless, and can be added to virtually anything. Delivered in small amounts over time, it arouses no misgivings as its victim's health fails in minute increments. My agent believes Sir Erasmus must have been dosed for some time, which accounts for the skin discolorations, for those are an early sign of poisoning, but then a larger, lethal dose must have been administered, as his end came swiftly and, to outward appearances, with no warning."

"You don't think his poisoning could have been accidental?"

Mr. Higgindorfer tipped his head to one side, considering. "Occasionally one sees accidental poisonings because of a contaminated well, but in those cases, entire families, whole villages even, suffer the effects. In Sir Erasmus's case, he was the only one in the home who succumbed."

An ugly suspicion crossed his mind. "Then you believe—"

"I believe someone close to the baronet helped him to his end." Higgindorfer rose to his feet and gave Edward a stiff bow. "I leave it to wiser heads than mine to discover who that someone might have been. Good evening, my lord."

Once Higgindorfer shuffled out, Edward sank into the other wing chair. *Someone close to the baronet, he says.*

Higgindorfer thought Anne was culpable. He didn't say so, but he might as well have. A man's widow was the logical suspect. Besides, Edward had thought of her first, too.

But could she have been so miserably unhappy with Sir Erasmus that she'd have stooped to poison to be rid of him?

No, he decided. Anne might not conform to society's notions of proper behavior in every area of life—*and God be praised for that or I'd never have had those blessed stolen moments with her*—but however many rules she might give the back of her hand to, it wasn't in her to harm someone else. Edward would stake his hope of heaven on it.

As he crossed the room toward the door, a flash of movement caught the tail of Edward's eye. He glanced over to see the floor-length curtain sway again. Someone was hiding behind that thick damask panel.

Which means they've heard far more about Anne and me and the death of Sir Erasmus than anyone should.

The ancients believed the enemy of one's enemy is one's friend. With a friend like that, who can say with certainty who the real enemy is?
—from the journal of Edward Lovell, Earl of Chatham, Viscount Bredon, and holder of a smattering of lesser titles and honors he forgets about with regularity

Chapter 17

Edward stared at the curtain for a few moments, hoping he'd only imagined seeing it waver slightly. When it moved again, he crept across the room. Then he suddenly threw back the damask panel, grabbed the man hidden there by his collar, and dragged him out.

It was Reginald Dickey.

Edward raised his fist to deliver a blow to the sneaking, conniving weasel.

The man cringed and held up his hands to shield his face.

"Please, my lord, if you must strike, aim for my gut, I beg you," Mr. Dickey whined. "I can live with a bellyache, but I'll be crushed if you ruin my nose. Its aquiline curve is the spitting image of my father's. My face buys me dinner as often as my wit."

Dickey was so ridiculous and pitiful, Edward didn't have the heart to thrash him. The urge was still strong, but he wasn't the sort to strike someone who didn't intend to give as good as he got. Edward released him with a shove that made Dickey stumble back a few paces.

"Confound it, man. What in blazes are you doing skulking about?"

"Skulking is such an ugly word," Dickey said testily. "I may stroll. I may saunter. I've even been known to sashay from time to time, but I never skulk."

"Very well, what are you doing so far away from the party?"

"Well, my original plan was to steal a kiss from Miss Finch here in this lovely deserted parlor." Dickey tugged down his waistcoat and adjusted his collar. "But that most excellent scheme was spoiled by the fact that the parlor has been far from deserted. I only just managed to hide myself when Lady Howard and her stepson and his wife barged in for a rather tumultuous family tête-à-tête."

So, Dickey had been privy to Anne's being cornered by Sir Percival before Edward arrived. Her stepson had said or done something to make her cry. Whatever it was, Edward needed to steer Dickey's attention away from Anne as quickly as he could, so he turned his line of questioning back to Dickey's intentions toward Miss Finch.

"What makes you think Miss Finch would meet you here?" Edward demanded. "I haven't even seen you dancing with her this evening."

"No, you haven't, and that's by our design, by the way," he said with a grin. "A classic case of misdirection. Clever of us, wasn't it?"

"What are you talking about?"

"Oh, between me and Miss Finch, we had it all arranged. You see, after Lady Howard learned we had been corresponding by means of the post, she put an end to it—"

"As well she should."

"Agreed. No baron worth his salt would be pleased to learn his daughter was corresponding with a rapscallion like me," he said with a smirk. "But since when do I care what anyone thinks?"

"You'd better care what I think," Edward said. "I'm still of half a mind to break your nose."

Dickey cupped a hand over his prominent feature and went on with his explanation. "In any case, after Lady Howard delivered a momentary setback by forbidding my correspondence with Miss Finch, I discovered that Lord Finch should really pay his staff better. It was appallingly easy to bribe the lady's maid to act as our go-between. Our missives have flown back and forth as if by carrier pigeon, which incidentally was my next plan should the bribery of a trusted servant have failed."

Edward folded his arms across his chest. "So you've been courting Miss Finch without her sponsor's approval."

Dickey shrugged. "I don't know that I'd categorize our association as a courtship, but the young lady and I are having a rollicking good time of it, whatever it is."

Edward took a menacing step toward him. "If you besmirch Miss Finch's good name—"

"I may have enticed her to risky behavior, but one cannot be held to account for his intentions, only his actions. No harm has come to Miss Finch through me," Dickey said, hand on his chest with every affectation of earnestness. "And if you'll pardon my impertinence, my lord, of the two of us, I am not the one who has actually played fast and loose with a lady's reputation this evening."

He has me there. But fortunately, Dickey was too interested in sharing the cleverness of his own romantic exploits to focus on Anne and Edward's.

"At any rate, Miss Finch and I orchestrated the entire evening. First, we arranged for me to partner with Lady Howard for the first dance, and then for Miss Finch to lure you into asking her for the second. Then once both of you were put off balance by those encounters, she and I were to make good our escape from the ballroom and meet here." Dickey sighed and shook his head. "But Robert Burns was right. 'The best laid plans of mice and men gang aft agley.'"

The man was well read, Edward had to give him that. Reginald Dickey was a prime example of what an investment in education could achieve no matter whether a fellow was to the manor born or conceived on the wrong side of the blanket. But Dickey's considerable and inventive use of his learning was only part of the man's appeal to the ton. He was a habitual dispenser of bon mots and laughter wherever he went.

Not that Edward cared for the type. Dickey's brand of fun was far too flighty for him to become one of Edward's regular companions. Cleverness for its own sake was as grating to his ear as a squeaky door.

However, at present, the squeaky door was preoccupied with his own doings, which meant Anne was safe from Dickey's clever tongue for the time being.

"But unfortunately, Miss Finch must have been waylaid by another hopeful suitor and is in danger of having her bejeweled slippers danced right off her little feet." Dickey affected yet another mournful sigh. "That's only conjecture on my part, you understand. There's been so much traffic in this parlor since I arrived, I've been trapped here. Even if she were caught in the clutches of a fire-breathing dragon, I couldn't go to her rescue."

"I doubt Lord Finch would see you as a knight in shining armor going to the rescue of any fair damsel," Edward said. "Much less his daughter."

"No, indeed," Dickey said without taking the slightest offense to Edward's statement. "And therein lies my greatest strength with respect to the feminine sex. In fact, I doubt even such an august personage as yourself could compete with me in this arena."

Edward snorted.

"I'm not jesting, my lord," Dickey said. "Oh, I wouldn't best you on account of my own attributes, though one can never discount the value of personal charm. But I'm quite aware that when weighed against someone with your title and breeding, your vast holdings and impeccable reputation, I barely move the scale. And yet, I'll wager Miss Finch will give *me* a kiss before she bestows one on you."

"And why is that, pray? Not that I've any intention of kissing Miss Finch."

"If you don't, you're the only bachelor in Town who doesn't," Dickey said, to all appearances untroubled by his myriad rivals for the young lady's favor. "But I'll share my secret with you, my lord. The bald fact is, women claim to want the white knight, but the man they really swoon over is the villain, the risk-taker, the breaker of the rules."

"That makes no sense."

"None at all," Dickey said agreeably. "And yet it's quite true. Ladies have this horrible affliction, you see. They believe those of us who don't fit Society's mold are merely misunderstood, or that we behave badly because we weren't shown enough love in our unhappy youths. Women in general have conceived the notion that I'm somehow redeemable."

"Silly creatures."

"Indeed." Dickey nodded. "I'm not, you know. Redeemable, I mean. In fact, I'm utterly *un*redeemable. My vision of heaven isn't harps and choirs, it's eating foie gras off a lady's fingers."

"And yet your villainous plans were for naught this evening," Edward said, vaguely amused by the man despite himself. "It seems the ladies have won this round."

Dickey sighed. "They have, but they had plenty of help from Fate." He held up his splayed fingers and ticked off the items that came between him and a tryst with Miss Finch. "First Lady Howard and her thoroughly unlikeable stepson force me to make a tactical withdrawal behind those curtains. Then you and Lady Howard render me the unwitting observer to the sorriest case of an interrupted love scene ever."

Edward bristled at the idea that Dickey had been present while he seduced Anne. But the man seemed anxious to press on with his litany of woes, so Edward didn't interrupt him.

"And finally, my lord, your man of business pops round, disrupting an evening of fun and frivolity by spreading evil rumors of murder and mayhem." Dickey pulled a handkerchief from his pocket and mopped his brow. "Ugh! What a night."

Then he took a few steps toward the door.

"Hold a moment." Edward had yet to figure out a way to keep Dickey from spreading gossip about Anne. "Where do you think you're going?"

"In search of a chamber pot. I freely confess I need to take a piss. In truth, my lord, the decorative urn in the corner is in serious danger if you do not allow me to withdraw forthwith."

Edward grabbed him by the collar again and backed the man up until his spine pressed against the curtains again. "Then the only thing in danger is the front of your breeches until we settle something."

"Come, my lord, there's no need for violence. We are both civilized men."

Edward didn't feel the least civilized. "If you repeat a syllable about Lady Howard—"

"You'll have to be more specific. Do you mean, for example, anything I might have heard of the conversation between Lady Howard and her stepson? Or the stolen moments that passed between you and said lady? Or perhaps the nefarious doings that your man of business hinted might be laid at Lady Howard's feet?"

Dickey had several arrows in his quiver of scandal. Edward wasn't sure he could secure them all before the man loosed them upon the ton.

"Well, you know me," Dickey said. "It's a rare item that reaches my ears without flowing through my mouth sooner or later."

Like a terrier with a rat, Edward gave Dickey a brisk shake. "I warn you. If you slander Lady Howard, I—"

"Lady Howard, Lady Howard! You really are concerned for her, aren't you? I thought perhaps you'd be worried about your own sterling reputation. Be easy on that score, my lord. I have no intention of doing her harm," Dickey said. "Despite the way she tried to thwart my pursuit of Miss Finch, I happen to like the lady."

"You like all the ladies," Edward growled.

"True, but some more than others," Dickey conceded. "Lady Howard is safe from me in the matter of Sir Erasmus's demise. You may depend upon it. I won't be a party to increasing whatever pain she might have suffered over her husband's death. Though I suspect she didn't suffer much."

Edward narrowed his eyes at the man, trying to discern whether he was telling the truth. He couldn't be sure. "If I hear the slightest breath of a rumor about Sir Erasmus's passing, I shall know whom to blame. And whom to punish."

"I said I would keep mum," Dickey said with a frown. "What must I do? Sign an oath in blood?"

"Don't tempt me," Edward said as he released his grip on Dickey's collar. "What did Sir Percival want with Lady Howard?"

"Actually, you ought to refer to her as the *Dowager* Lady Howard now," Dickey corrected. "At least, that's how Lady Howard the Younger demands *your* Lady Howard style herself so long as the Cornwallians are invading London drawing rooms. Oops!" Dickey clapped a hand over his mouth. "Pardon me, my lord. I forgot. You didn't wish me to repeat anything I'd heard."

"Don't try my patience. You know perfectly well I didn't mean you shouldn't tell me."

"Very well. Here is the gist of their exchange. First, the reason for the presence of Sir Percival and his wife in London. It seems the Crown is extending an olive branch to its German cousins, which by extension includes the current Lady Howard, who is related to the Schaumbergs."

That was an interesting political development, and while Anne probably disliked being labeled a dowager to her face, it wouldn't have upset her to tears. "What else?"

"The *Dowager* Lady Howard has been notified that because she received a small jointure upon her husband's death, she is not entitled to a dower portion from his estate each year," Dickey explained. "It seems she has been effectively cut off."

No wonder Anne was weeping. The support from her husband's estate hadn't been terribly substantial to begin with, as the share was divided between her and Sir Erasmus's mother. Now she was entitled to nothing. Edward was determined to see that she didn't suffer want even if he had to funnel moneys to her anonymously.

Provided he could find a way of generating moneys to funnel.

"But frankly, my lord, I don't see why the specter of Lady Howard's looming penury should disturb you," Dickey said with a sly grin. "It makes her ever so much more likely to succumb to your charms and agree to become your mistress."

Edward didn't think. He just acted. His fist flew out and connected with Dickey's jaw before the command to do so ran through his mind. Dickey's head snapped back and he crumpled to the floor.

A whiff of urine invaded Edward's nostrils.

He knelt to discover that although Dickey was insensate, he was still breathing. The man would rouse soon. However, in the relaxation of losing consciousness, his bladder had voided itself.

Edward didn't regret laying the man out. Dickey had besmirched Anne's honor, after all, but Edward didn't feel the need to add insult to injury. He rose to go in search of a servant who could find a clean pair of breeches to help Mr. Dickey out of his embarrassing predicament.

He would have to slip the servant a few coins to ensure a bit of discretion. It was the least Edward could do when it was his blow that had caused Dickey to wet himself. And if he could trust the man's veracity, Edward had learned a great deal of useful information from him.

At least Dickey was telling the truth about one thing, Edward thought ruefully as he closed the parlor door behind him. *He did need to piss.*

Storytellers like to use stock phrases such as once upon a time, *and* happily ever after *to fill a void in their prose. My favorite idiom is* And it came to pass. *I call the wording to mind whenever I hope something hasn't come to stay.*

—Lady Howard writing as Mrs. Hester Birdwhistle

Chapter 18

The retiring room was empty.

There's a mercy. It was also the first bit of luck to come Anne's way all evening. She hurried over to the small vanity that held a pitcher and ewer and poured out a little water. She wet her palms and brought them to her burning cheeks.

She almost expected to see steam rise.

The whole time she'd threaded her way through the crowd and up the stairs to this quiet enclave, she'd been afraid her guilt would shout plainly from her heated face.

She ran a finger over her bottom lip. It still tingled. Her insides still pounded. Years ago, she'd made the mistake of listening to her body instead of her head. She ought to have learned her lesson, but all it took was a few kisses, and Edward had reduced her to a quivering light-skirt again.

What a hopeless wanton I am.

Anne had always been intoxicated by her senses, whether she was playing the harp, lost in the tangle of ethereal notes, or dabbing a bit of perfume between her breasts, drunk on the sweet smell, or dancing by herself in the silvery darkness of a starlit night. She reveled in the shivery sensation of new experience, the heady joy of a fresh adventure. Her only consolation was that the part of her sensual nature that would get her into trouble only seemed uncontrollable when Edward Lovell was about.

She needed to avoid him at all costs.

"There you are!"

Anne turned away from the vanity to see Martha framed by the doorjamb.

"I've been looking all over for you," the girl said. "It's nearly time for the supper dance."

"Is it?" The evening had flown.

Martha's eyes were bright and her cheeks flushed. She'd clearly been enjoying herself.

"Are you all right? You almost look feverish." Anne put a few fingers to the girl's forehead. Her temperature seemed normal, but her face was rosy and her smile so wide, it threatened to split her face.

"Stop fretting. I'm fine," Martha said. "Can you believe it? I've danced every dance. I can't even remember the names of all my partners, but there was a new gentleman queued up to beg the next dance from me each time I was escorted off the floor."

"Of course there was," Anne said, grateful that Martha was so intent on her own doings that she didn't notice Anne's discomfiture. "I told you you'd be much in demand."

"Come, now." Martha rolled her eyes. "We both know my dowry is what's in demand. But as long as it means I don't end up as a pitiable wallflower like poor Miss Tilbury, I don't care."

Anne frowned at her. It surprised her that Frederica Tilbury should be ignored.

"Of course, Freddie has a fairly substantial dowry as well," Martha mused. "It's fair odd that she shouldn't be dancing as much as me."

"There, you see," Anne said, glad to be able to focus on something besides Edward and how utterly undone he made her feel. "It is you and not your dowry that is making you the belle of the ball."

"Or maybe the gentlemen here tonight value their hearing," Martha said slyly. "Miss Tilbury has been playing the piano in public a good bit of late."

"That's unkind."

"But not untrue. Honesty is the best policy. Isn't that what you're always telling me?" Then Martha's mouth lifted in an impish smile. "Of course, Freddie may have been hugging the wall by choice just because a certain vicar is not here this evening."

"Reverend Lovell?"

"The same. Didn't you notice how smitten she seemed to be with him at Lady Ware's dinner party?"

Obviously, Martha read people as well as she read piano scores. She narrowed her eyes at Anne, and then her brows drew together in concern.

Martha put a few fingers to Anne's forehead, mimicking her earlier maternal gesture. "You seem a bit warm. Are *you* quite well?"

"I'm fine." Anne turned away from her, hand to her cheek.

"You haven't been dancing," Martha pressed on, "so you can't say that's why you're all hot and rosy."

"I danced," Anne said defensively. "You were right there when Mr. Dickey asked me."

"So I was," she said with a grin. "He dances well, doesn't he? I noticed the two of you talking during the cotillion. He's ever so amusing, isn't he?"

"Mr. Dickey's charm has never been in dispute," Anne said, grateful for the turn in their conversation away from her. "Only his eligibility. And his sense of propriety. Have you been dancing with him?"

"No." Glumly, she plopped down onto a cassock. "I haven't even seen Mr. Dickey since he danced with you. But to be fair, I had little enough chance to look for him. Every other man in the room seemed determined to tread on my toes at least once."

"Good. As you're all danced out, you've no need to dance with Mr. Dickey."

"Oh, pish. You're no fun." Martha leaned forward, propping her chin on her fists. "Come to think of it, I haven't seen you since I danced with Lord Chatham either. Where have you been?"

"I've been...in conversation with a number of people." That was true. As far as it went.

"How deadly dull!"

Anne shrugged. "It's what adults do."

"Pity. What a waste, in fact." Martha stood and crossed over to the mirror above the vanity and turned one of the strands of hair that had escaped her coiffure around her finger, hoping to make it curl. Unfortunately, when she released the lock it still hung as straight as a horse's tail. "You adults can do anything you please, and it pleases you to do nothing."

What Anne had done with Edward in the parlor was the exact opposite of nothing. When she'd given a bit of her body to him, she'd let him back into her heart, into her soul. He'd nearly led her to ruin the last time. No good could come of it now.

"We can't do anything we like," she said crisply. "If we wish to keep Society's good opinion, propriety demands we follow the rules."

Yes, she was being hypocritical, but if she would only listen to her own advice, she'd do better next time.

"Ugh!" Martha said with a grimace. "If it means you're only allowed to stand around and talk, I'm beginning to think having Society's good opinion is overrated."

Anne clapped a hand on her forearm. "Don't. A lady who loses her reputation has lost everything."

Martha rolled her eyes. "Now you're just being melodramatic. Even if I were to do something that warranted society's censure, I'd still be myself. I'd still be the daughter of a very rich man. I'd still play the piano exceedingly well. A reputation is nothing more than a vapor."

Yet it was the only thing Anne had, and she'd risked it with Edward tonight. She'd been beyond stupid. Only the fact that they'd been caught by one of Edward's loyalists had saved her from scandal.

What if Lady Ackworth had happened upon us while Edward's hand was up my skirt?

Anne had been dismayed at the thought of becoming a governess or paid companion. But if she lost her good name, even those less-than-desirable ways of keeping body and soul together would be lost to her.

Edward might still offer to make her his mistress, but even though a dark part of her cheered this line of thinking, such an arrangement would make her feel...so much less than she was. She had no doubt she'd be cosseted and adored, but she'd still be nothing more than a plaything. And when her looks failed, Edward would no doubt be generous in pensioning her off, but then she'd be cast away. Used up.

From the moment she'd discovered Edward had left England for his Grand Tour, her life had been one misstep after another. Her choices made her more and more deeply dependent upon others' good graces. The only time she felt truly herself, truly free, was when she'd traveled incognito right after Sir Erasmus's death.

But even then, she'd been subject to a shrinking dower portion due to the poor management of her husband's heir. And now, she wouldn't even be given that.

"Goodness! What I'd give to look inside your head right now, Anne. I can almost see wheels turning and a bit of steam leaking from your brain." Martha circled round her, stopping to peer into her ears. "What are you thinking about so hard?"

"Nothing that concerns you." Anne straightened her spine and pasted on a brave smile.

"Well, in your many conversations this evening, did you at least happen upon something interesting?"

Plenty. But nothing she could share with Martha. Oh, wait. "It seems the Crown is going to be feting its German cousins soon."

"I already know that. I danced with Viscount Schaumberg. In fact, he asked me to come to the ball at Carlton House in a fortnight. He said he'd have the official invitation sent round tomorrow."

Anne blinked in surprise. Most debutantes would have led the conversation with the invitation to the hallowed halls of Carlton House. However, Anne wasn't sure it was a good idea for Martha to go. When King George IV was regent, the decadence and outright debauchery of his parties was the stuff of legend. She didn't know if the weight of the crown had had a settling effect on him or not.

"Oh, don't worry," Martha said. "I told him I couldn't attend without you! Please say we can go."

"We'll decide if and when a formal invitation arrives," Anne said. "For now, let us see if we can find a nice eligible gentleman to partner you for the supper dance. I believe I saw Viscount Mambry here earlier."

"Ugh! He's so old," Martha complained. "He has hair growing out of his ears and nostrils, but practically none on his head."

"With age comes responsibility. A woman needs a man who is steady and reliable."

"By that logic, we should all ride mules instead of horses."

"Don't change the subject," Anne said. "Age brings wisdom. It makes sense for a gentleman to be older than his bride."

This was sound advice. After all, Edward had abandoned her when he was younger. If only he'd been as old as Lord Mambry when she'd first met him, he wouldn't have been chafing to hare off to the Continent for his Grand Tour.

"How old is Lord Chatham?" Martha asked.

Anne bristled. "That's a bit off topic."

"No, it's not. I danced with him this evening. He'd certainly meet your standards of eligibility."

However one wanted to measure a man, Edward did well. A deep ache throbbed in her chest at Martha's sudden interest in him. Anne tilted her head, trying to count up the years. "Lord Chatham is thirty-two, I believe."

"Saints alive! He's handsome enough, I'll grant you, but the man is twice my age."

"And wasn't your father that much older than your mother when they first married?"

Martha snorted. "Yes, but it doesn't matter now. They're both old."

"Nonsense. They are in the prime of life." Anne knew Martha's mother was not yet forty, and her father's head of hair only sported enough gray at the temples to make him seem wise.

"I rather think the prime of life is very much younger than my parents' ages," Martha said. "Why couldn't I entertain a suit by a man in his early twenties, for example?"

"Most gentlemen in their twenties have not yet come into their inheritance, so their position in life is not settled enough to support a wife."

Martha fingered the lace at her bodice. "What if the gentleman I wanted was someone who didn't stand to inherit?"

"Someone like Reginald Dickey, you mean."

"Well, since you brought him up, yes. Why not?" the girl said defensively. "He's ever so much fun. And he likes me."

"Of course he does," Anne said dryly.

"I know what you're thinking, but it's not just for my dowry."

"How can you be sure of that?"

Angry tears gathered in the girl's eyes. "How can I be sure any man will want me for myself instead of for the pounds sterling Papa has hung on my neck?"

It was a fair question.

"You know as well as I that people often think I'm a bit...well, odd," Martha said. "Mr. Dickey doesn't. He thinks I'm unique, and he likes unique people."

"In that, he and I are in perfect agreement," Anne said, putting an arm around the girl's shoulders. "You are not a pattern sort of girl, and in my opinion that's good...up to a point."

Martha leaned her head onto Anne's shoulder and sighed.

"One shouldn't blindly follow the herd. You'll miss a good deal that way," Anne said. "But you also shouldn't strike out so far on your own that you find yourself beyond the safety of society should you need it."

Martha shook her head. "I don't understand."

"I pray you never do, my dear." Anne patted her head. "I pray you never do."

Folk line up to mark a great man's passing. But when a bairn dies before it draws first breath, only the mother mourns. Through the passing years, she catches glimpse of the child that might have been, hovering like a sweet wee ghostie just at the edge of her sight.
—John Fernsby, gravedigger and self-taught philosopher

Chapter 19

Though Edward tried to find Anne in the press of people, she seemed determined to elude him for the rest of the evening. By the time he returned to the ballroom, couples had already paired up for the supper dance. Anne was partnered with that old stick Viscount Mambry, who, despite his advanced years, could still manage a passable reel.

"Yoo-hoo! Lord Chatham, there you are," Lady Pickering called to him from halfway across the room. Then she raced to his side, elbowing any stragglers between them out of her way. "I see you aren't dancing, my lord, and there's still room to join the foot of the lines."

"Your eyesight is as acute as ever, madam."

"Isn't it lovely the way events conspire to solve these little dilemmas? You are in sore need of a partner, and my Eleanor dances a divine reel."

The girl at her side blushed like a poppy with measles.

"What a happy accident!" Lady Pickering exclaimed.

Accident, yes, but not at all happy.

However, Edward had been well and truly treed by this maternal bloodhound. He was duty bound to ask the girl to dance, which she accepted with uncontrollable giggling.

Then because the reel was the supper dance, he was obliged to escort her in to the meal and sit beside her for the many courses. Because a few "royal cousins" were present, Lady Ackworth had set a table worthy of such august company. In order to speak to all her guests, their hostess circuited the long table, which had been extended to stretch into the adjoining anteroom to accommodate the entire party. Lady Ackworth made a huge point of explaining that Lord Ackworth had suffered a headache early in the evening and had withdrawn from the festivities.

Whether his lordship had a headache or not, Edward thought he had the right idea.

The fine linen tablecloth was crowded with dishes. There were whole chickens, tongue, partridges, collared eels, prawns, and lobsters. Roast potatoes, savory Welsh rarebit, and gooseberry cheese were offered as well. These were followed by jellies and trifles, blancmange and peach compotes. French wine flowed freely.

Edward couldn't fault the menu. It was the company he found sadly lacking.

The topics about which Miss Pickering was most capable of conversing consisted of hopeful pronouncements about the weather and the finer points of doily-making. If she'd ever read a book or seen a play or had an original thought, she gave no evidence of it.

Edward couldn't wait for the dessert course to end. During the meal, he tried to catch Anne's eye, but she studiously avoided looking his way. Viscount Schaumberg and his cousin, the current Lady Howard, were seated on either side of Lady Ackworth, who presided at the head of the long board. Sir Percival had been placed a few seats down from his wife, clearly not important enough to warrant closer association with Lady Ackworth and her luminaries.

Anne had managed to be seated with Lord Mambry near the midpoint, about as far from her stepson and his wife as she was from Edward's end of the table.

After the ladies retired, the gentlemen were plied with port. Viscount Schaumberg crossed the room and pulled up the chair beside Edward.

"Chatham," he said gruffly. "Where do you stand on the question of your king's proposed trip to Scotland later this year?"

Politics was a minefield. Edward preferred to confine his opinions to the House of Lords.

"It will be the first time an English monarch has visited Scotland in two centuries. One might argue this trip is long overdue," he said, neither approving nor disapproving. "The Scots haven't forgotten what they see as injustice after their failed attempt to place their 'Bonnie Prince Charlie' on the throne, and to be fair, the Crown's retaliation after the Jacobite rebellion was harsh. But with his visit, the king no doubt hopes to improve relations with our Scottish cousins."

"So your King George, he goes to make amends for another king's sins. Better he should pay for his own." Schaumberg's brows lowered. "If he must gallivant about the world making peace with those who have been wronged by his house, don't you think he'd do better to visit Brunswick? After all, we were offended by his own deeds."

It was no secret that the continental branch of the British royal family was still seething over their Princess Caroline's treatment by her husband. In the first place, Prinny had only agreed to marry her in exchange for cancellation of the exorbitant debt he'd accumulated. Then he'd been cruel to her from the very start of their arranged marriage. Upon meeting his bride-to-be for the first time, he'd turned to Lord Malmesbury and reportedly said, "Harris, I am not well. Pray, get me a glass of brandy." The story had lost nothing in the retelling.

Princess Caroline had responded with equal disdain, though few could fault her after such a reception. With as much mutual hatred as the royal couple shared, how they'd managed to produce an heir was a wonder, but they somehow gave England a new princess. Prinny conspired to limit Caroline's access to their daughter Charlotte to only once a week, and then under strict supervision.

Years later, when Princess Charlotte died in childbirth, Caroline was abroad and had to hear of her daughter's death through a second party, not directly from her husband. Then to add insult to injury, when, upon the death of his father, the Prince Regent ascended to the throne to become George IV, he refused to allow his estranged wife to be crowned Queen at his side.

She died suddenly about a year later, after claiming to have been poisoned. Judging from the suppressed anger in Viscount Schaumberg's expression, he fully believed the accusation.

"I am not privy to the king's travel plans," Edward said. "But he did invite you to London in order to honor you. That seems a bit of an olive branch to me. He is hosting you at Carlton House, is he not?"

Carlton House had been George IV's home while he was Prince Regent. It was a wildly opulent structure in the heart of Pall Mall, constantly in a state of renovation, as the royal whim dictated, but never truly improved upon. Since his coronation, the king had grown tired of Carlton House and was considering a move to Buckingham, but it, too, would require a good deal of refurbishment to measure up to the ever-changing royal taste.

"Yes, yes. My cousin Sofia and her husband"—here he shot a scathing glance in Sir Percival's direction that told plainly how poorly he regarded his cousin's husband—"and myself. We are to be his guests of honor at

Carlton House. I am not fooled by this. He means to make a mockery of us, just as he did my poor cousin, the princess who should have died a queen."

"The British people were saddened by her death," Edward said. "Depend upon it."

"Only because they despise their king. She was, as you British say, the lesser of two evils." Schaumberg clapped a hand on his shoulder. "But I thank you, Lord Chatham. You, I do believe. Rarely have I met an Englishman who could see two sides of a question. You will be at this Carlton House, yes?"

"I have been invited." Edward knew he should defend his king from the German's verbal attacks, but in the matter of his treatment of his wife, the British monarch was indefensible. Then a realization hit him with the force of a blow.

So am I.

Like the Prince Regent, Edward had amassed debts in his youth, which his father had offered to expunge in exchange for his obedience in leaving for his Grand Tour immediately instead of finishing out the Season and asking Anne to marry him. After much prodding by his father, Edward had agreed to his sire's terms. He had been so sure a few years' wait would make no difference to him and Anne that he'd left blithely for the Continent, confident that she would still be there when he returned.

It had nearly killed him when Reginald Dickey told him she hadn't waited for him. As Edward went on traveling the capitals of Europe, he'd tried to convince himself that he hated her. By the time he finally returned home, he'd developed a thick scar over what was left of his heart.

Edward hadn't been as openly cruel to Anne as the king had been to his wife, but hadn't he been so privately selfish it amounted to the same sin?

And since he'd returned, he had never come out and asked her why she'd married Sir Erasmus so soon after he left. Edward had assumed she'd done it to spite him.

What if I was wrong? What if it was the very opposite of spite?

Something Miss Finch had said earlier that evening niggled at the back of his mind, and he had to run the truth of the matter to ground. Edward stood abruptly and gave the German viscount a brisk bow. "I beg your pardon. I have just remembered something which requires my immediate attention."

"But you will be at Carlton House, yes?" Schaumberg insisted. "I need to know there will be at least one Englishman who speaks the truth in that company."

"Yes, I will be there." Edward would make no claims for his honesty. In fact, if matters led him where he feared they might, he'd have to take what he learned to the grave.

For Anne's sake.

* * * *

"My lord, this is most irregular." The sexton at St. Thomas-by-the-Way lifted his lamp so its yellow light spilled out the church's side door. The man blinked sleepily up at Edward. "Why are you disturbing the peace of the House of God at this decidedly ungodly hour?"

"The hour is of no moment. I am here to examine your parish rolls," Edward said curtly. "Specifically the burial records."

"The vicar will have to be summoned for that."

Edward shoved past the man into the small vestibule. "By all means do so. I'll wait while you rouse your employer from his well-deserved slumber. However, I've five quid in my pocket for the wise sexton who will lead me to a quiet room where I can study those records undisturbed. Immediately."

The sexton's eyes widened at that, and he nearly dropped his lamp in his hurry to lock the door behind Edward. "As this is obviously a matter of importance to your lordship, I don't suppose it would do to wake the reverend. After all, he'll be rising to conduct services in a few hours. He needs his rest. This way, if you please."

Now that five quid danced in his imagination, the junior churchman was only too eager to be helpful. Once the sexton found the ledger for the year Edward had started his Grand Tour, the fellow left him seated at a small desk in the musty sacristy, alone with the dusty tome. Edward pulled the lamp the sexton had left closer, opened the book, and began reading.

The records were organized in columns, a month to a page. First the dates of deaths were notated, then the name of the deceased, followed by the name of their father, but strangely enough, not their mother.

Toward the bottom of the page for September, Edward found this entry written in a spidery script:

29 September, one abortive female, Sire—Sir Erasmus Howard, Remains interred: outer ring near far wall, fifth plot.

An abortive. That term might be applied to an unformed blob of flesh that had been expelled early or it might be used to describe a stillborn babe, if the family didn't want to pay the higher price for burial a stillborn required. Either way, a child was buried in the second plot where Anne placed flowers when she visited her husband's grave.

So Anne had been pregnant but hadn't carried a baby to full term. She had married Sir Erasmus in August of that year, so naturally any issue would be claimed as his. Edward wasn't surprised to see her husband listed as the father of the deceased babe.

He didn't know much about the mysteries of how a child's body was knit together in the womb, but given the relatively short length of time Anne had been married before the untimely end of the pregnancy, he was surprised that the ledger listed the baby's sex.

A question burned in his gut. He'd know no peace until he had the answer.

As God is my witness, if Anne is willing to give me a second chance, I swear I won't need a third.
—from the journal of Edward Lovell, Lord Chatham

Chapter 20

After a week of trying to attend events where Anne and her protégé were likely to be, Edward had finally enlisted the help of several lookouts. He ordered a small army of street urchins to be stationed on the corners near their house. When Lady Howard and Miss Finch went out, his sentinels raced to report their activities, but invariably, Edward missed them at the gallery opening or recital or lecture. Or if he did manage to find them, the venue was entirely too public to permit him private speech with Anne.

And only complete privacy would do for this conversation.

At last, a boy came from John Fernsby, the gravedigger at St. Thomas-by-the-Way. Her ladyship was come to pay her respects at her husband's grave with an armful of flowers, the messenger said. She usually passed an hour in the churchyard when she visited, Fernsby's messenger relayed, so if his lordship would only hurry, he might yet catch her.

"Is she still here?" Edward asked as he leaped from his horse's back almost before the gelding came to a stop. Fernsby, who'd turned from gravedigger to gardener for a change, was pulling out some ivy that threatened to overpower one of the listing headstones.

"Last I looked, your lordship," Fernsby said, doffing his cap. "Soon as she turned up, I sent a boy round to fetch you like you asked."

Edward flipped a shilling to the man, who caught the coin and slipped it into his pocket. "Is anyone with her?"

"Usually, she has a young lady at her side," Fernsby said, "but not this time."

Edward passed the reins of his side-stepping horse to the gravedigger. "See to my mount and there'll be half a crown for you."

Fernsby tugged at his forelock in respect and led the horse to the other side of the church, where it could munch at the grass without denuding someone's grave.

Twilight was falling, deepening the shadows between the church wall and the taller building next to the enclosed yard. Edward didn't see Anne standing over her husband's grave, the one marked by an ornate stone in its place of honor near the church itself. Instead, she was seated on the stone bench in the far corner under the arbutus tree. Near her, a single rose rested on an otherwise unmarked grave. The Lent lilies Miss Finch had said were planted there were past blooming and the remaining green stalks stood in spiky disarray. But the location of the grave matched the entry in the church rolls.

Outer ring near the far wall. Plot number five.

The mound was small. A mere bump in the grass was all that betrayed the resting place of the undersized body beneath it.

When Miss Finch had first told him that Anne always brought a flower for another grave, he hadn't considered the possibility that it would be for a child. Edward removed his hat as he drew near.

She was weeping. Not loudly. Not sobbing. That wasn't her way, but tears glistened on her cheeks and lashes.

"Anne," he said softly.

She startled at her name and looked up. Then she swiped her cheeks. "Goodness! What you must think of me. It seems every time you happen upon me of late, I'm a soggy mess."

"I haven't happened upon you of late. If I didn't know better, I'd say you were avoiding me." Edward had suspected she didn't want to see him, but she still had a debutante to trot out so eligible beaux could press their suits in all the oh-so-proper and approved ways. She must have known she couldn't avoid him forever. "Where have you been?"

"Martha and I have been attending plays in small theatres and musical evenings in private homes and such." Anne laced her fingers and placed them on her lap. She was trying to seem nonchalant, but she squeezed her hands together so tightly, her knuckles went white. "It's not as if we have been in hiding."

Silence stretched between them. It was a quiet hour of the day for the city. Folk of the middling sort were making their tired way home after a day's work. The ton had not yet emerged for an evening of play. Only the rustling of the tree's leaves broke the deep quiet.

"Anne," he said softly, "what are you doing here?"

"My husband is buried in this churchyard. Is it not proper for me to pay my respects?"

"Yes, of course." Edward ran the brim of his hat round and round through his fingers. Finally, he motioned with it toward the grave with the single cut flower. "Who's buried there?"

Her chin trembled. "My daughter."

"I'm so sorry, Anne." *More sorry than I can say.* "Would you like to talk about her?"

"No." She looked away. "I'd rather not discuss this with you."

He didn't say anything. Instead he simply sat down beside her on the bench. When the silence became unbearable, he asked, "What was her name?"

"I said I didn't wish to discuss it." She gave a disgusted snort.

Good. He'd rather see her annoyed than sorrowful. "What if you *need* to talk about it?"

Her lips tightened in a thin line. "You never learned to take no for an answer, did you?"

"No, and I've no intention of learning now. Her name?"

Anne sighed. "She didn't have one. Not officially. But I've always thought of her as Lily."

It made sense for the child not to be named. Sir Erasmus might have been willing to put cash on the nail for a burial, but no one paid for an abortive to be christened.

Edward cast about for some way to get Anne to talk about the child. "I'm surprised she wasn't buried in Cornwall."

"Why? People tend to be buried where they die, Edward. We were in London when I...when we lost her."

But if Edward remembered Sir Erasmus correctly, the man had a pompous streak. Even though the babe never drew breath, if the child was his, why was she buried on the edge of the churchyard in an unmarked grave?

Edward reached over and covered her hand with his. She didn't pull away. "Anne, is there something I should know?"

She was trembling now. "You're going to make me say it, aren't you?"

"Let me help." He took her hand and cradled it between both of his. "After I learned that you frequented this churchyard to leave flowers for two graves, I paid the sexton to look away so I could study the church rolls. There is an entry in the fall of 1816. A female abortive is all it says, though Sir Erasmus is listed as the father."

"I lost the child very early," she said woodenly. "I'd barely felt a flutter, but I knew there was life in me. I hadn't even told Sir Erasmus that I was bearing. Then when...it happened, my husband wouldn't pay to have her christened. Why go to all that expense for a soul that never saw the sun, he argued. But he did allow me to use my pin money to have her interred here. Quietly." Anne studied the tips of her shoes with absorption. "We never told anyone."

"Sir Erasmus is named as the father in the church rolls. Was he?"

She met his gaze. "No."

"Anne, if I'd known—"

"You'd have defied your father and asked me to marry you?" She pulled her hand away from him. "We both know you wouldn't have, Edward."

"How can you say that? I loved you."

"Did you? I seem to remember you loved the idea of larking about the Continent with Lord Rowley far more."

The Grand Tour was as much a part of a gentleman's education as matriculating from Oxford or Cambridge. The polish, the fluency in language, the understanding of how other cultures operated that Edward had gleaned from his travels stood him in good stead now. It was unfair of her to have expected him to forgo that rite of passage. Especially because she hadn't told him she was carrying his child.

"I didn't have all the information. You're not being fair."

"What was not fair was asking me to wait for you when I knew I could not," Anne said.

"You told me you would."

"I told you what you wanted to hear." Her tone was unspeakably weary. "Don't you see, Edward? I had to say I'd wait because I knew I couldn't take away your choice to go."

"I'd have stayed if I'd known." He liked to think he would have, but he'd been younger and more headstrong then. And far more stupid.

"Perhaps you would have stayed and made an honest woman of me," Anne said, her tone clipped now and edgy. He actually preferred this feistier version of her over the worn, tired Anne. "And perhaps you wouldn't have resented me at first, but eventually you would have."

"Not if you were bearing my child."

Her eyes glistened with tears she struggled not to let fall. "But I didn't, you see. What if you had given up your Tour and married me against your father's wishes?" She turned away from him, but he could tell from the way her shoulders shook that she had lost her battle with those tears. "I'd have lost Lily all the same."

He rested his palms on her shoulders. "You can't know that."

"I know I can't go back in time to find out." She turned and glared at him. Then her face crumpled. "Poor Sir Erasmus. I *used* him. He might not have been the most admirable of husbands, but I'm not very proud of the way I went into the marriage either."

Spoken like a woman who would never have resorted to poison to rid herself of the man. The last of his uneasy suspicions faded. "Did he suspect the child wasn't his?"

She shook her head. "He never saw her. Never knew she couldn't possibly have been his."

Edward burned with guilt over putting her in such an untenable position. For the first time, he felt grateful to Sir Erasmus for marrying Anne and unwittingly shielding her from public shame. "It was a mercy he never discovered the truth."

"I paid dearly for that mercy. I lost you. I lost our daughter and I defrauded the man who gave me the protection of his name. Oh, what a mess I've made of everything."

"No, you haven't. This was my fault. You did the best you could in a difficult situation. One for which I was responsible. One for which I'm sorrier than I can say. Anne, I'd give anything if I could go back and make it all right."

"You can't."

"You're right. We can't go back. We can only go forward." He dropped to one knee and caught up one of her hands. "I bungled this the first time and I can't promise I'll get it right now, but if you'll marry me, I vow I'll live every day trying to make it up to you."

She tilted her head at him. "Really, Edward? You think just because you're feeling guilty, it means now is a good time to propose to me?"

"No, it's not that. I mean, yes. I do feel guilty. I should, don't you think?" He didn't pause long enough for her to weigh in on the subject. "But that's not the reason I'm ruining the knee of these trousers." He squeezed her hand. "I love you, Anne. No matter where I've gone, or what I've done, it's always been you for me. You are the woman by which all others are measured and found wanting."

"Oh, my. That's a bit theatrical." She stood, looking vaguely amused. He ought to have been insulted that she found his proposal funny, but he would rather have her laughing than crying. "How many times have you rehearsed this?"

"Not enough, evidently," he admitted, "but I've imagined you as mine as many times as there are hairs on my head. I just never actually thought about how I'd go about asking you."

"Good. Because I'd hate to think you planned on a graveyard as a suitable place for a proposal."

"You're not taking me seriously."

"No, I'm not." She tugged her hand away from him. "I wasn't the right girl for you when you were Lord Bredon. And now that you're the Earl of Chatham, I'm certainly not the right one."

"You are the *woman* for me," he said adamantly, "and I still love you. I still feel like Bredon."

"But you're not. I know you were only considering Martha because of the size of her dowry. Be honest with yourself, Edward. Your estate is in trouble. And you need a wife who brings more to the marriage than a small grave and empty hands."

Edward rose to his feet, put his hands on her waist, and pulled her close. "What I need is you. I don't care about the rest."

"Yes, you do." She rested her forehead on his chest. "Because you must."

"Anne, I know you've been cut off by Sir Percival. Let me provide for you. If you don't love me, at least say yes so I can care for you."

"Oh, Edward, that's what makes this all so pitiably difficult. I do love you."

If the skies had parted and he'd been given a glimpse of paradise, he couldn't have been more thrilled. "Then say yes."

She shook her head. "We're doomed to repeat ourselves, you and I. I couldn't take your Tour from you before. I can't take Chatham from you now."

"Don't fret about that."

"Can you honestly tell me you haven't considered asking the House of Lords for permission to sell off some of your entailed properties? That's what Lady Ackworth says."

"I swear that woman claims to know when a gnat bats its eyelashes," he grumbled. "But she's wrong. I'm not that desperate. Not yet, at any rate. Let me worry about Chatham."

"Then you must let me worry about you, Edward," Anne said. "I can't accept your proposal."

"You mean you won't."

"If you like."

"No, I don't like. I don't like the way we're going about this at all." He reached to cup her cheek. To his relief, she didn't pull away. In fact, she inhaled a hitching breath when he ran his thumb over her lips. "Neither do you."

"How could you know that?" she whispered, her mouth barely moving.

He bent his head until his lips were within inches of hers. "A man just knows."

Then to his very great surprise, she slipped her fingers under his lapels and stood on tiptoe. Eyes wide open, she closed the distance between their mouths.

Wifely duties, we are taught, often require a woman to endure the act of marriage with gritted teeth and grim determination, all the while reminding ourselves that the joy of bearing children is worth any momentary discomfort. Yet ladies of independent means sometimes seek out sensual experiences, not for the purpose of procreation, but with languid abandon for the sheer joy of the act. However, be advised that when one joins one's body to another's, one surrenders a piece of one's heart which will never be recovered.

—from *Confessions of an Unconventional Soul* by Lady Howard, writing as Mrs. Hester Birdwhistle

Chapter 21

I deserve to go to hell.

Edward's kisses melted her so thoroughly, she almost didn't care.

Her fingers fluttered down his chest, slipping beneath his jacket. His chest was corded with strong, hard muscles beneath his fine lawn shirt. He cinched her tighter to him and she felt a hard bulge in his trousers. Warmth pooled between her thighs. She arched into him and rocked slowly.

He growled into her mouth.

The deep ache that lived in her secret place began to throb. She was hollow. Empty. Needy.

Anne had been taught it was wrong for a woman to even have such needs, much less act upon them. She'd been raised as a lady, strictly schooled in what was right and what was wrong. Nature, however, had played a cruel trick on her.

She was a secret voluptuary. She reveled in her senses, and Edward Lovell knew how to make them sing.

His strong arms tensed around her. Then his hands slid down her back to cup her bum, fondling her through her thin gown and chemise.

No. I can't let it happen again.

Edward would insist on marrying her this time, but it would still all go wrong. He'd abandon his principles. He'd bankrupt Chatham. He'd let down his younger brothers and fail to provide for his tenants and retainers. He'd be forced to relinquish the stewardship of the estate he held so dear. His honor would be gone.

All for her.

And when all was said and done, he'd hate her for it.

She wedged her hands between them and pushed against his chest with all her might. "No."

Edward released his hold on her, but his intense gaze held her prisoner. She couldn't move.

"No to what?" he said, his face fierce, his chest heaving. "You want me, Anne, I know you do. As much as I want you."

More, probably.

"You can't deny it." His voice was ragged with need.

"No, I can't," she admitted. "I do want you. And I will love you till my last breath, but I can still say no."

"No to my proposal?"

"No to this...this...whatever this madness is between us," Anne said, backing away from him. She'd be sucked back into his arms if she didn't escape his dangerous pull soon. "No to you."

"Anne—"

She didn't wait. She lifted her skirts and ran.

* * * *

Anne was grateful Edward didn't try to follow her. Her insides were such a jumbled mess, she didn't think she had the strength to tell him no again. The brisk walk back to the Finch town house settled her a bit, but now instead of feeling roused and frustrated, she was bone-tired.

And so profoundly sad it was as if the emotion had been invented specifically for her. Her chest ached so, she imagined her heart might leap from her chest and flop about on its own because she'd taken such poor care of it. Surely no one had ever felt so hopeless. So unspeakably hollow.

Anne found Martha in the parlor, standing with her hands clasped behind her back. The low table before the settee was set with a lovely tea, complete with a plate of ladyfingers and cucumber sandwiches, a steaming kettle, and cups and saucers for two.

"You're back early," Martha said quickly, her eyes darting about the room. "I didn't expect you to return for another half hour or so."

"And yet you've arranged for tea. How thoughtful," Anne said, grateful for something as ordinary as taking tea, something as mindless as pouring out and mixing in the right amounts of milk and sugar. It would allow her to go through the motions and behave as if she were still a living, breathing person, even though she seriously doubted it. She removed her bonnet and pelisse and handed them to their maid, Betsy, who dropped a quick curtsy and scurried away. "Thank you, Martha, dear. I'm in sore need of a cup."

"Why?" Martha asked. "You usually seem calm after a visit to Sir Erasmus's grave."

"There were...too many people in the churchyard." Anne realized her mistake as soon as the words were out of her mouth. Martha would want to know who was there, so she scrambled for a way to misdirect her. "I couldn't think properly with others present."

That was true enough. Edward drove all rational thought from her mind.

"That's why you go there?" Martha asked. "To think?"

"To remember, then." She sank into her favorite chair opposite the settee and sighed.

"Why don't we move into the music room?" Martha said. "I've been working on a new sonata. I'd appreciate your opinion of it."

"Perhaps later," Anne said, wondering why Martha didn't sit and let her pour out. Or maybe she'd let Martha do it. The girl needed the practice, after all. One didn't serve tea gracefully without performing the homely ritual often. "After supper, I'll be pleased to listen to—no, we can't," she interrupted herself with a sigh. "We are expected at Lady Daly's for a card party this evening, aren't we?"

"I already sent round a note, begging off."

Anne could have kissed her, but it wasn't like Martha to turn down a chance to gad about. "Why?"

Martha scuffed the toe of her shoe against the Aubusson rug. "I don't really care for cards."

"Then you should concentrate on conversing with those at your table." Heaven knew the girl needed practice speaking to others in ways that didn't lead them to believe young Miss Finch was decidedly odd.

"That's just the problem. The other players," Martha complained. "I'm not allowed to choose my own tablemates, and if I don't like the ones I've been seated with, I'll still be stuck with them until I've played the requisite number of hands."

"How will you know whether you like them unless you talk to them? Sometimes, people will astonish you." Anne had certainly been astonished by Mr. Dickey at Lady Ackworth's ball. The fellow had been unusually humble and quite candid about his unique situation among the ton while he partnered her for the cotillion. She couldn't help but feel for him.

Anne leaned forward to help herself to some tea, but noticed that the cups were already full. Martha had already poured out two servings. Now the girl plopped down on the settee and twisted her fingers together. One knee jittered up and down.

"Why are you so fidgety, Martha?"

"Fidgety?" The knee went suddenly still. "Me?"

"Yes, you. You're as nervous as a cat. And why have you already poured—"

The curtains on the window that looked out on the street wavered a bit and Anne noticed the polished toes of a pair of shoes peaking from beneath them.

"Martha, I need you to go to your room immediately."

"But why do I—"

"If you utter another syllable, you and I shall board a coach bound for your parents' country estate first thing in the morning." When Martha opened her lips to object, Anne stopped her with, "Try me in this, young lady, and you will be severely disappointed."

Martha's mouth closed with a click of her teeth. Making a low growl in the back of her throat, she flounced from the room and stomped up the stairs. Anne remained silent and motionless until she heard the girl's door slam overhead.

"Whoever you are," she said, "you have been discovered. I suggest you slink out from your hiding place and face the consequences."

"I never slink," came a familiar voice.

Anne wasn't surprised when Reginald Dickey stepped from behind the curtain. But she was surprised to see that he sported the yellowing remains of what must have been a spectacular shiner around his left eye. Someone had knocked him silly.

"Mr. Dickey, will you have tea while we discuss what I'm to do with you?" Anne said, deciding civility would serve her better than a screeching fit. "It seems Martha has already poured yours up."

"Lady Howard, I know how this must look—"

"Do you?" she said sharply. "Because it doesn't seem so to me. If you wished to ruin Miss Finch's reputation, you could hardly do better than to visit her privately when her chaperone is unavailable."

He made his way to the settee and sank onto it cautiously. "It's not like that. As soon as I realized you were not at home, I asked Martha to call her maid into the parlor, to stand in your stead, as it were."

So that's why Betsy was in the parlor when I arrived.

Usually ladies' maids didn't have any duties which required their presence in the public portions of the house. Betsy's province was the bedchambers of the ladies she served and the belowstairs areas where she did the mending and laundering of her mistresses' wardrobes. Anne should have known something was wrong the moment she saw Betsy on the ground floor.

"Still, that does not excuse your behavior," Anne said sternly. "Betsy may make an admirable lady's maid, but she is hardly a suitable chaperone for Miss Finch."

"Any port in a storm." Mr. Dickey flashed her his most winning smile.

She sent him a withering stare in return.

"But the fact that I even thought to ask for a chaperone ought to tell you that my intent was not to do Miss Finch harm," he said, clearly scrambling to make Anne believe him.

She did not. Her trust in the male of the species was at a particularly low ebb at the moment.

"Your intent does not signify," Anne said with a frown as she handed him his tea. "Intent and outcomes are rarely the same thing where you are concerned, Mr. Dickey."

"But this time they are." He took a noisy slurp. Anne hoped the cup had gone cold. "I wouldn't harm Martha for worlds."

"Do not let me hear you speaking of her in the familiar again!"

"Miss Finch, then." Dickey took another sip. Clearly the tea was not cold enough. "I would cut off my right hand before I hurt her."

"There are some who would pay to see such a sight, Mr. Dickey."

"Lady Howard, how can I convince you I wish only the best for her?"

"You can leave her alone. You are not an eligible parti, Mr. Dickey."

He sighed deeply. "Merely because of the accident of my birth."

It did seem unfair, but Anne's task was to see Martha suitably wed. The bastard son of a great man, even an acknowledged bastard, did not qualify. "I am sorry, but yes."

"If I were the earl's legitimate son, you wouldn't be upset to find me courting Mar—Miss Finch."

"I would if you tried to woo her when I was not available to chaperone," Anne said. "Surely you must see that your mere presence here endangers her."

"Point taken. In the future, I shall endeavor to plan my visits with Miss Finch to coincide with your schedule."

"No, you won't. You aren't attending, Mr. Dickey," Anne said, trying to do her best imitation of Lady Ackworth. "You may *not* court Miss Finch."

"So the children truly must pay for the sins of their father." Dickey punctuated his statement with a snort.

"I don't make the rules, sir. And frankly, you do not suffer from an infraction of them. Indeed, it seems to me as if you float along in life as carefree as a bubble, despite your present histrionics."

"Histrionics!"

"Spare me your outrage. You and I both know that a man may thumb his nose at propriety when it suits him, but if a woman doesn't follow the rules, she is the one who pays and most dearly." When he didn't argue back, Anne went on more gently. "If you truly care for Miss Finch, you will cease from addressing your attention to her."

"I can't," he said, his shoulders slumped in misery. "I love her, my lady. She's the only person who allows me to be myself, not the jovial clown the ton expects me to be."

"Oh, I rather think you are exactly what you seem, Mr. Dickey."

"Then it's plain to see I have you fooled."

"That, sir, is precisely what I'm trying to avoid."

Mr. Dickey set his tea cup down and met her gaze steadily. "Let us agree to set aside the question of my courting Miss Finch for the moment."

"Agreed, but only if you regard it as a settled question."

"I don't," he said, "but I feel I must take this opportunity to tell you of some rumblings of trouble that have come to my attention."

A tingle of apprehension raked Anne's spine. She'd tried so hard to shield Martha from unkind wagging tongues. "Do these rumblings concern Miss Finch?"

"No, my lady. They concern you."

Chapter 22

"I have little interest in gossip, Mr. Dickey," Anne said primly. "Even less if the gossip is about me."

He examined his nails for cleanliness and then, apparently satisfied, buffed them on his lapel. "This doesn't exactly fall under the category of gossip. It's more like hitherto undisclosed truth."

"Mr. Dickey, if you think to blackmail me into allowing you access to Miss Finch, you have severely underestimated my resolve to protect her." Anne wished he were near enough for her to give his sly face a resounding smack. "I will not allow you to besmirch her good name."

"No, no. There's no besmirching involved. As if I'd stoop to such a thing. Besides, this has nothing to do with Miss Finch. We agreed to set aside discussing that young lady at present," he said, raising his hands in mock surrender. "I only offer the information I possess as a...a warning of sorts."

Anne narrowed her eyes at him. "Do you threaten me, sir?"

"No, of course not. It would never enter my mind to do such a thing. I may not be a gentleman in the purest sense of the word, but I'd never threaten a lady." His brows tented and nearly met over his aquiline nose. He seemed genuinely distressed by the notion. "I merely hope you will know how to protect yourself in light of this information."

That sounded ominous. Her nerves fired off small bursts of alarm. "From what do I need protection?"

"Enquiring minds," Mr. Dickey said. "Certain parties have decided to interest themselves in the death of your husband."

"That makes no sense. Sir Erasmus died years ago."

"Under mysterious circumstances," Dickey added.

"No, he succumbed after a brief illness."

"Some take leave to doubt that. The word 'poison' has been bandied about." Anne was shocked to her toes. "Poison?"

"Arsenic, to be specific. There seems to be some empirical support for the notion. A couple of women who worked for Sir Erasmus's funeral furnisher have described seeing what seemed to be signs of poisoning on his body."

The small bursts of alarm graduated to full-blown panic. "Did they report their findings to the authorities?"

"No, which does give you the teeniest bit of leeway to manage this situation. That and the passage of time. Those two facts bode well for you."

"Me?"

"My lady, look at the evidence dispassionately. Poison is a woman's cudgel. It is intimate, yet nonviolent. It requires proximity to deliver, but may be accomplished covertly." Mr. Dickey ticked off the reasons poison was a feminine weapon on his fingers. "As to who might have done this murder, if indeed it can be established as murder so long after the fact, it would only be natural for gossiping tongues to lay the blame at the merry widow's feet."

"I am not a merry widow," Anne said, trying to keep her inward shaking from being outwardly visible.

"Not at present, I'll grant you. In fact, your countenance is the exact opposite of merry."

She stood and paced the length of the room to distance herself from him. "And why shouldn't it be, as you plainly intend to spread this malicious lie throughout the *ton*?"

"Not a bit. This is one juicy morsel I've sworn to keep," Mr. Dickey promised with upraised hand. "I only tell you now so you are forewarned that someone has hired inquiry agents to ferret out the details of the deed."

"Who?"

"The man who gave me this black eye to seal my silence on the matter. It was Lord Chatham." Mr. Dickey stood as well. "Good evening, my lady. I shall see myself out."

As soon as Mr. Dickey cleared the doorway, Anne's knees threatened to buckle.

Oh, Edward.

How could he suspect her of such a thing?

However, Anne knew perfectly well why. She just didn't want to admit it, even to herself. She *had* wished Sir Erasmus dead on numerous occasions. Not openly, of course, but in her heart, she'd longed for his demise. It was hard not to.

Her husband regularly flaunted his mistresses in her face, squiring them openly about Town and making her an object of pity. He made cruel comments about how fortunate it was that Anne had lost the baby, as it would have upset his son Percival to have a younger rival. Worst of all, even though he availed himself of numerous other women, her husband forced himself on her with sickening regularity.

Sir Erasmus's death had been the best thing that had happened to her since Edward had larked off for his Grand Tour.

Anne had been set free. She poured her bitterness into Mrs. Birdwhistle's scandalous pamphlets and followed her own whimsical advice to foreign shores. She might never have returned to conventional society if the need to conserve her dwindling funds hadn't sent her back to England.

And now Edward thinks I murdered my husband.

Anne wished with all her heart that she'd stayed abroad. She should have found a little town in the south of France and set herself up as an English teacher. She might not ever have seen Edward again, but that would have been preferable to having him suspect she was a killer.

A hard knot balled her stomach.

She sank into her chair and wrapped her arms around herself, as if she might hold herself together that way. Finally, shock over the idea that her husband had been murdered cleared. Then she realized Edward couldn't believe she had poisoned Sir Erasmus.

He wouldn't have asked me to marry him if he thought I was capable of administering arsenic to my spouse.

Which meant his inquiry into the death was related to something else. Perhaps he meant to uncover evidence that would exonerate her.

Or find the real killer.

Because if she hadn't done it, someone else must have. Anne cast about in her mind, trying to retrace her husband's steps for the last few months of his life. His health had never been terribly robust, but he'd been failing considerably while they overwintered in Cornwall. He blamed his frequent stomach complaints on too much underdone mutton. Then once they returned to London in the early spring, Sir Erasmus rallied and became quite disgustingly cheerful.

Anne had chalked it up to the fact that his mistress was in close proximity when they were in Town.

Now she needed to consider who might have stood to gain from his death. Besides her.

Mr. Dickey was right. She *was* the natural suspect. Her unmourned husband was still disrupting her life from beyond the grave.

What a tangled web it all was.

It was her own fault. She never should have married Sir Erasmus under false pretenses. Edward was right. She ought to have told him she was bearing his child. He might have resented her in time, but if he'd known, they would have faced the consequences of their rash actions together.

However, at the time, what they'd done hadn't seemed rash. Loving Edward was magical. The exquisite torment, the ecstasy of learning him by heart—she could no more have wished to undo it than she could fly.

But she had shouldered the burden of her imprudent decisions all by herself over the years.

She was so utterly tired.

Still, her mistakes might not be for naught, she reasoned. Not so long as someone else could learn from them.

She rose and tucked an errant strand of hair behind her ear. Then she headed for Martha's bedchamber.

Once she was there, Anne sat down on the foot of the bed.

"Martha, you broke the rules with Mr. Dickey this evening."

"We were only having tea," Martha whined.

And Anne had only thought she'd steal away to meet Edward for a few breathless kisses in her family's garden.

"Seemingly innocent situations can turn not so innocent very quickly. Sit beside me, dear." She patted the counterpane. "I'm going to tell you the story of a foolish young woman who thought she could break the rules with impunity. It is not pretty hearing and I cannot promise I will not have to stop to dry my eyes several times. But I can promise you that every word of it is true."

Martha lifted a skeptical eyebrow. "How do you know it's true?"

"Because the foolish young woman was me."

The French say there is no perfect marriage for there are no perfect men. I am proof of that adage, yet it seems to me that marriage is the only perfect solution.
—from the journal of Edward Lovell, Earl of Chatham, Viscount Bredon, and desperate lover of Anne Spillwell Howard

Chapter 23

Mr. Price rapped softly at Edward's study and then, as the door was ajar, leaned to peer in at him. "My lord, Mr. Higgindorfer is here to see you."

Edward sighed. Just because he was expecting the man didn't mean he was looking forward to the meeting. "Very well, Price. Show him in."

The dour old man of business shuffled in, pulled the Chatham ledger book from his satchel, and balanced the book on the edge of Edward's desk. It seemed about to topple off. Edward took the precarious placement as Higgindorfer's not-so-subtle metaphor for the instability of the Chatham estate's financial situation.

"What gloom and doom do you bring me this time, sir?"

"About the estate, no perils of which you are not already aware." Higgindorfer sat in the chair opposite Edward without waiting for permission. "Your credit is spread thin, your taxes are going up, and an unseasonably dry spring threatens to destroy your tenants' crops."

Always a ray of sunshine. "Have you any words of advice?"

"Only two, my lord." The old man leaned forward. "Marry well."

Though Edward had considered this very option, he didn't appreciate Higgindorfer's proposing it so baldly. "It is not the most dignified of ways to improve one's finances."

"Perhaps not, but it is often the most practical." Higgindorfer leaned back in his chair and tented his hands over his belly. "To that end, it has come to my attention that there is a pamphlet being circulated at White's that names specific debutantes and lists the approximate dowry payments their future husbands might expect."

"Yes, yes. *The Bachelor's Bible*." Edward waggled his hand in the air as if he might wave the suggestion away. "I'm acquainted with the tome."

"Then you are aware that a certain Miss Finch would seem to answer our financial dilemma." When Edward didn't respond, Higgindorfer went on. "There is no shame in a marriage of convenience, Lord Chatham. Why, there is even royal precedent for it. Did not His Majesty the king accept a bride not of his own choosing in exchange for Parliament canceling his debts?"

"And look how well that marriage turned out. A dead heir, an uncrowned queen, and ugly rumors that Princess Caroline of Brunswick's death was hastened by poison."

Higgindorfer cleared his throat with a wet harrumph. Even the old man of business seemed to agree that the king's behavior toward his wife had been reprehensible. In fact, one of the reasons George IV was planning a trip to Scotland was that his popularity among the English was at such a low ebb. The Scots could scarcely think worse of him.

"Perhaps His Majesty isn't the best example," Higgindorfer conceded, "but the royal marriage did solve his debt problem, at least for a season. However, I have every confidence that once Chatham's debts are retired, your stewardship of the estate will see to it that they do not return. And if things take a turn for the worse, you must admit, my lord, that an alliance with a gentleman as wealthy as Baron Finch would stand Chatham in good stead."

"But the alliance you propose isn't with the baron. It's with his daughter." *His awkward, decidedly odd daughter.*

"At the risk of being impertinent," the old man said, his voice even more gravelly than usual, "I must point out that you are being deliberately obtuse."

"No, I understand you perfectly, Higgindorfer. I just don't agree that marriage to the Finch girl is my only option. Let us set the question aside for the moment." *Forever, if I have anything to say about it.* "Have you anything to report on other issues?"

"As a matter of fact, yes. Some new developments have come to the fore touching upon our enquiry into the death of Sir Erasmus." Higgindorfer shifted uncomfortably in his seat. "I very much fear that the investigative agent I engaged was not as discreet as I'd hoped. Apparently, his poking about has come to the attention of a local magistrate, who has now decided to interest himself in the matter."

That was unfortunate. It was one thing for Edward to search out the truth. Whatever his agents uncovered, he'd counted on being able to control the information if something damning about Anne was revealed. Having a magistrate involved complicated matters considerably. "Has the magistrate uncovered anything of interest?"

"Indeed he has. A canvass of local shopkeepers was made. It seems the apothecary near the Howard town house keeps scrupulous records. According to his ledger, someone purchased a quantity of strychnine on the Howard account about a fortnight before Sir Erasmus died."

"Strychnine?" Edward said, surprised. "I thought you said the discolorations on the baronet's body pointed to arsenic."

"They do and would seem to indicate non-lethal doses delivered over some time. Administered in such small amounts, arsenic will build up in a body's system. It is nearly undetectable as an instrument of murder because it is slow acting, often mimicking simple gastric distress until the victim is finally carried off. Strychnine, by contrast, kills quickly. In Sir Erasmus's case, the evidence suggests that someone had been dosing the baronet with arsenic, but apparently grew tired of waiting for that agent to have the desired effect. The killer switched poisons."

"Did the chemist remember who ordered the strychnine?"

"Only that it was a woman."

"This proves nothing. It might have been anyone connected with the Howard household. Why, the housekeeper might have bought the poison to control vermin."

"Except that Sir Erasmus is dead, not a nest of rats," Mr. Higgindorfer said. "My lord, I know you have interested yourself in this unfortunate situation because of your previous association with Lady Howard—no, no, there's no need to deny it. I well remember how smitten you were with her that Season before your Grand Tour. The attachment was a source of great concern to your father."

Edward stared at him stonily.

"It would distress him even more if he could see that you are still involved with a woman who threatens to drag the Chatham name into such sordid doings."

"My father, God rest him, is past such concerns."

"Nevertheless, I needn't point out that this new development does not bode well for Lady Howard," Higgindorfer went on.

"She did *not* murder her husband."

Higgindorfer raised both hands in mock surrender. "I'm not saying she did, but you must admit, the appearance of nefarious doings could hardly be stronger."

"This only proves someone is trying to make it appear as if she is guilty."

"Then I must say, they are doing a bang-up job of it, my lord." Higgindorfer gave him a searching look. "Do you wish me to continue having inquiries made into the situation?"

"No."

"I am greatly relieved, my lord."

"Don't be. I only call a halt to our investigation because it has caused official interest to be taken in the case. Let us not help that magistrate make an innocent woman's life more difficult."

"I very much fear that ship has sailed," Higgindorfer murmured.

"What do you mean?"

"I mean there are those who do not consider the lady innocent."

"It would be highly unusual to charge a member of the ton with murder," Edward said. It was common knowledge that there seemed to be two sets of laws, one for the common folk and another for the titled few. It might not be fair, but the double standard had been in effect time out of mind, and for once, Edward was grateful for it.

"But Lady Howard is merely the second wife of a rather minor baronet. Sir Erasmus was landed gentry, not a peer," Higgindorfer explained. "There are those of a liberal persuasion running amok in our lower courts. Many would jump at the chance to try a member of the upper crust, even one clinging to the bottom-most rung of nobility, for a capital crime."

Edward stood and turned his back on Higgindorfer. The view out his window was usually a soothing one. Beautiful people strolled on the well-kept street. There was order. Elegance. The appearance of politeness. Yet Edward knew it wasn't only the masses who would welcome seeing a minor member of the ton face a murder charge. Beneath its thin veneer of civility, Polite Society would be secretly gleeful. They might profess shock over the scandal of an upper-class murderess, but they'd lick up every drop of a trial as if it were the sweetest cordial.

So must the hordes of Rome have cheered when Christians were torn to pieces by wild beasts.

"Then in light of this new revelation, are you sure there is nothing else you wish me to undertake in the matter of Sir Erasmus's death?" Higgindorfer asked, his tone surprisingly gentle.

"No." This was something Edward would have to fix himself.

"Very well," the man of business said. "Back to the matter of the drought at your country estate."

"Sell the mill in Essex," Edward said quickly. "It is not entailed; therefore I may do with it as I wish. I am within my rights to sell it."

"But my lord—"

"You heard me. Sell it." Edward sat back down in his leather desk chair as if in doing so he could draw upon the power of all the previous earls of Chatham who'd made decisions from there. "And send word to my land agent at Chatham that he's to assure our tenants they will not be held accountable for rents they are unable to pay due to a poor harvest. We will provide them with whatever they need for the rest of this year and seed to begin afresh next spring."

"But, my lord, by selling the mill you are giving up a property that is currently providing you with income in order to shore up one that is not."

"It is not the property I'm shoring up. It's the people, Higgindorfer," Edward said testily. "Some of those families have been farming Chatham land since the time of my grandfather's grandfather. Am I to turn them out simply because it didn't rain?"

Higgindorfer's jaw dropped. Then he seemed to collect himself and closed it with a snap. "My lord, that's...extraordinarily generous. But I'd be remiss in my duties if I didn't add that it's also more than a little foolhardy."

Because it was Higgindorfer who said it, Edward was prepared to let the insult slide. Besides, the man was right. Once a gentleman of property started down the road of selling off an estate's assets, it was hard to predict where the selling would end.

"Nevertheless you will see to it, Mr. Higgindorfer," Edward said firmly. "Let me know once the sale is accomplished and our tenants are safe."

"As you will, my lord." The old man gathered up the unread ledger and stuffed it back into his satchel. "May I say your decision demonstrates great nobility of spirit...if not great business sense."

Trust Higgindorfer to deliver a compliment with a backhanded swipe.

"If there's nothing else, then, I'll be on my way." Higgindorfer was halfway to the door when he stopped himself. "Oh! There is one more item. I understand you've accepted an invitation to Carlton House. Have you settled on a gift for the king yet?"

"No." It was a sorry fact that although King George IV was arguably the wealthiest man in the kingdom, his subjects were expected to lavish gifts upon him at every turn. "Find something suitable, would you? A snuffbox perhaps."

Higgindorfer shook his head. "Not a snuffbox, my lord. The cousins of the late princess are joining forces to present the king with a superb one. Sir Percival Howard and his wife, in concert with Lord Schaumberg, are said to be offering His Majesty an exquisite gift from Brunswick. The snuffbox in question is said to be most singular in both design and historicity."

"Oh?"

"As I understand its provenance, the snuffbox belonged to the late Princess Caroline's great-grandfather. Apparently, the two sides of the royal family are about to make peace." He took another few steps toward the door. "In light of this ultimately positive development despite His Majesty's misadventures in marriage, perhaps your lordship will reconsider a marriage of convenience to resolve our difficulties."

"Out," Edward thundered.

"Yes, my lord. Very good, my lord. I shall not bring up the matter again."

"See that you don't." Once Higgindorfer latched the door behind him, Edward released a long sigh. The old man was right. A marriage was exactly what was wanted to solve the difficulties Higgindorfer had revealed to him.

But it certainly wasn't the marriage his man of business had in mind.

No matter how independent a lady might wish to be, there comes a time in her life when she must bow to the truth. In this world, a woman's best, sometimes only, protection is the love of a good man.
—Lady Howard writing as Mrs. Hester Birdwhistle

Chapter 24

The longcase clock chimed nine. The parlor was awash with soft light at this time of the morning. Anne took another sip of her hot chocolate and tucked her feet up under her, while Martha perused the on-dit section of the *Times*.

"This reporter was astounded when Lady Ackworth, normally the arbitress of correct behavior, had to be physically ejected from the opera last evening," she read aloud.

Anne sat up straight and leaned forward. "Really? Why?"

"The *Times* says she arrived late and demanded to be seated after the second act began. She must have made a terrible scene."

"That doesn't seem very sensible of her," Anne said. "Everyone knows it's bad form to demand admittance once a performance has begun."

Martha ran her finger over several lines of the paper. "It appears it wasn't missing the opera that upset Lady Ackworth. It was the fact that her chair was already occupied by a certain Mrs. Phoebe Beauchamp."

"Oh, dear." Anne understood Lady Ackworth's dismay. Mrs. Beauchamp was a notorious high-flyer. Her appearance at the opera in the Ackworth box was an open acknowledgment that Lord Ackworth had acquired a new mistress and he wanted to tweak his wife's nose with it.

"I don't understand," Martha said, tipping her head to one side. "Aren't there several chairs in the Ackworth box? Surely there was room enough for both Lady Ackworth and Mrs. Beauchamp."

Anne marveled at the girl's innocence but decided she wouldn't disabuse
her of it. She'd already told Martha more than most young women knew
about what passed between men and women when she'd opened the door
to her own past as a cautionary tale. Instead of being horrified by Anne's
experience, Martha had been both sympathetic and wise. She'd promised to
put Anne's example of what not to do to good use. She would be circumspect
in her behavior and give no one cause to accuse her of being fast.

"And if Mr. Dickey tries to draw me into a compromising position
again, I shall box his ears," Martha had promised firmly.

Anne had assured her there was no need for violence, but the girl's
promise to behave with propriety gave her great comfort. For the first time,
she began to relax a bit in her role as sponsor and guide.

She and Martha were both lounging in comfortable undress, that was,
morning gowns in soft fabric which covered them quite adequately but
weren't fashionable enough for jaunting about town. After they finished
off the last of their croissants and jellies for breakfast, they would repair
to their chambers to don more ornate day dresses. Anne and Martha were
scheduled to be "at home" to anyone who cared to pay a visit today. And
if no one called, they would spend the afternoon reading or sewing or, in
Martha's case, playing the piano.

Leisurely mornings with Martha were a lovely benefit of Anne's current
situation. While chaperoning a lady, she could live like one, too. However,
once Anne helped Martha make a suitable match, she'd have to seek
employment that might require actual labor during these drowsy hours.

The peace of their morning was suddenly disturbed by Edward Lovell
barging into the parlor. James, their tall, handsome footman, followed close
on his heels. Anne suddenly wished she were wearing something more
substantial than pale pink muslin.

"Beggin' your pardon, Lady Howard," James said, his features
screwed into a distressed frown, "but his lordship wouldn't wait to see if
he'd be received."

"Then it is not your fault he has burst in here like a highwayman."

"I'm not bursting anywhere," Edward growled. "I've simply no time
for foolishness."

"And you consider common courtesy foolishness, Lord Chatham? Our
'at home' hours won't start until eleven. Leave your card now and return
then. Perhaps at that time, you'll be admitted. James will show you out."

"James will show himself out if he knows what's good for him. This is
not a social call," Edward said, his expression fierce. Anne didn't blame

her footman for backpedaling toward the door. "Miss Finch, leave us, if you please."

"No, Martha, stay."

"Trust me, Lady Howard. This is a conversation best undertaken in privacy." Then he turned to Martha. "You may leave the parlor door ajar, if you fear for your sponsor's reputation."

Anne narrowed her eyes at him. He was being such a bully she almost didn't recognize him. "Martha, do not stir from that spot."

"Actually, my lady," Martha said as she sidled toward the door, "I believe I left my embroidery upstairs. The light is so lovely in the morning. I'll just fetch my needlework and return."

"Take your time," Edward told her.

"Well, it might take me a while to find it at that, my lord," Martha said. "I haven't worked a stitch in a fortnight, but I'm sure the sampler is in my bedchamber somewhere."

Anne stood, her hands fisted at her waist. "Martha, stay right where you are."

"I shall..." The girl's gaze darted back and forth between them, and then rolled heavenward as if seeking guidance there. "I'll return," she finally said, "sooner or later."

"Later is better." Edward watched Martha until she closed the door behind her. The latch made a loud snick.

So much for Martha being concerned for my reputation.

Then Edward turned and looked at her. The ferocity left his features and all she saw was longing. "Anne," he said softly.

Just her name. That was all, but it was enough to send shivers over her entire frame. Why did he insist on torturing her this way?

She lifted the shield of politeness before her and straightened her spine.

"Well, Lord Chatham, you now have my complete attention. Will you take tea?"

"No. But I will take you." He closed the distance between them and caught her up in his arms. Before she could object, he covered her mouth with his in a kiss tinged with desperation.

Her heart ached with it as well. The longing was so deep, she feared she'd drown in it, except that Edward was there to hold her up. She stopped struggling and let herself sink into him.

She'd love this man till they were both dust, but at every turn the world conspired to keep them apart.

Mia Marlowe

When he finally released her mouth, he cradled the back of her head with his palm and pressed her head to his chest. The kiss that started almost as an assault had ended with tenderness so sweet it made her ache.

"Oh, Edward," she whispered.

"Please, Anne. Don't fight me anymore," he said softly. "You know I love you. I asked you to be my wife, didn't I?"

She pulled away so she could meet his gaze. "In a graveyard," she said with a grimace.

"Well, this is not a graveyard. It's your perfectly proper parlor. Let me get it right this time." He knelt. "Anne, will you do me the supreme honor of becoming my wife?"

"Oh, do stand up, Edward." Didn't he realize it didn't matter where he asked her? The facts hadn't changed. She'd still cause him to risk Chatham, which meant risking all that he was. It was almost cruel of him to ask again. There was still no way for her to accept. "You look ridiculous."

He rose to his feet, a sheepish expression on his handsome face. "Here I thought a woman's fondest hope was bringing a man to his knees."

"I don't need you to grovel," she said tartly.

"I never grovel, but I *am* asking. Please, Anne." He caught up one of her hands. "Marry me."

She swallowed hard. "Is Chatham still in danger from its creditors?"

He frowned at her. "I've made arrangements to settle those issues for the time being."

"But not for long—"

"Nothing is ever long in this life. Come, Anne." He brought her hand to his lips and kissed her knuckles. Little tendrils of pleasure raced up her arm. "Haven't we wasted enough time?"

She pulled her hand away and turned from him. It would be easier to keep saying no if she didn't have to look at him. "You're trying to confuse me."

"No, I'm trying to make everything clear." He slipped his arms around her and pulled her close so that her spine rested against his chest. Then he bent his head and she felt his warm breath on her neck. She nearly melted into him. "I made the mistake of putting my own selfishness before you once. That will never happen again. No matter what, you come first."

"An earl is not at liberty to say such a thing. Your first duty is to your estate." Even so, she couldn't bring herself to pull away from the string of baby kisses he was pressing along her neck. "You know it and I know it."

"I only know I love you." He turned her around and embraced her. "And I'd beggar myself and all of Chatham to keep you safe."

"I am safe. Perfectly safe." This time when she extricated herself from his arms, she crossed the room to put some distance between them. "Granted, my situation is not ideal at the moment, but I'm exploring a number of options once my contract with Miss Finch's parents is at an end." She lifted her chin and gave him her bravest smile. "I'm like a cat, Edward. I always land on my feet."

"Anne, I'm not talking about reduced circumstances. You are in real danger."

The only danger she was aware of was that she was sorely tempted to let him lift her skirts and take her right there in the oh-so-proper parlor. But he seemed so certain she was at risk, she had to ask, "From what?"

Edward raked a hand through his hair. "I'd hoped you'd agree to marry me for myself, but I can see I shall have to tell you all and trust to your instinct for self-preservation."

Now he was scaring her in earnest. "What do you mean? Has something happened?"

"Sit," he said. "This may take a while."

Once she perched on the settee, and he took the chair opposite her, he told her about his inquiry into Sir Erasmus's death, and the subsequent interest of the local magistrate. "The apothecary remembers it was a woman who bought the poison, Anne. And she charged it to the Howard line of credit."

"Whatever else you think of me, I swear, I did not do this."

"Of course not." Edward shot her an indignant look. "Give me credit for being a good judge of character, at least. If I thought you'd killed your first husband, why would I want you to marry me? Today. Right now." He fished in his pocket and came out with a pair of rings and a common license issued by the vicar at St. Thomas-by-the-Way. "We can be married before noon. The vicar is expecting us. Then you'll be my countess. That magistrate might have been emboldened to charge the widow of a baronet, but he will not dare to threaten the Countess of Chatham."

Anne let it all soak in for a moment. "So you only wish to marry me to protect me?"

"No. I'm too selfish for that," Edward said, leaning forward. "I want to build a life with you, Anne. Yes, there may be problems. I'd be lying if I said there wouldn't be. Yes, my man of business would rather see me paying court to your protégé, but *you* are the one I love. Living without you as my wife is no life at all."

Her whole being yearned toward him, but she held herself motionless, forcing herself to stare at the tea service on the table between them. "But if I say yes, I may be Chatham's undoing."

"If you say no, you'll be my undoing."

Anne raised her gaze to meet his. Edward's soul shined through his eyes, and it was a beautiful one. Strong. Sure. Faithful.

"Nations rise and fall. Fortunes are won and lost," he said softly. "The only thing we take with us when we leave this life is the love we share while we are here. Please, Anne. Share your life, your heart, yourself...with me."

"Edward, are you sure?"

"It's the only thing I am sure of."

"Then, yes," Anne said softly. "I will marry you."

His smile was like a sunrise. He leaped to his feet and pocketed the license and rings. Then he took both her hands and raised her to stand before him. "Quickly, then. The license is only good until noon. Do you wish to have Miss Finch stand up with you?"

"Yes...no. Hold a moment." Anne's mind raced furiously. Her euphoria about marrying Edward dissipated as the cold reality of what he was sacrificing for her settled in. If he was forced to slice up Chatham piecemeal because he ought to have married an heiress, she'd never forgive herself. "I don't think this marriage should become public knowledge."

"Why not?"

"Because the main reason you're doing this is so I'll have the protection of your name should I need it," she said. "But we don't know for certain that the magistrate is going to press charges against me."

"That's not why I asked you to marry me." He frowned down at her. "I want you for your sweet self. If becoming my countess will shield you from prosecution, I consider that a side benefit."

"But what kind of countess will I make if I put my own needs ahead of your estate's?" She took a step away from him, and when he reached for her, she straight-armed him. "No, Edward. The only way I'll take vows with you is if you promise to keep our marriage secret until we see if it is needed."

"It's needed. By God, if it was any more needed, I'd have you on the floor with your skirts up this very instant."

Part of her throbbed at the thought, but she tamped the feeling down. "That's another thing. If we wed, we must take care that the marriage can be annulled once we discover I am not in danger in the matter of Sir Erasmus's death."

"Annulled?"

"Yes," she said shakily. "That way you can still marry an heiress and save Chatham."

"Anne, what must I do to convince you I don't care about that?"

"Maybe not now in the heat of...the heat we're in, but you will later."
He studied her silently for a moment. "You already have my heart.
Marriage will only mean you have the rest of me, too. If you think I would
wish to take back my vow to you, you really don't know me at all."

"Perhaps I don't, but I do know myself. And I can't allow you to sacrifice
everything for me," she said gently. "So to that end, we need to maintain
grounds for an annulment, which means not...I mean, we can't..."

"Be together."

"Not as husband and wife." She'd already learned the hard way that
even one coupling with Edward was enough to make life spring up in her.
Lily's small grave was testimony to that. "Those are my terms."

Edward scowled at her for a moment, and then sighed. "Very well. I'll
take you any way I can have you. But we must away right now. The sooner
you are my wife in the eyes of the church, the sooner you will have my
protection should it come to that."

She nodded. "I'll just go change into something more suitable."

"You're suitable just as you are."

That was debatable. The simple column dress didn't have a stitch of
embellishment, and her hair probably needed attention, too.

The long case clock chimed ten.

"There's no time," Edward insisted. "If this marriage truly is just for
form's sake as you claim, then why should what you're wearing matter?"

"I suppose it doesn't."

Anne rang for James and told him to bear a message to Miss Finch that
she and Lord Chatham had an errand to run together, but that she would
be back in time to attend Miss Finch during their at home hours.

"Oh! And tell Betsy to bring down my long cape and the feathered
bonnet." It was one thing for Edward to see her in her old gown. It was quite
another for a passing member of the ton to catch her looking so shabby.
And whatever state her hair was in would be hidden by the outlandish
bonnet that had become her trademark.

So with a sorry turnout on her part and a sorry countenance on his,
Lady Howard née Anne Spillwell and Edward Lovell, Lord Chatham
went to their private nuptials at St. Thomas-by-the-Way. And if either of
them was happy, they gave no sign of it to those they passed on the street.

An errand. For the love of God, she called our wedding an errand. Of no more import than a trip to her milliner or a visit to the butcher's shop for a lamb shank. If I wasn't so besotted with the woman I'd have stormed out then and there, but where Anne is concerned I'm weak as water. However, if she thinks to keep this marriage ripe for an annulment, she has another think coming. A husband has rights, and I mean to claim them. Fortunately, I know just what to do to make sure she is as weak as I.

—from the journal of Edward Lovell, Earl of Chatham, Viscount Bredon, and frustrated husband

Chapter 25

The brief service at the church really couldn't be called a ceremony. There was no music. No flowers. No witnesses save the sexton and the taciturn gravedigger. But when the last "amen" was said, Edward and Anne were pronounced man and wife. Their names were entered into the parish rolls along with the signatures of the witnesses, such as they were. John Fernsby was illiterate, so he merely marked an *X* in the ledger to indicate he'd been present to solemnize their vows.

Once they were back in the Chatham carriage, Edward ordered his driver to take them home to Lovell House.

"No," Ann said firmly.

Edward tried to convince her to come home to Lovell House with him, but she stubbornly clung to her demand that he take her back to the Finch town house.

"Did you or did you not just promise before God to obey me?" he said, softly enough that his driver couldn't overhear.

"I did. And you, my lord, promised to comfort me. I will be comforted by your adherence to our agreement to keep this marriage secret."

"Anne—"

"Did you not accede to my terms before we went to church?"

"I did, but—"

"No buts. The former promise supersedes the latter. You agreed to a secret marriage and that is what we have."

If Anne had been a man, she'd have made a top-notch barrister. Well, Edward knew a bit about law, too. "You know I am within my rights to—"

"My first husband was not shy about asserting his husbandly rights without my consent. I came to despise him for it." She glared at him, daring him to oppose her further.

Sometimes a man needs to know when to take the field and when to retreat.

In the end, she handed him back the silver and gold ring he'd slipped on her finger during the ceremony. He stuffed it in his pocket. Then he returned her to the Finch town house and left her there.

It was all wrong. They were meant to be together. She loved him and he her. *Let all else be false in this world and that much be true.*

He knew they were well and truly married with every fiber of his being, and he ached to make her completely, irrevocably his. Somehow, he'd crack her resolve. He just needed the right time and place.

And the patience to wait for the opportunity to present itself.

* * * *

A week passed during which Edward's faith in his ability to be patient was sorely tested. He saw Anne plenty of times during those days, but she was always surrounded by other matrons and their darling daughters. He was never able to cut her from the flock of other females long enough to even speak to her alone.

However, Edward held out hope that the king's grand fete would be the perfect venue for his assault on Anne's carefully guarded heart and even more closely barricaded body. There were hundreds of rooms in Carlton House. Surely he could find a way for them to be alone in one of them.

But after he arrived on the appointed night, he began to wonder if his plan was possible. He surrendered his topper to one of the small army of footmen and, because he heard music already under way, made his way to the Grand Council Chamber, which had been set aside for dancing. If Anne was already there, she wouldn't be far from the gathering of music and nimble feet.

The walls of the expansive chamber were covered in crimson silk with gold embellishments at the cornices. Candelabras were suspended above the dance floor, which highlighted the elaborate arabesque designs that had been chalked on the wood. A circlet with the king's initials occupied pride of place in the center of the room.

The ballroom was edged with "conversation stools" for those who preferred to watch the dancers. Even though the first dance hadn't been called yet, the press of people made the space uncomfortably warm, and almost every one of the stools was already occupied.

Edward despaired of finding Anne among the throng.

But he did find his favorite sister and his best friend, Lawrence Sinclair, Lord Ware. As soon as Caro spotted him, she waved him over.

The Countess of Ware was dressed in an elegant cream silk gown, shot through with gold threads. A fascinator with spangles sparkled in her perfectly coiffed hair and her cheeks were rosy with good health. However, no amount of fashionable distraction could hide the prodigious bump under the front of her gown.

"Oh, I'm so glad you're here, Teddy. Where have you been keeping yourself?" she said as she kissed the air beside his cheek. "We haven't seen you since the night of our dinner party."

"I've not been in hiding," Edward said as he shook hands with Sinclair. The Earl of Ware was as well turned out as his very pregnant wife, his vest fashioned of the same fabric as her gown. Clearly, Edward's sister was marking her territory. "Frankly, I'm surprised to see you here, Caro."

"I know. It's most irregular." She laid a hand over her belly in a protective gesture. "But when the king commands Lord and Lady Ware to attend him, they must come. Besides, I've been dying to see something besides the four walls of my own parlor for weeks!"

"But remember what the doctor said. No dancing. No exotic foods," Sinclair reminded her. "You must not overexcite yourself."

"Good heavens, Lawrence. I'm the size of a small country. I'm not likely to *over* anything at the moment." She swatted her husband with her fan, but her eyes were intensely fond as she smiled up at him. Then her gaze jerked toward the dancing master, who strode to the center of the floor and announced that the king's ball was about to commence. "However, just because I can't dance, that doesn't mean that you can't, dear. Look. There's Lady Howard and Miss Finch, over by the credenza with the very large china dog. Why don't you ask her to dance?"

"Lady Howard?" Sinclair's brows drew together.

Caro delivered a not-so-surreptitious elbow to his ribs. "No, silly. Miss Finch. You can't very well ask a debutante's chaperone to dance and leave the poor girl standing about to twiddle her thumbs."

"If *The Bachelor's Bible* is correct, Miss Finch is anything but a poor girl," Sinclair said.

"You know what I mean. Now off you go, Lawrence, before I decide you need to dance with me."

"Caro, you promised to take it easy."

"And I will, if you'll dance with Miss Finch," she said. "A couple of stools have just opened up. Teddy and I will just sit there and watch while you and Miss Finch cut a few capers."

Sinclair helped her settle onto one of the conversation stools, kissed her cheek, and then grimaced at Edward. "No one can gainsay the will of a woman who's with child."

"Precious few can gainsay my sister even when she's not."

Sinclair laughed in agreement, and then went to do Caro's bidding before she chose a partner for him for the next dance, too.

Edward sat down beside her.

"Hold a moment. You'd best not get too comfortable." Caro placed a hand on his forearm. "Surely you don't think I'm going to allow you to molder here beside me like some overripe hunk of cheese, do you?"

Edward thought it prudent for someone to be near Caro in case she needed anything. He'd hate to see her waddling off to fetch a cup of punch for herself. "Well, no, but—"

"But nothing," she interrupted. "See there, Teddy. Lawrence has just taken the dance floor with Miss Finch, which leaves the lovely Lady Howard standing all alone." Caro lifted a suggestive brow at him. "Such things ought not to be."

"No, indeed." Edward leaned over and kissed Caro's cheek. "You are my favorite sister, you know."

"Of course I am. And I would be, even if you had twenty sisters," she said with a grin. "I shall be fine here. Go dance the lady's slippers off."

* * * *

Anne was pleased that Martha had not languished long among the wallflowers before she was invited to dance. However, even though she liked Lord Ware very much indeed, she couldn't help wishing Martha's first dance of the evening was with an eligible gentleman instead of a happily married one. Still, Lord Ware was doing his best to show Martha to good advantage as they twirled around the room. Someone else was bound to notice her.

Please God, let it not be Reginald Dickey.

"Good evening, my lady."

The masculine voice at her side made her startle and turn toward the sound.

It was Edward. She'd been so intent on watching her charge, she hadn't noticed his approach. He bowed to her correctly and she responded with a deep curtsy. "My lord."

"And master," he whispered. "Try saying them together."

She snorted at him indignantly.

"I thought perhaps you might like to give me a pet name," he said, a wicked grin making him look even more handsome than usual. "Lord and master will do. I'm given to understand a wife will sometime refer to her husband thusly."

"Only if she wants something from him."

"Ah." He nodded in understanding. "And don't you want anything from me?"

"What I chiefly want, *Lord Chatham*, is for you to leave me in peace."

That was a lie. As big a faradiddle as she'd ever told in her entire life. She hadn't had a moment's peace since she'd exchanged vows with him last week. While Martha played the piano, she thought of Edward. When she was supposed to be engaging in conversation with the visitors who stopped by to see them, she thought of Edward. And when she lay down in her bed for the night and silver light fingered its way through her shutters and across her counterpane, oh! how she thought of Edward. But she couldn't admit such things to him.

"Very well, no terms of endearment, then," he said. "Will you at least do me the honor of a dance?"

She cocked an ear to the music and suddenly recognized it as that blasted Boccherini tune in three-quarter time. The same one that had led them into such disasters in the past. "But it's a waltz."

He tipped his head as if he, too, were hearing it for the first time. "I believe you're right. Don't fret. I'll take care not to tread on your toes."

That wasn't what troubled her. When she waltzed with Edward, he took command and she let him. Who knew what sort of madness he'd lead her into?

"It's just a waltz," he said softly. "Let me at least hold you for a while, wife."

A sob rose in her throat. She wanted to truly be his wife so badly. It was all she'd ever wanted. Even when she'd been gadding about the capitals of Europe, soaking up new places and new sights as Hester Birdwhistle, she was really just trying to fill the Edward-sized hole in her heart.

"Yes, my lord." *And master,* she added silently. "I'll waltz with you."

When you spend a good deal of time watching the sea, you begin to understand inevitability. Like the tide, some things are simply going to happen, and there's no way to stop them without ripping apart the very fabric of the universe.

Or your own heart.
—Lady Howard, writing as Mrs. Hester Birdwhistle

Chapter 26

Anne and Edward waltzed around the perimeter of the room once. It felt so right, so *meant*, for him to hold her close, to release her for an under-arm turn and then to catch her up once more without losing a step. They moved as one being, as if their thoughts, their breaths, the very beats of their hearts were in perfect synchronicity.

That was why, when Edward waltzed her out the doorway and into a dimly lit cloak closet, Anne didn't question it. She just kept dancing to the Boccherini tune, even though the music was much softer now.

She still didn't protest when he danced her through an open doorway into an even more remote space off the cloak room that was probably used as a lumber room to house the empty trunks of the king's overnight visitors. There were no trunks crowding the space, so evidently no guests were in residence at Carlton House at present, though few of the revelers would leave until the sun was shining through the long windows. Still holding her close, Edward reached behind him to close the door, which latched with a loud snick.

Then he simply held her.

Anne was grateful for the warmth of his body.

They stood together without speaking, snugged next to each other. Being alone with Edward there in that quiet space seemed so dreamlike,

Anne touched him lightly, slipping her fingers beneath his lapel to feel the heat of his chest through his fine lawn shirt. It reassured her that this was no dream. He was really there.

Edward's heart pounded under her fingertips.

The tiny room was lit by a single gas sconce, but Anne wondered if she were glowing a bit herself. Edward drew a deep breath and released it slowly in contentment. His happiness wrapped itself around her mind, caressing, soothing, calming her fears.

They swayed almost imperceptibly to the distant music. There was something so blessedly ordinary about letting him hold her like this. It was a simple pleasure meant to be enjoyed by a husband and wife.

"The moon is full tonight," Anne finally said, breaking the silence. "It was simply enormous when I arrived."

His mouth twitched in a smile. "I remember another night with a full moon."

That magical night was all Anne could think of, too. In her parents' garden, he had taken off his jacket and had laid it on the ground to keep the dew from chilling her. He wouldn't have needed to. His body heat would have kept her warm.

"It's been so long, Anne," Edward said, his voice ragged. He kissed her temple, her cheeks, her lips and finished with a lingering kiss below her ear. "How I've missed you."

She nestled in his arms. "I thought about that night so often after you went away. About how you made me feel there in the garden."

His hands slipped down her back to her bum. "How did I make you feel?"

"Safe." *Among other things.* He'd flooded her senses almost to the point of drowning, but on that night she was firmly convinced that Edward would always be there for her.

"I'm sorry I didn't live up to that, but I'm here now and I'm not going anywhere without you. This isn't exactly a romantic garden, but I *will* keep you safe this time." He kissed her brow. "I promise."

"I know you will," Anne said, feeling jittery and feverish all at once, as if someone had loosed a jar of bees in her belly. A lovely, primal thing was about to happen. And she wanted it to. She would no more stop it than she would stop the earth from spinning.

"Don't be afraid," he said as he began to part the front of her gown.

"I'm not."

When she'd first purchased this style of gown with its long row of pearl buttons marching up the bodice, its main benefit was that she could get into it by herself without the assistance of a lady's maid. This was an important consideration for a lady who didn't expect to be able to afford a servant soon. Now the gown's main delight was how easily Edward could tease the tops of her breasts without being stopped by unyielding fabric.

"There's just one more thing," he said.

"What's that?"

He ran his thumbs along the top of the lacy chemise he'd just exposed, skimming over her breasts. Then his hands drifted down past her ribs and the curve of her waist. With obvious effort, he interrupted his exploration of her frame to dig into his own pocket. "You need your ring."

"What?"

"Don't worry. No one needs to know it's your wedding ring. You don't even have to tell anyone it's from me," he said. "But I'll know you're wearing it. And even if it means nothing to you, it means everything to me."

It meant the world to her, too. She was just reluctant to admit it.

He pulled a small leather pouch from his pocket and handed it to her. "Open it."

Anne loosened the drawstring and dumped the contents into her palm. There were the two rings from their wedding ceremony, his and hers. He plucked the larger plain gold band from her hand and put it on his left ring finger. Then he picked up the delicately embossed silver and gold circle that was hers.

"I'll still keep our marriage secret if you insist, but I want you to wear this for me," Edward said as he placed the ring on the third finger of her right hand. "When you're ready to claim me before the world, you can switch it to your other hand."

"When, not if?" she said with a smile. "You sound very sure of yourself."

One corner of his mouth curved up. "Don't I have reason to be?"

"Perhaps." He was doing everything he could to please her. Anne reasoned she ought to return the favor, just a little. She ran her beringed hand down his chest to his flat belly. His breath hissed in over his teeth. "You are a very stubborn man, you know."

"I prefer to think of myself as single-minded," he admitted.

She stood on tiptoe and nipped his earlobe. "And what is your single mind focused on right now?"

"Can't you guess?"

"Not without a hint." She ran a hand over his groin and found him erect and straining against the superfine fabric. "Ah! Good hint."

"That's cheating," he said.

"Want me to stop?"

"Merciful Lord, no!"

His laughter warmed her to her toes. They sank down onto the thick carpet in a hailstorm of kisses.

* * * *

"Now, Edward?"

Her voice sounded tight, as if she were speaking through clenched teeth. Indeed, when Edward turned his head to look over the hills and valleys of Anne's lovely prone form, he saw that her jaw was tight.

"Not yet." He nuzzled her again, drunk on her scent, desperate to draw their loving out, desperate to sink into her sweet body and find release.

She gave a little sob and twisted her fingers in his hair.

"Not yet, Anne."

"When?" she asked again, arching herself into his mouth. He devoured her for a moment, only pausing when she began trembling almost uncontrollably.

His body tightened in response to her need.

Without even realizing he'd done it, he moved up to cover her with his body and found himself knocking at her gate, poised to slide into her.

"If I...say it...will you..." she whimpered, "my lord and master."

Finally! He rushed in with one long stroke and she molded around him, her breath coming in short pants. He held himself motionless, willing the urgency to subside so he could revel in the joy that was Anne a little longer. Only a little. He wouldn't last much longer with his heart pounding in two places.

When he looked down at her, at the soft gape of her mouth, and the way her brows tented, he knew he couldn't keep her dancing on the edge any longer. He had to give her release.

He covered her mouth with his and loved her with his tongue. She moved beneath him, urging him in deeper with little noises of desperation that threatened to shred his control.

A little longer, please.

She turned her head away. "I can't wait any—"

He felt the deep contractions start. She was his. His forever. "Now, love, now."

Edward arched his back, driving in as deep as he could as his life shot into her in steady pulses. Pleasure, sharp as a blade, sliced through him.

Her whole body convulsed under him. She was like a being aflame, pulsing dim, bright, dim, bright. Then, when it was finally over, he laid his head between her breasts and rested in the quiet joy that settled over them.

"Oh, my Anne," Edward said as he inhaled her scent.

"Oh, my lord and master," she returned, running her fingers through his hair.

He raised his head and grinned at her. "You must want something, my love."

"Not a thing. I'm just finding I like calling you that," she said with a deep sigh. "As long as I have you, I have everything I could ever want."

"Well, maybe a bed would be nice," he said. "Would you like that?"

"What wonderful ideas you have, husband."

"An even better idea would be to announce our marriage to the world tonight."

"I think—no, wait." She pushed against his shoulders and he rolled off her. "Martha. I forgot about her completely. Edward, we have to find her."

"I'm sure she's fine."

"What if she's off in a closet with Mr. Dickey someplace?"

"Dickey? Impossible. The last time I saw him, I...discouraged that scoundrel from accosting you and your protégé."

"You may not be as persuasive as you think." She sat up, her fingers flying to pull her skirts down to cover her ankles and then to button the front of her gown. "Mr. Dickey seems to be quite smitten with Martha. Even after you gave him that shiner, he continued to pursue her. She promised me she'd box his ears if he tried to compromise her, but...well, I'd be the first to understand how a woman's best intentions can go awry."

"Especially when she's with a man with evil intentions."

"Is that a confession, Edward?"

"An admission." He took her hand and helped her to her feet. "I came here fully intending to seduce my wife this night. If it was evil, I don't care."

"A tad wicked perhaps, but not evil." Anne cupped his cheeks and gave him a quick peck. "And I hope to give you another opportunity to seduce me again in the very near future, but for now, please help me find Martha."

"She's probably dancing and you will have worried for naught." Edward opened the door, led her through the cloakroom, and checked to see if anyone was looking their way. The dancing had progressed to a raucous reel, so he tucked Anne's hand into the crook of his elbow and escorted her back into the brightly lit ballroom.

But contrary to Edward's prediction, Miss Finch wasn't bobbing and weaving in the long lines of dancers.

And neither was Reginald Dickey.

The problem with hiding my intellect behind wit is that even when the situation is deadly serious, no one takes me seriously.

—Mr. Reginald Dickey, who's mortally tired of being a source of amusement to the tittering masses of empty-headed Polite Society

Chapter 27

The reel came to its conclusion and the gentlemen escorted their ladies back to the edges of the dance floor. Anne and Edward weren't mistaken. Miss Finch was not amongst them.

"Perhaps Caro saw her leave the ballroom," Edward suggested. "Normally, she loves to dance, but in her delicate condition, she's only allowed to watch."

Anne stood on tiptoe, trying to see over the throng. "Where is your sister?"

The dancing master strode to the center of the room and called for a quadrille. Dancers began to reassemble on the floor in squares of four couples each.

"Caro is over there by—no, she's gone, too," Edward said, fisting his hands at his waist in consternation. The strings began to play again and the quadrille commenced in a blur of pale silk and dark superfine as the dancers moved through the prescribed figures.

"Do you see Lord Ware? He's tall enough to stand out in the crowd," Anne suggested. "Likely your sister is with her husband."

Edward shook his head. Then he spied Reginald Dickey coming back into the ballroom through the wide archway across the expansive space from them.

"Come." Without waiting for a reply, Edward grabbed Anne's hand and started off, cutting across the dance floor, dodging around the quadrille squares, narrowly missing the couples who were concentrating on the series of intricate steps.

Before they reached Dickey, he seemed to spy them and, to Edward's surprise, the man waded into the crowded sea of dancers to meet them. Standing in the middle of the dance floor on the now faded initials of the king, Edward crossed his arms over his chest.

"Mr. Dickey, do you know where we might find Miss Finch?" Anne asked. Edward wished she hadn't used such a polite tone, but that was his Anne. She'd defer to the devil if civility demanded it.

"Upstairs in one of the bedchambers," Dickey said.

Edward caught him up by his lapel and gave him a shake.

"It's not what you think," Dickey said, his arms flailing.

"Perhaps it's exactly what I think."

"Even if it were, my lord, do you really want to accost me in so public a manner?" he stage-whispered furiously. "If I had compromised Miss Finch, and let me hasten to assure you I haven't, thrashing me about like this is the best way to trumpet the news of the lady's undoing."

The weasel had a point. Edward released him. "Explain yourself."

"Lady Ware's time has come upon her. She is about to give birth. And Marth—I mean, Miss Finch—is with her."

"She ought not to be there," Anne said. "A birthing chamber is no place for an unmarried girl."

Dickey wrung his hands. "It all happened so fast. One minute, I was cooling my heels on the edge of the dance floor, waiting for Lord Ware to turn Miss Finch loose so I could claim a dance, and the next thing I knew, he and Martha were hustling Lady Ware out of the ballroom."

"So you followed them," Edward said.

"I had to see what was what, didn't I?" Dickey said defensively. "Come. I'll take you to them."

Edward and Anne followed Dickey through the dancers' maze of movement until they reached the arched doorway and filed out of the ballroom. Then they mounted the grand stairs that wound up to the next story of Carlton House. The stairs seemed to go on forever.

"However did a woman in labor manage all these steps?" Anne wondered.

"She didn't," Dickey said. "Lord Ware carried her. It was hopelessly romantic, the way her arms draped around his neck and the train of her gown flew out behind them. Frankly, I'm surprised he didn't trip over the silly thing and go tail over teakettle all the way to the basement."

"I'm only surprised Sinclair didn't try to take her home," Edward said gruffly.

"Lady Ware said there was no time," Dickey explained as they reached the next story and made their way through a labyrinth of rooms. "The babe, it seems, is planning to make its appearance rather quickly."

"That's good," Anne said. "I'm told a quick labor is often a sign that all is going well."

The long wail of a woman in deep pain reverberated through the ornately paneled door, calling Anne's hopeful pronouncement into question.

The whites of Dickey's eyes showed all the way around his irises. "Lady Ware is in there, my lady. I'll just wait here in the anteroom, shall I? I mean, in case I'm needed to fetch anything."

"Do that." Edward knocked on the door.

There was no response.

He knocked again.

"Come in if you must," a voice made hoarse by wailing tried to call. "But for the love of God, stop pounding on the door."

Definitely the voice of my favorite sister.

Edward and Anne entered the chamber to find Caro propped upright by mounds of pillows in the center of a four-poster bed. A furiously pacing Sinclair was wearing out a small oval in the rug near the fireplace. Miss Finch, her face as pale as parchment and her eyes wide, was perched on the edge of the bed, holding his sister's hand.

A birth pain must have come on Caro again, for she made a noise in the back of her throat that sounded like a trapped animal. Miss Finch gave a muffled squeak of her own as his sister squeezed the girl's hand with a grip of iron.

"Please, my lady," Miss Finch said softly. "I play the piano with that hand."

Caro released her fingers and scrunched a helpless pillow instead.

Once the pain passed, Edward decided to try to keep things light. "Well, Caro, trust you to steal the attention away from the king at his own party."

"He hadn't even made an appearance by the time I had to leave his miserable party. This is His Majesty's fault, you know," Caro grumbled. "If the king hadn't insisted we attend this...benighted...fete, I'd be in my own bed with my own midwife assisting me."

Caro didn't actually say *benighted.* Her words were a bit garbled when another pain came upon her, but Edward had a good guess as to which vulgar expression his sister might have used where his mind had substituted *benighted.*

"Are there no servants available to help?" Edward asked.

"There are servants aplenty on the lower floor, offering canapés and trotting to and fro," Miss Finch said shakily. Clearly, this peek into a birthing chamber was an eye-opener for her maidenly soul. "But we didn't encounter anyone on this level of the house."

"Besides, Lady Ware ought to have a doctor to attend her, not a chambermaid," Anne said, as she hurried to the other side of the bed from the one where Miss Finch was situated. "Surely there's at least one physician in attendance this night."

"I'll find and fetch him," Sinclair said, his concerned face as pale as the bed-curtains, but the way his eyes blazed, Edward had no doubt he would bodily drag a doctor to his wife's side if the man didn't come willingly.

"No, let me go," Edward offered, hoping to make good his escape before the situation became even more uncomfortable.

"Please, I need something to do," Sinclair said, his expression tight. "Watching Caro suffer and not being able to help her is worse than a beating."

"Well, it's no stroll through Vauxhall for me either, you know," Caro said, panting softly.

Sinclair leaned over to place a kiss on her damp forehead. "I'll be back soon, dearest, with someone who can help you."

"No, Sinclair, I'll go," Edward insisted.

"I'm her husband, Bredon."

"But—"

"Oh, why don't both of you go?" Anne said, clearly exasperated with them. "Honestly, men are beyond useless sometimes."

Edward had never loved her more. "If you insist, my lady."

He and Sinclair made a hasty retreat as Caro wound up for another long wail.

Once outside the door, Sinclair bolted toward the grand stairs and Edward would have followed, but Dickey caught him by the arm.

"A word in your ear, my lord."

"Not now, man. My sister needs a doctor."

"Our king may need a physician as well unless something is done," Dickey warned. "I have...overheard certain conversations that lead me to suspect there may be a plot to do His Majesty harm this very night."

"Are you coming, Bredon?" Sinclair called from the head of the staircase.

"No. Go on ahead," Edward called back. "Divide and conquer. We'll both seek out a doctor, and surely one of us will succeed."

Sinclair flew down the stairs. Edward hoped he didn't take a tumble and break his neck, but if Sinclair had managed to climb them while bearing a wailing pregnant woman, he would likely make it down by himself.

"You're making me shirk my brotherly duties at a critical time, Dickey." Edward glowered down at him. "This had better be worth it."

"Trust me. It will be, if we take action."

"Let me be the judge of whether or not we do anything with this information." Edward suspected Dickey was trying to send him off on a snipe hunt. "How did you happen to overhear this treasonous conversation?"

"You know me, always a gadabout. I arrived early at the fete and was wandering in and out of some of the rooms here in Carlton House to while away the—"

"Looking for a likely place to steal away with Miss Finch later, no doubt," Edward finished for him.

"Yes, I'll admit it if you like. I planned to lure the lady away from the festivities so I might have her to myself for a while," Dickey said. "But not to do her ill. The truth is, I love Martha, and no amount of beating from you or threats from Lady Howard will change my devotion to her."

"Or to her dowry," Edward said cynically.

"Her money doesn't matter a pinch to me," Dickey protested. "In fact, I don't care if her father cuts her off without a farthing. The duke may not have given me his name, but he's been abundantly generous with his funds. I am more than capable of providing for a wife."

A wife? Dickey's intentions at least seemed honorable. "We can debate your romantic situation another time, Dickey. What about the king?"

"Oh! Yes, I thought I'd discovered the perfect trysting spot, but alas! the space was invaded by Sir Percival and Lady Howard the Younger. And don't worry, my lord. I would never use that appellation for Sir Percy's wife in the company of *your* Lady Howard. The implication being that she is Lady Howard the *Elder*, you know."

Frustrated by the man's inability to stay on topic, Edward thundered, "Dickey, by all that's holy, out with it, man."

"They didn't know I was in the room because I ducked behind the drapes and heard them talking about—oh! You'll be relieved to know I have discovered that Sir Percy and his wife were the ones behind his father's death. As it turns out, Lady Howard the Younger was the woman who purchased strychnine at the apothecary shop a few weeks before her father-in-law's death. Lady Howard the Elder is blameless. Again, I mean to give no cause for offense. In fact, your Lady Howard can't be more than a few months senior to her stepson's wife, can she?"

"The king, Dickey." Edward was relieved by the news proving Anne's innocence, but Dickey was once again off topic. "You said they present a threat to the king."

"You'll be pleased to know I overheard them rehearsing their entire scheme."

"What scheme?"

"Why, the one to poison the king, of course."

In the birthing chamber, a woman passes close by the gates of Death, near enough to feel its icy breath. Our churchyards are filled with the graves of young mothers who slipped through that gate, instead of creeping quietly by it.
—from the journal of Lady Howard, née Anne Spillwell

Chapter 28

Lady Ware bit her lower lip, trying to keep from crying out, but she lost the battle. The pain was too intense.

"What are we to do?" Martha wrung her hands in distress.

Anne was just as panicked as Martha, but someone needed to remain calm. At least outwardly. "Once this birth pain passes, we shall help Lady Ware out of her gown and between the sheets."

"How is that going to help?" the pregnant woman demanded once the contraction subsided. "And for pity's sake, Anne, we've known each other for a long time, and now you're about to watch me give birth. Call me Caro or I promise I shall become very difficult."

"God save us from that," Anne said with a forced smile. She took Caro's hand. "We'll help you undress because you'll be more comfortable out of that gown. Besides, it's so lovely, I'm sure you don't want to ruin it."

"I very much fear that ship has sailed." Caro shook her head ruefully. "There I was, happily watching my husband dance. I taught him how, you know." She smiled at the memory and then sighed. "In any case, all of a sudden I discovered I was sitting in a puddle."

"Your birth waters have burst," Anne told her. "It's perfectly normal."

"If you say so," Caro said. "If I'd had the slightest inkling that such an embarrassing thing could happen, I'd have defied the king and never left home tonight."

"No one can predict when a child will decide to come," Anne said in a soothing tone. "You couldn't have known this was your time, and in any case, giving birth doesn't always start with a bursting of the waters."

"I didn't even know it was possible. My own mother never even mentioned such a thing. What a pity we women are kept in such ignorance about our own bodies," Caro said with a sigh. "My gown is likely ruined already. Still, I expect you're right. This will go easier if I'm in my chemise."

Caro scooted to the edge of the bed and stood shakily. "Hold a moment, please."

Beads of perspiration popped out on her forehead. Anne knew another pain must have overtaken her. They were coming so close together. Surely that boded well and this would all be over soon.

"Martha, see if there's fresh water in that pitcher on the commode," Anne said gently.

Martha skittered across the room, obviously glad to put a little distance between herself and the drama being played out near the bed. "There's plenty of water."

"Pour some in the ewer and bring it to me. If the housekeeper here at Carlton House is worth her salt, there should be some linens in those drawers. Bring a cloth or two as well."

Like the men, Martha seemed steadier now that she had something to occupy her hands instead of letting Caro squeeze them to pieces. They managed to help Caro out of her ball gown and stays, stopping when another pain came upon her so she could concentrate on breathing. After Anne helped Caro slip off her pantalets and peel off her stockings, she knelt to wash the stickiness of the birth waters off Caro's legs.

"I'm sorry this cloth isn't warm," she murmured.

"It's fine," Caro said. "How kind you are, Anne. You're just what Teddy needs, you know."

"I doubt that," she said with a shake of her head. She might still prove to be Chatham's downfall. "But your brother is all I need."

"I'm glad to hear it. Oh!" Another sudden pain seemed to grab Caro and she grabbed Anne's hand. Her knuckles ached before it was over, but once it was, Caro released her. The pregnant woman closed her eyes.

"I'm so tired already," Caro said as Anne helped her into the bed. She sighed as Anne pulled the fresh sheet up over her. "I wish I could go to sleep and not wake until it's over."

"I doubt you can sleep, but you should close your eyes and try to rest between the pains."

Caro's eyelids fluttered closed.

A small chair was situated next to the cold fireplace. Anne pulled it close to the bed and settled into it so she could keep watch over Edward's sister.

Anne had been alone when she lost Lily. The heavy cramping began one night right after she'd retired for the evening. She should have rung for her lady's maid, but she didn't want to believe it was happening. By the time she did call for help, there was nothing to be done.

And perhaps there never had been. Just as dawn had painted the sky grayish pink, Lily slipped out of Anne's body, unimaginably tiny and perfect, with all her fingers and toes, but no heartbeat. It was too soon. Lily wasn't ready. She'd had no chance.

Anne had feared that God was punishing her for making a child with Edward and then trying to cover her sins by marrying Sir Erasmus.

A hard lump throbbed in her chest.

Tears gathered. She sniffed and blinked them back. The last thing Caroline Sinclair needed was for Anne to be weak-eyed around her. She'd weep for Lily tomorrow when she visited her grave again.

And she'd pray that God was kind. That He wasn't the sort of deity who visited the sins of the parents on their children. That Lily was safe in His care until Anne might someday join her again.

Suddenly blinking and sniffing wasn't enough. She hurried to the commode in search of a square of linen with which to dry her eyes. Martha was standing there. The girl had moved a stack of cloths to the top of the small chest of drawers and was busily folding, unfolding and refolding them again and again.

"This settles it, Lady Howard," she whispered. "I shall never marry."

"Nonsense."

"I mean it," the girl insisted. "I intend to cross my legs and never uncross them for any man."

"Don't speak like that. Women have been bringing babies into this world since the Garden. It's as natural as...as breathing."

"I don't care," Martha hissed. "I'm never going to have children. I've *seen* things."

Oh, precious lamb. You haven't seen anything yet.

* * * *

"Who is planning to poison the king?" Edward demanded.

Reginald Dickey laced his fingers together and cracked his knuckles.
"Sir Percival and his wife—I'll just call her that, shall I? It'll save us from
confusing her with your Lady Howard."

"Dickey, you're trying my patience. And it is not a wise thing to do.
Stick to the facts. You say you know that my Lady Howard is innocent in
her husband's death?" Edward was loath to fall into the scoundrel's way
of speaking, but it seemed the only way short of pummeling him to get to
the truth. "I'm certain she is innocent, but why are *you* sure she did not
murder Sir Erasmus?"

"When they were talking, you see, Sir Percival's wife said it was a good
thing they still had strychnine left over from his father's death. It saved
them from taking the risk of purchasing more."

Edward was relieved to hear Anne vindicated but wished Dickey
would get to the point. "How are they planning to deliver the poison
to His Majesty?"

"That's just the thing. They aren't," Dickey said. "Sir Percival's wife's
cousin—oh, my! That is awkward, isn't it? Maybe it would be easier for
me to just call her Lady Howard—"

"Dickey!"

"In any case, it's her cousin, Viscount Schaumberg, who will be giving
a snuffbox to the king. Oh, the treachery!"

Higgindorfer had said something about a snuffbox Schaumberg
planned to give the king. It was said to be quite ornate and full of familial
significance. "So Schaumberg is a party to this assassination plot."

"No, no. He apparently doesn't know anything about it. You see, the
viscount may be grim and cheerless—he is German, after all—but I believe
he truly wants to see the two sides of the Hanoverians reunited in peace,"
Dickey said. "Lady Howard the Younger, however, still seems to harbor a
grudge over the death of her cousin, the king's unlamented wife."

"But if Schaumberg doesn't know anything about it, how will they use
him to poison the king?" Edward asked.

"Oh, they were arranging it right then. It seems Schaumberg and his
entourage are not as diligent about guarding their personal effects as they
should be. Our conspirators had gained temporary possession of the box
and laced the snuff with strychnine."

"While you watched through a slit in the draperies?"

At least Dickey had the grace to look chagrined as he nodded.

"Ever courageous, I see."

"What would you have had me do?" Dickey said defensively. "Leap out
from my place of concealment and accuse them on the spot?"

"It's what any loyal subject would be expected to do. You did have Sir Percival and his wife dead to rights."

Dickey's lips turned down and he cocked his head. "I'm as loyal a subject as you'll ever find, but these people are planning to murder a king. I am not a violent man by nature. I have no affinity for either firearms or fisticuffs. My chief weapon is my wit. But a cutting parody composed on the moment, however clever the rhyme scheme, wouldn't have stopped them. Do you honestly think they'd have hesitated for a blink to do away with me?"

"'Cowards die many times before their deaths,'" Edward quoted.

"With apologies to Shakespeare, if I'd opposed them then, I very much suspect I'd have died to no purpose," Dickey said. "Now, as I have shared my clandestinely discovered knowledge with you, this coward has used his fear to live *and* save a king."

Edward had to acknowledge Dickey's logic, if not the strength of his spine. "Pray God you've not left it too late." Edward strode away in a serpentine jaunt through several rooms to the head of the grand staircase. Dickey came to heel like a trained spaniel and followed close behind. "What else did Sir Percival and Lady Howard say?"

"Only that they had to be careful to return the snuffbox to Schaumberg's pocket without his realizing it had ever been missing," Dickey said. "Apparently, Sir Percival has nimble fingers. He didn't seem to think it would present a problem."

"Did they mention when the gift would be presented?"

"At midnight, His Majesty will entertain a chosen few guests in the Blue Velvet Room before he makes an appearance to the general throng and leads them in to supper. It promises to be a grand affair," Dickey said, kissing his fingertips in the French style. "I happened to wander down to the lower suite of rooms where the table has been spread from the bow room, through the antedining and the main dining rooms and down the full length of the Gothic conservatory. The king's staff of decorators has conceived an artificial stream burbling from one end to the other down the center of the long table, with real fish swimming in—"

"Dickey, if the king is assassinated, it will hardly matter how his table is set. Back to your point."

"Ah, yes, the midnight audience with a select few. Do you, by chance, know the location of the Blue Velvet Room? I confess, there are some areas in Carlton House that are so well guarded, my attempts to penetrate them have been unfruitful."

"I have had cause to speak with the king in the Blue Velvet Room on two previous occasions." In fact, Edward was one of those invited to attend the king in the private audience room at midnight, but he hoped to negate the threat to the king before then.

"Good. It's easy to become turned around in Carlton House," Dickey said as they walked together down the Grand Staircase. "In any case, as I understand the king's program, gifts to His Majesty are to be presented there at that time."

"I sent mine ahead of this evening. It should already be waiting for His Majesty." Edward wasn't sure what his man of business had decided upon, but if Higgindorfer had chosen the gift, he was certain it would be regal, appropriate, and as cost-efficient as possible. "But you think Schaumberg will carry the snuffbox in with him?"

"According to the conspirators, yes." Dickey nodded. "Schaumberg will give him the snuffbox at midnight and invite him to share a pinch on the spot to seal their reconciliation."

"No wonder you don't think the German is privy to the plot," Edward said. "We'll have two dead men if this scheme goes to plan."

"And even though Sir Percival and his wife expect to be there in that inner circle, the fact that Schaumberg was seemingly willing to die to take down the king will be patently obvious to all who are there," Dickey said. "He will be posthumously blamed for the king's death."

Edward nodded. The baronet from Cornwall and his wife had neatly covered every contingency. From somewhere deep in the bowels of the massive residence, a prodigious clock began to chime the hour. Holding his breath, Edward counted each deep toll and only exhaled when the clock stopped at eleven.

"We've enough time," Dickey said.

"But we're not in the right place. Come," Edward said. "If we can find Schaumberg before midnight, we can save him as well."

"I shall also keep a weather eye out for a physician," Dickey promised. "We mustn't forget your sister in her hour of need."

In the heat of discovering a plot against the king and a way to make sure Anne wasn't charged with her first husband's death, Caro's predicament had completely slipped Edward's mind. He was ashamed that he'd forgotten her while Reginald Dickey hadn't. Perhaps there was more substance to the ton's ill-born darling than he'd suspected. So Edward said something to the man he never thought he would.

"Thank you, Dickey. If you can bring a physician to my sister's side, I'll be in your debt."

It was probably a man who first admonished the English to keep a stiff upper lip in adversity. Clearly, it wasn't one who'd spent any amount of time in a birthing room.
—Caroline Lovell Sinclair, Lady Ware

Chapter 29

"Lord Ware hasn't returned with a doctor," Martha said quietly during a lull in Caro's labor.

Anne bit her lip and shook her head.

"Neither has Lord Chatham," Martha whispered.

"Carlton House is a large residence and there are hundreds of people here tonight," Anne whispered back, trying to project an outward façade of calm. "It will take time to find a doctor in this throng."

"Not even Reginald has come back," Martha said sorrowfully. Even though she'd used his Christian name, Anne didn't have the heart to correct her. "Are all men cowards?"

"Don't assume the worst. I'm sure they are trying."

"Very trying," Martha muttered.

Anne didn't disagree. Their whispered conversation was interrupted by Caro's next wail. They flew to her bedside to hold her hands and encourage her through the deep contraction. When it was over, Caro collapsed back on her pillows and closed her eyes again.

"I think the pains are coming less often," Martha said as she tenderly wiped the pregnant woman's brow. "That's a mercy."

But Anne knew it wasn't. Her experience with Lily had taught her that as the time of the actual birth approached, the pains should be coming with more frequency, not less. This was not a good sign.

"Martha, as the gentlemen have apparently failed, I think you should go and try to find help," Anne said. "Ask a footman if you have to. He'll know whom to call."

"Me?" Martha blushed to the roots of her hair. "You want me to tell a footman that...well, isn't it rather indelicate for me to speak to a man, even if he is a servant, about such things?"

"This is no time for missish prudery. But very well, then. Tell the first woman you see," Anne said testily. "Tell Lady Ackworth for choice. She'll know who's there and where to find the best help for Lady Ware."

"But then what?" Martha's brows nearly met across her nose in a despairing frown. "I...I must confess I have a terrible sense of direction. Carlton House has me completely turned about. There are hundreds of rooms and alcoves, twists and turns. I could never lead anyone back to this particular chamber."

"But you managed to find your way here, didn't you?"

"Yes, but then I was with Reg—I mean, Mr. Dickey. And we were following Lord and Lady Ware at the time," Martha said. "Once I set foot outside that door, I have no idea which direction to go to return to the ballroom or how to show someone the way back here once I find help."

Anne sighed. "Then I'll have to go."

"And leave me here alone with her?"

"Take your choice."

Clearly conflicted, Martha's lips tightened in a thin line. In the tense moments that followed, Caro shifted in the bed and moaned softly, but didn't cry out.

"I'll stay," the girl finally said. "But what should I do if the child comes and you aren't back yet?"

Anne explained what little she'd learned about birthing and what Martha might have to do for the baby and its mother. Martha's mouth gaped, but she nodded gravely when Anne asked her if she was up to the task.

Caro cried out again, her voice weaker now. Martha hurried to her side, but she called to Anne over her shoulder. "Do what you must, but come back soon."

With a nod, Anne scurried away, closing the door softly behind her. Instead of heading back down to the heat and light and press of people in the ballroom, Anne began to search for one of the nearly hidden doors that concealed an inner staircase designated solely for the use of servants. If she found one and followed it down, surely there would be a few matrons belowstairs who had seen a babe or two safely into the world.

Finally next to an alcove, neatly concealed with cleverly joined wainscoting and silvered wallpaper, Anne discovered one of those hidden doors. The narrow stairway was dimly lit by occasional gas wall sconces. It wound both up and down so far, Anne could see neither the topmost story nor the subbasement, for the stairway disappeared into shadow in both directions. She started down, hoping to run into a servant on the way up. Instead, she heard footsteps coming from above her, quickening their pace as they drew near. When she reached a landing, she started to turn around to discover who it was, but suddenly a pair of hands circled her neck and began to squeeze.

She couldn't draw breath. She couldn't cry out. Though she hadn't seen her attacker, she assumed it must be a man because when she clawed at his hands, one of her fingernails was bent back by a heavy signet ring. She kicked backward as hard as her narrow column dress would let her. He yelped when her heel connected with his shin, but his grip around her throat didn't lessen.

Darkness gathered at the edges of Anne's vision. The long tunnel before her grew ever dimmer. Then, just as she recognized the cloying scent of lavender her attacker had slathered on himself, the suffocating blackness claimed her and she winked out completely.

* * * *

Even more people had arrived for the King's fete since Edward had last visited the ballroom. All the large public rooms were as crammed as one of Lady Ackworth's routs. The violinists were playing for all they were worth, but it was a wonder the dancers could keep time with the music. The constant buzz of myriad conversations, punctuated by raucous laughter, conspired to cover the chamber ensemble with mindless cacophony.

"This party has degenerated considerably," Dickey observed. "Someone has undoubtedly spiked the punch."

Edward shot him a glare.

"It wasn't me," Dickey protested, hands raised in mock surrender.

"We need to spread out. You take this room. Wait. Hold a moment." Edward clapped a hand on his shoulder to stop him because Dickey had uncharacteristically obeyed his first command with alacrity. "I think that's Sinclair heading into the adjoining chamber. I'll follow him. You stay here and try to find Viscount Schaumberg or a member of his entourage."

"Or a doctor," Dickey added.

"Preferably both."

Edward began to shoulder his way through the press to where he'd last caught sight of his friend disappearing into another room. He found him moving along the perimeter of the cavernous space, trying to weave through the heavy knots of guests who were standing about chattering like geese.

Edward caught his friend by the elbow. "Sinclair, what are you doing, man? Haven't you found a doctor yet?"

"One of the footmen thinks Dr. Brimble has been drawn into a card game being played in one of the rooms set aside for that purpose."

"Which room?"

Sinclair snorted. "The footman didn't know. If Brimble's a whist man, he's in the small study on the third floor, northeast corner. If he fancies a game of loo, it's being played in one of the basement suites of rooms near the library. The footman couldn't say which game called to Dr. Brimble, and the man was so terrified he'd be caught not attending to the guests down here, he wouldn't break away from his duties to assist me." Sinclair drew a shaky breath. "Oh, God, Bredon. If something happens to Caro, I..."

"Stow that rot. My sister can weather any storm. We Lovells are made of stern stuff," Edward said with more confidence than he felt. "I'll take the third floor. You check the basement."

For the moment, the threat to the king receded into the background as Edward pushed his way through the next few rooms, heading once again for the Grand Staircase.

* * * *

True to Dickey's suspicions, a decidedly alcoholic fume emanated from the punch bowl. He resisted the urge to sample some of the improved stuff and continued his circuit of the room. As usual, he smiled and nodded and scraped the occasional bow as he passed by the titled idiots. They were so smug, so arrogant. With no personal accomplishments or merit, but simply by virtue of the accident of their births, they were absolutely certain of their own superiority.

How he loathed them.

A man should be judged on his actions. Preferably on his intellect and the fruit of his wit.

Careful, Dickey. Such democratic ideas will get you branded a political upstart.

Then he happened to catch sight of one of the minor visiting nobles who'd accompanied Viscount Schaumberg.

It's easy enough to pick the Germans out. They all look perpetually constipated.

The men from Brunswick appeared desperately uncomfortable in their clothes. They all seemed to have collars that were too tight which shoved the skin of their necks up. To Dickey, they looked a bit like sausages that had sprung a leak.

Their tailor deserves to be shot.

Dickey hurried over to the German. "I say, my good fellow, I need to speak with you on a matter of some urgency."

The German glared down at him.

Why must these Teutonic types always be so blasted tall?

"*Was ist das?*" the man said, clearly bored by it all.

"*Das ist...*" Dickey had reached the extent of his German. "Your lord is in grave danger."

When the man narrowed his eyes and cocked his head quizzically, Dickey decided the fellow's English was no better than his German.

He tried again. "Viscount Schaumberg...*ist...ist...*" From deep in his schoolboy days, the German word for *peril* rose to the surface. "*die Gefahr.* Your lord *ist die Gefahr.*"

The burly German's brows lowered. He grabbed Dickey by the nape of his jacket and frog-marched him out of the room. Several people laughed and pointed as they passed by, no doubt thinking this was just another of Reginald Dickey's self-deprecating jokes. Though he pleaded loudly, no one came to his aid. The German dragged him down the Grand Staircase, not stopping at the basement level but continuing to descend into the bowels of the great house.

"But I was only trying to help," Reginald protested miserably.

Clearly, doing good is not all it's cracked up to be.

They say before one dies, one's life passes before one's eyes. I shall try to live in such a way that when the time comes, it will be an enjoyable reprise with as few regrets as possible.
—Lady Howard, writing as Mrs. Hester Birdwhistle

Chapter 30

Anne had the sense of being held underwater. In another moment, her lungs would burst for want of air. Determined to live, she clawed her way toward the surface, but the elusive world of light and air remained just out of reach. Finally, she could bear it no more. She surrendered to her burning chest and inhaled.

She fully expected a lungful of murky liquid, but instead sweet air flooded her being. Her eyelids fluttered open and she discovered that she hadn't been submerged after all and was perfectly dry. She was, however, bound, gagged, and stretched out on a long settee in an unfamiliar anteroom.

"Why did you bring her here?" a woman said in a fierce half whisper.

Anne immediately shut her eyes again. Instinct warned her that feigning senselessness was the best way to learn what had happened to her. And likely the safest.

"Where else should I take her?"

The second voice belonged to her stepson, Sir Percy. The woman must have been his wife.

"Why didn't you finish her in the stairwell and simply leave her there?" the current Lady Howard demanded.

"Because if I had, we'd have another suspicious death connected to our family," Percy said. "This way, we can fashion an outcome that will satisfy the magistrate who's looking into my father's death."

"Ah! I have it. We only need for your stepmother to sign a confession and then arrange for her demise to look like a guilty suicide."

Fear coiled around Anne's spine and radiated through her whole body, but she willed herself to remain motionless.

"How clever of you, dear," Percy said. "Do we have any strychnine left over from the snuffbox?"

"Enough. It won't take much. The dowager is on the smallish side." There was a brief period of silence, as the conspirators seemed to weigh the merits of their plan. Finally Lady Howard the Younger spoke again. "But won't it seem suspicious if your stepmother dies of poison on the same night as my cousin and the king?"

"You're right. That would be too much of the good thing. And how on earth can we persuade her"—Anne assumed Percy had gestured in her direction—"to write and sign a false confession?"

Anne opened her eyes just enough to peer beneath her lashes. Her stepson's wife pulled a small derringer from her reticule.

"Where did you get that?" Percy asked.

"Never you mind. I've had it for a long time, in case you're worried someone might connect it to a recent purchase. And before you ask, yes, I know how to use it. Rest easy, husband."

Anne heard the longcase clock chime the half hour.

"It's nearly time for the private audience," Percy said. "Should we leave her here and come back to deal with her during the panic that will surely attend the king's death?"

"No, you go on ahead while I take care of matters here."

"But the king will be expecting you in the audience chamber. You're the late princess's cousin, after all."

"Tell His Majesty I am indisposed. Men never inquire too closely into a lady's maladies. Besides, in his arrogance, the king believes it is with his late wife's male relatives he must reconcile. He is wrong to underestimate the resolve of the female of the species. Considering the shabby way he treated his wife, isn't it fitting that a woman's plan will bring his sorry reign to an end?"

"With a little help from your loyal husband," Percy reminded her.

"Yes, of course. If you hadn't agreed to let me switch your father from arsenic to strychnine, the dose I decided on for His Majesty would have been much more art than science. Finally, the death of Princess Caroline of Brunswick will be avenged this night." Lady Howard the Younger brandished the small weapon menacingly. "Then in a fit of remorse over the murder of her husband, your stepmother will put a bullet in her brain."

* * * *

Edward finally found the whist room, but no one named Dr. Brimble was playing there. He hoped Sinclair had had better luck in the basement with the loo players.

Or perhaps Dickey had been useful for once and located a doctor for Caro in the ballroom. Edward was comforted by the fact that Anne was by his dear sister's side. Anne was levelheaded in a crisis and not easily dismayed. Plus, she had given birth herself, albeit too soon. She would know what ought to be done for Caro.

The small grave in the St. Thomas-by-the-Way churchyard weighed on Edward's conscience. Guilt gnawed at his gut because Anne had gone through losing the child alone. He'd never be able to make it up to her, but that didn't mean he'd stop trying.

"Merciful Lord, be with her now," he murmured under his breath as he left the whist players to their games. He'd meant to return to the chamber where Caro was struggling to give birth, but then he heard the large clock chime three-quarters of the hour. Carlton House was ponderously large, and given that the state rooms were crammed to the rafters with guests, it might take all of fifteen minutes for Edward to make his way to the private audience in the Blue Velvet Room.

And how much good could he do in a lying-in room in any case? Anne would likely shoo him away.

"King and country before all," he muttered, and started back down the Grand Staircase.

* * * *

Martha wrung out the cloth she'd been using to bathe Lady Ware's face between contractions. They didn't seem to be coming as often now or as hard, but Lady Ware was weakening with each pain. It occurred to Martha that this was not how things were supposed to be.

"I wonder," she said tentatively, "if perhaps you might push a bit with the next one."

"What do you think I've been doing?" Lady Ware whined.

"Oh! Well...then maybe you should try *not* pushing and see if that helps."

"You have no idea what you're asking," Lady Ware said wearily. "I want to push. I have to—oh!"

The pain seemed to take her by surprise.

"Try not to push, my lady," Martha said. "Here! Squeeze my—no, not my hand—my arm, instead of pushing."

Surprisingly enough, Lady Ware seemed to listen and tried to do as she suggested. Together they gritted their teeth through the contraction, Lady Ware, because she was fighting the urge to push, and Martha, because the countess's grip made it feel as if a boa constrictor was wrapped around her forearm.

This will undoubtedly leave a mark.

When the pain subsided, Lady Ware lay panting for a moment. Then she put both hands on her distended belly. "I believe something just happened."

"What?"

"Something feels different. The babe has shifted into a new position. Oh! Here comes another one." Lady Ware grabbed her arm again.

"So soon?"

"Yes," she said through clenched teeth. "Should I push this time or not?"

"I don't know. *I don't know*," Martha said frantically.

"I'm going to push."

"What should *I* do?" Martha wailed.

"Get ready to catch!"

* * * *

Instead of fifteen minutes, it was closer to twenty before Edward could fight his way through the rout to the quieter section of Carlton House where the king's private apartments were. By the time he gained admittance, the ceremony had already begun. Viscount Schaumberg was down on one knee, proffering a truly magnificent gold snuffbox nestled on a velvet pillow to the king.

"Rise, Cousin," the king said. "Let us seal our newfound amity by taking a pinch of snuff together."

"No!" Edward shouted and dove for the box of poison. He managed to knock it and Viscount Schaumberg to the ground. The snuffbox bounced, sending a shower of white powder on the thick carpet with each rotation.

"What is the meaning of this outrage?" the German shouted.

Edward scrambled to his feet and waved off the servants who had hurried to clean up the spilled snuff. "Be careful how you handle that stuff," he ordered, and then turned back to Viscount Schaumberg, who was lumbering to his feet. "Lord Schaumberg, your gift to the king has been tampered with by Sir Percival Howard and his wife. That snuff is poisoned with strychnine."

"Ridiculous," Percival said in a pinched tone.

"No, it's not," came Reginald Dickey's voice from behind Edward. The fellow strode to the center of the room, accompanied by several of Lord Schaumberg's retainers. "I was present when Sir Percival and Lady Howard conspired to taint the snuff with poison."

"No, you weren't," Sir Percival said. "That room was empty."

"Aha!" Dickey pointed at him with dramatic flair. "Then you admit to conspiring."

"No, I didn't," Percy said, taking a step or two backward. "I just said you weren't in the room when we..."

"Conspired?"

"Confound it, man! No one was there!" Sir Percival didn't seem aware that he was failing to deny Dickey's charge.

"Just because you were unaware of my presence, it does not follow that I wasn't tucked neatly behind the damask draperies." Dickey turned his attention to the king, scraping an elegant bow to his sovereign. "Your Majesty, I am witness to the machinations of Sir Percival and his wife, and in their conversation, they did also admit to the murder of his own father by the same method. In fact, I believe one of Your Majesty's finest magistrates is looking into the untimely demise of Sir Erasmus as we speak."

"Bind him." The king gestured toward Sir Percival. "And find Lady Howard at once as well."

"I'll go," Edward offered.

The report of small arms fire sounded, but the pops were muffled and seemed to be coming from above their heads on an upper story of the great house. Sir Percival's smile was wickedness incarnate.

"You'll likely find the *Dowager* Lady Howard in a room that reeks of gunpowder," Percy said. "My wife, however, is clever enough never to be found."

"Where is she?" Edward demanded.

Sir Percival shook his head.

"Your Majesty, give me five minutes with the blackguard and I'll have the location of the other traitor out of him."

The king nodded. "It seems to us that you have earned that right, Lord Chatham. Do with him as you will."

With more violence in his soul than he'd thought possible, Edward stalked toward Sir Percival.

The will to live against all odds is sometimes mistaken for courage. It is instead the deep animal instinct to keep moving, keep breathing, and not to surrender without a fight.
—Lady Howard the Elder

Chapter 31

It didn't take five minutes. In less than one, Edward had wrung the location of his wife out of Sir Percival. As soon as Percy gave up the room where he'd left Lady Howard, Edward fled the king's private audience chamber without so much as a by-your-leave. A number of the king's guards were hard on his heels.

He pounded up the stairs and flew through the maze of chambers till he came to the small anteroom Percival had described. Edward burst through the door.

A woman was lying on the floor with another on her knees beside her. The kneeling woman turned her face toward him.

It was Anne.

"Hurry!" she said, directing her attention back to the prone woman. "Lady Howard has been shot."

"You evil witch!" Percival's wife screeched as she thrashed from side to side, clutching her shoulder. "You're the one who shot me!"

"Yes, I am. But in fairness, you were quite intent on shooting me as well. In fact, I believe the gun was still in your hand when it discharged," Anne said with eerie calmness, as she pressed a wadded bit of her petticoat to her stepson's wife's wound. "And now you must keep still or you'll bleed to death. Edward, dear, did you ever manage to find a doctor for your sister?"

His throat was so constricted he couldn't answer. Instead, as the king's guard bore the shrieking Lady Howard away, Edward just pulled

Anne close and held her. She'd had to fight for her life, but she was only trembling slightly.

"What happened?" he finally managed to say.

"Sir Percival had bound and gagged me," Anne said. "Lady Howard made the mistake of untying me."

"You are a veritable lioness."

"You'd do well not to forget it, husband."

"How could I?" Edward bent to kiss her softly. He wanted to snatch her up and carry her off to a tower. Somewhere he could protect her and keep her safe from the dangers and heartaches of this world. But when she grasped his lapels and deepened their kiss, he knew she'd never be the kind of woman who wanted to be safe. Anne would always jump into life with both feet.

And in his heart of hearts, Edward knew he wouldn't want her any other way.

But he did wish she were more easily sidetracked.

She was the first to pull away from their kiss. "Edward, you distracted me. Did you or did you not find a doctor for Caro?"

"I...I think Sinclair managed it. Let's go see."

She gave him a sidelong look of derision. "Do let's."

He negotiated the labyrinth of rooms back to the chamber where Caro was without getting turned about. When they reached the room, they discovered that Sinclair had in fact dragged Dr. Brimble from his loo game, but the men had arrived at the birthing chamber too late to be of help. By the time they arrived, the baby had been delivered and was nursing contentedly. The doctor had examined both mother and her new baby boy and pronounced them healthy and sound.

"As if he'd lifted so much as a finger to make them that way," Martha said as she took the tightly swaddled newborn from its mother and lifted the child toward Edward. "Your nephew, my lord."

He took the little bundle and held it gingerly, as if he feared it might crumble in his arms. When the baby squirmed, Martha said, "Hold him tighter, my lord. He likes that."

Edward obeyed and the child quieted once again, his sweet little body totally relaxed. "Remarkable," Edward said softly so as not to wake him. "He's beautiful. I must congratulate his parents."

He handed the baby back to Martha, who took him with ease, cooing and patting his little bum.

"Just look, Anne," Martha said in hushed tones. "Lady Ware has made a whole new person."

"I rather think she had a little help," Anne said.

"Yes, yes," Martha agreed. "I'm sure Lord Ware had something to do with it."

"I'm sure he did, but I was thinking about God." Anne ran her finger down the newborn's soft cheek. "If the Lord hadn't sent you to help Lady Ware, who knows what might have happened? But I'm sure you must have been distressed. For that, I am sorry."

"I'm not. It...it was a miracle, really," Martha said, as she dropped a kiss on the sleeping baby's forehead. "And you know what? I think maybe I would like to be married someday after all."

"Tempus omnia monstrat." Time shows all things. It's the Lovell family motto. Thank God, it's also true.

—from the journal of Edward Lovell, who, no matter how many honors are heaped upon him, still thinks of himself by the name he grew up with—Lord Bredon

Chapter 32

The newly created Marquess of Rothberg returned to Lovell House after a long conference with his man of business. The meeting, necessitated by Edward's new title, could only be held in Mr. Higgindorfer's office, owing to the vast quantities of ledgers and paperwork involved.

By way of a reward for Edward's decisive action in saving the king, and incidentally Viscount Schaumberg as well, from inhaling poisoned snuff, His Majesty had conferred the lapsed Marquessate of Rothberg upon him. The honor was considerable and there was much pomp and circumstance surrounding Edward's elevation, especially after he had revealed his secret marriage to Anne well in advance of the ceremony. Edward had never been prouder than when a marchioness's coronet was placed on Anne's lovely head.

But apart from the honor of being named a marquess, the conferment of a new estate might prove a double-edged sword. If Rothberg was as light in the pockets as Chatham, his financial woes would be doubled.

Anne met him in the foyer. "We can't go into the parlor just now."

"Why?"

"Lord Tintagel is proposing to Martha in there," she said with a sly smile. At the same time the king had rewarded Edward, he'd acknowledged Reginald Dickey's contribution to foiling the assassination plot. Sir Percival's baronetcy was stripped from him and he and his unhappy wife were tried, convicted, and summarily deported to New South Wales. The king conferred the Cornish baronetcy on Dickey, but not without first elevating the title and estate to a barony. Reginald was created the first Baron Tintagel, the name of the new estate having been purloined from the largest village within its confines. Lord Tintagel might yet be a bastard, but he was also now a peer.

"She'll accept him, won't she?" Edward asked.

"In a heartbeat. I rather suspect we'll be making a trip to the country soon. No doubt Martha's parents will want the wedding performed in their home parish."

"There's a good deal to be said for unions solemnized at St. Thomas-by-the-Way."

He bent to kiss his wife, but she turned her head at the last moment and his lips only brushed her cheek.

"Don't keep me in suspense, Edward. What did Mr. Higgindorfer say about Rothberg? Has revealing our marriage made things worse for you?"

"If it had, I still wouldn't care." He pulled her close and kissed her thoroughly. When he released her, her lovely eyes had gone all soft and doelike. He promised himself he'd benefit from that later. "If I have to petition the House of Lords and sell every square inch of land I own, I'd still count myself a rich man because I have you by my side."

"Oh dear." Anne's dreamy expression faded and her brows drew together. "It must be worse than I thought."

"No, Anne. It's better than I could have wished. Rothberg is a rich estate in a well-watered area near Wales. By all accounts, the manor is a bit old fashioned. It goes back to the days of the Tudors, but because the land is so productive, the rents are lavish. You'll be able to renovate to your heart's delight. The estate also boasts a productive iron and copper mine. The income from the mines alone means that Chatham is saved. And so am I."

She sagged into him, resting her head on his chest. "Oh, Edward."

"You saved me, Anne. I don't deserve you, but God has given me everything I could ever want. I'll never ask Him for more."

"Oh, I'm hoping you'll want a little more. You see, dear," she stood on tiptoe and whispered into his ear, "I'm pregnant."

THE SINGULAR MR. SINCLAIR

Don't miss the first charming novel in Mia Marlowe's House of Lovell series, available now!

**"A delightful Regency romance, full of passion, humor, and love."
—*USA Today* bestselling author Ella Quinn**

Lord and Lady Chatham were blessed with five sons and only one daughter. But when it comes to Caroline, one is more than enough...

Caroline is about to embark on her *third* Season and her parents fear she'll be permanently on the shelf if she fails to make a match this time. Unfortunately for them, that is precisely what Caroline wants! Curious and adventuresome, Caroline longs for a life of travel, excitement, and perhaps even a touch of danger...

If only she can remain unmarried until she turns twenty-one, Caroline will inherit her grandmother's bequest and gain her freedom. It's not a staggering amount, but it's enough to fund her dreams without a husband's permission. She has her future all planned out—until Lawrence Sinclair appears on the scene...

Intense, intriguing, and handsome, the man reminds Caroline of a caged lion. In fact, the more she knows of him, the more questions she has. And when she learns how dangerous he really is, he may just become her new fascination—the one she can't resist...

"Mia Marlowe is the mistress of saucy historical romances."
—*Books Monthly*

"Mia Marlowe is a rising star!"
—*New York Times* bestseller Connie Mason

"Mia Marlowe proves she has the 'touch' for strong heroines, wickedly sexy heroes!"
—Jennifer Ashley, *USA Today* bestselling author of *Lady Isabella's Scandalous Marriage*

"Her three-dimensional characters truly steal readers' hearts and keep the pages flying."
—Kathe Robin

Meet the Author

Mia Marlowe learned much of what she knows about storytelling from singing. A classically trained soprano, Mia won the District Metropolitan Opera Auditions after graduating summa cum laude from the University of Northern Iowa. She and her family have lived in nine different states, but she now calls the Ozarks home. Learn more about Mia at www.miamarlowe.com.

Printed in the United States
by Baker & Taylor Publisher Services